This book is dedicated to my great aunt, Mrs. Oneva Estus. She was the inspiration for the main character, Lucela, because of her loving nature, strength, and ability to show love through her quiet demeanor. 'Aunt Neva', as she was affectionately called, could always be counted on for kind words of encouragement and a hot, wholesome meal that comforted the soul. She was known for her culinary skills, not just within the family, but even throughout town.

My own grandmother passed when I was just a toddler, but Aunt Neva quickly filled her loss within the family. Until I was around five, she allowed my mother and me to share her home. My aunt was originally from the South, and therefore maintained many of the region's customs, especially in regards to food. Each day began with a hearty breakfast that my own children would have been envious of: fresh squeezed juice, milk and cereal, bacon and eggs, and toast with homemade jelly---on a routine basis! Around noon I would receive a filling lunch that was always hot, whether soup and a cheese sandwich, or a burger and fries. Dinner was always served around five o'clock and consisted of meat, potatoes, vegetables and hot pastry, such as rolls or cornbread. I didn't always care for my vegetables, but would usually eat them with the promise that I could eat as many oatmeal cookies as I wanted that Friday or have an extra slice of cake on Sunday. (Desserts were usually provided on the weekends). Finally, supper occurred about an hour before bedtime and was usually a lighter meal, maybe a roast beef or ham sandwich with a glass of milk.

I was a very inquisitive and rambunctious child. (In today's world I would have definitely been medicated and labeled as ADHD!) However, I knew, even at a very young age, that within her home I was truly loved. She never criticized my constant questioning or lively ways. In fact, in hindsight I realize that she actually encouraged it because she knew that it was stemming from intellect and not unruliness. After learning to read at age three, my aunt would ask me to read the "funny papers" to her while eating breakfast. By the age of four I had advanced to newspaper articles, reading headlines and captions under pictures while my aunt busied herself preparing meals.

The kitchen was Aunt Neva's sanctuary and I was permitted to intrude. There was a stepstool (that probably hadn't been used in years, since Aunt Neva was a rather tall woman) that became my constant seat and allowed me to peer over her shoulder until my anxiety could no longer be contained and I decided to plop myself on the counter to get a closer look, just long enough before being admonished and told to get down because sitting on the counter "wasn't ladylike." I appointed myself as her official "helper" and would look forward to special occasions and holidays so that I could run about locating spices and ingredients, while taking a "pinch" here or there of cookie dough, pie crust, and other delicacies. Although I don't recall her ever using a cookbook, Aunt Neva's meals were always perfect and she always managed to measure the exact same ingredients each time. In fact, almost forty years later, I can still recreate many of the dishes that she fixed from memory. (I spent A LOT of time watching her prepare meals!)

As with most children, the parents, grandparents, aunts, uncles, and others that have contributed to their lives are usually valued most once the child has grown into adulthood and realizes the effect of their impact on their lives. Now that my children are grown, I can acknowledge that much of what I have taught them is because of her loving influence. While they were growing up, I would often encourage them to creatively express themselves, and although I did not have Aunt Neva's patience, I often used my culinary skills to show love. (My children often joke about how a spanking was usually followed by some kind of special treat, as a way to assuage my guilt.) My aunt never had children of her own, but she definitely served as a "mother" to not only me, but many people within my family and the community.

What made my aunt special was her ability to show love in a consistent and quiet way. She was the epitome of the old adage, "Actions speak louder than words." She knew that sometimes a caring touch, a hot meal, or a special dessert could brighten someone's day. I remember arriving home from school on many occasions, feeling dejected at having been ridiculed for being so "different" and having her wipe my tears and soothe my heart with a big hug. She would tell me, "Eat your lunch. You'll feel better." While eating lunch I'd slyly tell her, "Aunt Neva, I'd feel a lot better if I had some oatmeal cookies." She'd look at me and smile before reminding me to be sure to wash my hands and face before taking my nap. About an hour later, I would awake to the fragrant smell of vanilla and cinnamon. Upon entering the kitchen I would see a glass of milk and a small plate of cookies waiting-- *just for me*. As I nibbled on the cookies, Aunt Neva would sit down and share a story with me that would not only teach me a lesson about dealing with the difficulties I faced that day, but would make me feel that in spite of it all, *I was special and I was loved*.

My aunt passed away when I was a young mother, during my late twenties. She was born in the South less than 50 years after slavery and lived a long life. In fact, she passed on her 90th birthday. Around the holidays, I often think fondly of her, usually while I am preparing celebratory meals. Sometimes I can picture her in my mind, frosting a cake, buttering cornbread, or mixing dressing in a pan with her large, loving hands before allowing me to lick the spoon, sample a corner from the cornbread, or taste a pinch of dressing. She would always ask for me for my approval, and I took my duties as her helper very seriously. I now realize that she was patronizing me, probably to keep me from feeling guilty about my large appetite and hyperactive impatience at waiting for the meal to be complete.

There is a passage in the Bible that is often quoted regarding the example of a virtuous woman. Although the long passage provides many examples to support the woman's virtuosity, one scripture aptly describes my aunt: *"She openeth her mouth with wisdom; and in her tongue is the law of kindness."* Although Aunt Neva was a woman of few words, she had the ability to share great wisdom and understanding, and I can honestly state that I never heard her curse, gossip, or say an unkind thing to anyone. Every day, I strive to follow her example of Christian love. Honestly, I fail at times, but I encourage myself by acknowledging that she faced many injustices in her lifetime that I never have and yet triumphed above them. With her as my guardian angel, surely I can accomplish what she did and so much more.

Although the main character in this story was *inspired* by a real life individual, the characters, location, and events that take place in the text are purely fictional. Any similarities to real life events or individuals are purely coincidental and in no way meant to discredit or offend anyone.

Lucela sat looking out of the window, sipping her morning coffee from her cracked china cup. The light brown liquid slowly seeped onto the saucer, like a finger that had just been pricked by a pin. A lone tear traveled down her leathered brown face before finally settling into the crevice of her deep dimple. She absently wiped it from her cheek and abruptly rose to her feet in a defiant manner, almost knocking her chair over. She retrieved her large butcher knife and placed it on the counter. This would be the last tear she would cry over Abe.

CHAPTER ONE

Lucela and Abe had met at a church picnic twenty years ago. She was going on thirty, he twenty-five. He'd shown up with his cousin, having just left the army and looking sharp in a crisply pressed uniform. In hindsight, Lucela realized that he must have looked like a fool to wear such a get-up on a 90 degree day, but at the time she viewed him as a good catch--and in their small town the pool of available, unrelated men was extremely small. Besides, as a domestic approaching the "old maid" years, not too many were biting at her hook. Before her fast cousin Myrtle had a chance to sashay around Abe, her Aunt Saxie grabbed him by the arm and sat him down at their family's table next to her other, less flamboyant niece. "Sit right on down, Son. I see you's been busy fightin' for Uncle Sam and gettin' by on that mess hall food. Bout time you had a good, home-cooked meal 'stead of that gov'ment grub. My niece, Ceel here, one of the best cooks in the county. Lemme have her fix you a plate. What you say yo' name was?"

"Abraham Lincoln Jessup, ma'am. I'm Sis. Hawkins' nephew; James is my cousin. But everybody calls me Abe. I sure 'preciate yo' generosity. Been a mighty long time since I've had a home-cooked meal, let alone a good one."

"Well, I'll have Ceel fix you right up. She makes the best coconut cake around. Always goes first in the Cake Walks. You like coconut cake?"

"Yes, ma'am! That's my favorite." And with that he turned and smiled at Lucela eagerly. Smoothing her dress, Lucela shyly got up from the picnic bench and began preparing a plate for him: the first of many she would place in front of him for many years, and the one she was the most eager to fix. Upon returning to the table, she placed a napkin his lap and laid his plate on top of the table as if he was a king before setting a large glass of sweet tea next to it. Abe picked up his glass, took a long, desperate swallow then winked at Lucela. "Staying here might work out after all," he thought to himself. Lucela blushed bashfully then sat down next to Abe, anxiously waiting to refill his glass or heap another serving onto his plate. Staring at his handsome face took away her appetite, so she sipped on a single glass of lemonade all afternoon.

After Abe finished his third piece of coconut cake, he grasped Lucela's moist hand and asked her if she would like to go for a walk. She complied with a smile while Aunt Saxie and the other elderly women from the church nodded approvingly. They ventured down by the pond and Lucela quietly listened while Abe told her his life story. He'd been raised by his grandfather, after his mother abandoned him at the age of five. He'd grown up hard, helping his grandpa peddle bootleg whiskey in the backwoods of Arkansas. Although he had five other brothers and sisters, he didn't really know them since they'd all been raised apart, scattered among relatives like a litter of puppies.

After eating most of his food, Abe took sip of tea to clear his throat before finally conversing with Lucela. "Shoot, your

Auntie had it right when she said it had been a long time since I'd had some good cookin'. But she had it wrong puttin' it off on Uncle Sam. Growing up, Granpa and I had to shoot everythang we ate; kill it before it killed us: possum, squirrel, rabbit, deer, once even bear, you know? But by the time I came along Gramps was through foolin' wit' women, so a woman's touch was always missing from our house. Jus' us two batchin' like single men. Thas' all I know. By the time I joined the Army after he died, I thought I was livin' the life. At least I didn't have to hunt for my own food, even if it came out of a can." He laughed at his joke, like he had just delivered the punch line on a frequently told tale. Lucela joined in to release the giddy butterflies that were floating in her belly. "You don't say much, do you? You always so quiet, Lucela?"

"Naw, not always. I just like lettin' people talk without interruptin' em. Thas' jus my way, I guess. Plus, I like hearing you talk." Lucela giggled as Abe stroked her arm lovingly, then turned to her and smiled. She gazed into his hazel eyes, "cat eyes" that contrasted with his dark chocolate skin. It was the first time she'd ever received so much attention from a man in her twenty-nine years and it was a new sensation. At that moment, the butterflies she felt escaped from her stomach and fluttered down until they settled in her privates, causing a tingling of excitement and anticipation that caused her to lose her breath. Maybe this was what Myrtle used to talk about feeling when she was with her various "men friends." She knew that at twenty-nine, she was not a prime catch, and that few offers would come her way hereafter. Her aunt always said that sometimes you have to "move while the water's troubled." Lucela felt the ripples Abe was causing in her, and decided she would grab hold of him before the tide took him away. At that moment, she vowed to "hook her catch" before he got floated downstream, even if he was just a big fish in a very, very small pond.

Like Abe, Lucela had been raised by family instead of parents. Her mother had died in a house fire when she was seven, trying to save her infant brother, Charles. She had never known her father, but had been told that he was a full-blooded Cherokee, thus explaining her long, coal-black wavy hair (that she usually wore in a tightly rolled bun) and her reddish-brown skin tone that tanned like a shiny new copper penny in the summer sun. Her Aunt Saxie, who was widowed and childless, welcomed Lucela into her home and raised her as she would have raised her own: God-fearing, virtuous, home-trained, and domesticated. At the age of twenty-nine, Lucela was still a virgin, attended church every Sunday, was polite and helpful to others (especially her elders), and the best cook in her church—even among the Mother's Board. She had courted a few gentlemen in her younger days, but had always fallen by the wayside when they sought out the affections of others who were willing to submit to their physical demands. As a result, Lucela was now the only unmarried woman among her age group within the church, and with the exception of her twenty year-old cousin Sallie Mae, was the only childless woman within her family. Just like her aunt, she worked as a maid for a prominent White family in the town, a job she secured due to her outstanding culinary skills.

Through the years, Lucela filled the maternal void in her life by showering the children in her family with affection the only way she knew how: through cookies, cakes, and pies. Her young cousins anticipated their birthdays not just for the presents, but for the special cakes she would bake for them. No matter what their requests, she would always find a way to come through. When four-year old Ruth Anne asked if she could make her a Mickey Mouse cake, Lucela complied with a two layer chocolate cake, frosted in vanilla and decorated with a "Mickey Mouse" created from chocolate chips and a maraschino cherry nose. Ruth Anne liked the cake so much, she cried when the candles dripped onto Mickey's ears and refused to let anyone cut it. Aunt Saxie was highly amused when the child ceased her incessant thumb-sucking to authoritatively lisp to everyone to "Let Mickey stay priddy!" thus forcing the guests to indulge only in ice cream. After she had opened her gifts, Ruth Anne pushed them aside to walk over and climb into Lucela's lap. Once seated comfortably in her familiar spot, she removed her thumb and whispered, "Thanks, cuthin' Ceel for my buthday cake. It's priddy!" She kissed Lucela on the cheek then tenderly stuck her tiny thumb in the deep cavern of one of her prominent dimples. Lucela reached down and playfully tugged at one of her short, red-ribboned pigtails. After erupting in a giggle, she returned the thumb to its usual location. She immediately noticed a slight taste of saltiness, but her young mind was unable to comprehend that it had been flavored by Lucela's tears. Many thought they were an expression of joy, but they were actually coming from a different place. Lucela's maternal longings were no longer concealable.

During their walk home, Aunt Saxie spoke her mind. "That Ruth Ann somethin' else, ain't she? No bigger than a junebug and tryna give orders! If that ain't Harvey's child, I swear. He coulda spit that girl out! She sure got a thang for you, Ceel. You know you her favorite cousin. If I didn't know better, I'd swear Rosie was jealous. Done spent all that money on them toys and that baby done fell in love wit' the cake!" Lucela smiled slightly, but couldn't laugh due to her heavy heart. Aunt Saxie felt the cool distance between them in the darkness. "Ceel, girl, your time's gon' come. I feel it. You jus' gotta do it right, get babies wit' a man of your own that will raise 'em right. You don't wanna end up like Myrtle wit' a houseful and ain't none of 'em matchin'. I'm not sure she even know who to put 'em on, so she jus' struggle to feed 'em by herself. You know I raised you better than that. And yo' mama, my sister Lottie, God rest her soul, wadn't that kinda woman neither. Myrtle take after her Daddy's peoples. She brings so much shame on yo' Auntie Gladys. I know she'd give anythin' to have a daughter like you. Childless or not, you still a woman who can hold her head high in this town, without any shame. When the right man comes along, ain't gon' be nothing no man 'round here can say 'bout you that will cause him to look away cause you ain't been passed around."

"Yes, ma'am," Lucela murmured. She wanted to say more, but was afraid she wouldn't be able to utter another word without unleashing a flood of tears.

Saxie halted her footsteps, reached out, and gently touched her niece's arm. She lowered her voice to a notch slightly

7

higher than a whisper and spoke in a slow, measured tone, as if she were speaking to a young child. A warm summer breeze moved between them, as if it were sent by God himself to provide comfort. "Ceel, the Bible say *"They that wait on the Lord, he renew their strength."* You jus' gotta wait and be strong. Your time will come."

That afternoon, as she gazed into the sunset while resting her head on Abe's shoulder, Lucela's thoughts drifted back to Aunt Saxie's words from last summer. *"My time has finally come,"* she thought. *"Thank you, Lord."*

CHAPTER TWO

After a two-week courtship, Lucela and Abe were married in a small ceremony at Mt. Nebo Baptist Church, the same church she had been christened and baptized in. Lucela proudly wore new satin shoes, her blue birthstone ring, and her mother's pure white wedding dress--a sacred treasure that had been salvaged from the fire. Sticking to the tradition, she borrowed Saxie's pearls, a gift she had received upon retiring from Dr. Miller's family after 50 years of service that spanned three generations.

Amidst the sea of congratulatory hugs and best wishes, Lucela felt as if she had finished a long race and won the blue ribbon. She had snagged a man who was not a product of the local community, and she was extremely pleased. Unlike her cousin Ellen, whose husband couldn't hold a job for more than three months, or her friend Alfreda, whose husband drank away each paycheck, Lucela felt fortunate to have chosen a financially stable man. Abe had served his country and now received a monthly pension due to his slight war injury. Lucela anticipated a long life ahead of them that included children and marital bliss.

As he reveled in the celebration that consisted mainly of Lucela's family and friends, Abe felt like a fox that had surveyed a pasture and caught the fattest sheep. Although she was a little older than his previous girlfriends, Lucela had a lot to offer. She lived in her own house (well actually it was Saxie's, but she was already well past 70) was employed, and had squirreled away a nice savings through her frugal lifestyle. In addition, she treated

9

him like a king and seemed to be happy just being in his presence and catering to his every need. He envisioned a long life ahead that included her servitude and eternal devotion.

Lucela's marital bliss was interrupted not long after the rice had been thrown. Her dreams of leaving her job to venture into motherhood ended after Abe received his first pension check and she realized that it was barely enough to cover one utility bill. When she suggested he look for a job to supplement his meager pension, Abe refused, saying he "didn't want to mess up money he was sure he'd have for money he might get for only a little while." Noticing her disapproval, he added that "his leg still bothered him and he didn't think he'd be able to handle standing on it every day." Yet he managed to stand around the pool hall on a regular basis, from sunup to sundown. And she'd heard from Myrtle that his limp didn't prevent him from chasing a few women around. Yeah, that old leg was just fine when Abe wanted it to be. And he wanted it to be on a regular basis.

At first, Abe had only loving touches for her. However, due to her inexperience, she was timid and uncomfortable the first few times, and after a few months Abe appeared bored and disinterested when she reached out to him during the night. He would roll over on his side and sleep with his back facing her, like a stranger. Lucela feared that maybe their love life had fizzled due to her shy behavior, and had lately tried to create a spark between them after a long talk with Myrtle. She rushed home from work each day, bathed and freshened up with fresh perfume, an alluring outfit, jewelry, and even makeup. But when she was greeted each evening with barely a glance and the question, "What you fixin' fo' my dinner?" she knew that her efforts were in vain. Now her blue ribbon felt like a booby prize. The joke was on her.

Although Abe cared for Lucela, he felt like he'd had the wool pulled over his eyes. He'd been fooled into marrying the first girl he'd seen before he'd had a chance to survey his options. And as a new man in town, he soon realized that many options had awaited him. In addition, these options were more exciting and experienced in the ways of physical pleasure. Sure, Ceel was his wife, but he felt like an ornery boy two weeks after Christmas. While she was once a shiny new toy, she now appeared rusted and without luster. She spent her days cooking and cleaning for White folks all day, then came home too tired to cater to him. But Marianne Thompson found time for him. She catered to him with fresh meals (although still not good as Ceel's), hot baths, and warm backrubs: things his wife now had little time for. And if there was one thing Abe lived and longed for, it was a woman's touch---because deep-down he still felt like a helpless, motherless child.

When Lucela hadn't conceived in five years, she became desperate and despondent. She'd tried every home remedy and folk practice imaginable, some more outlandish than others. Old Mother Hines had told her to swallow a spoonful of molasses before bed, advice she took into consideration since Mother Hines was a mother of twelve with forty-five grandchildren. Her cousin Myrtle had told her to stop drinking Coca-Cola, since she

11

often douched with it to prevent pregnancy and knew Ceel wanted to stay fertile. Finally, Old Mama Delacroix, the Creole woman who lived by the river, had given her a dried kitten paw and told her to place it inside the sachet she kept in her underwear drawer. This remedy didn't work either and after a year she threw it out due to the odor it was causing in her bureau.

Lucela's maternal instincts turned inward and caused her to be melancholy and depressed. She no longer took joy in other's children, not because she was hateful, but because it constantly reminded her of what she longed for. During the christening of Sallie Mae's third child, a son, Lucela sobbed uncontrollably as if she were attending a funeral. Little Ruth Anne, now eleven years old, sat next to her and patted her softly with her left hand, while rocking back and forth and quietly sucking the thumb of her right one. Aunt Saxie, now barely mobile and senile, wiped the tears from her milky eyes. She knew the cause of her niece's outburst.

While Lucela became downhearted, Abe became resentful and bitter. Since she was approaching thirty-five he blamed her age and lack of sexual experience for their demise. "Back home, girls start poppin' out babies at thirteen. You done waited too long and all the ripeness done dried up in you. Can't no baby grow in there. I know, 'cause I still got plenty of sap left in me. Even with this bad leg." Although he was wrong, he was right. Abe had dropped a few babies around town, two with Marianne, a set of twin boys, and a girl with seventeen year-old Edna Willis. Out of respect for Lucela, he didn't parade the children around, but he visited with them regularly and tossed their mothers a few dollars

12

every now and then, usually after he'd left their beds. Since he knew the problem wasn't him, the love he had once felt towards Lucela turn into a deep hatred for her. Strangely, this hatred was not due to Lucela's actions or her ways, but due to Abe's hatred toward himself and the unconventional family situation he had once again been forced to accept. He'd married a woman who had supplied his needs, yet could not give him the children he desired. Sadly, Abe realized that this had always been his lot in life, to lack the true family he deeply desired, while having to settle for the "scraps" of kinship that remained.

In a town so small that it had one movie theatre and two grocery stores, word traveled quickly. Lucela knew about the "outside" children Abe had sired before they were even born. She had decided to keep these facts to herself, especially since she had accepted her fate of being barren. Since both women were wild-spirited and loose, their families had not pressed the issue of Abe acknowledging paternity, especially since the twins were Marianne's fourth pregnancy, thus making her a mother of five. Also, neither regularly attended church, so Lucela did not have to face the horror of sitting through another emotionally draining christening that would also cause her some embarrassment. However, one Easter Marianne did decide to drag her brood out to church. Despite her discomfort, Lucela later admitted to Myrtle that she did find it amusing watching Abe sweat profusely each time one of the chocolate-colored identical boys would turn around and stare at him with their inherited "cat eyes." With the exception of Abe's age, the three of them looked like a set of triplets.

"Girl, I was holding that laugh so tight I almost busted open! Abe was sweating like a turkey at Thanksgiving and them two boys was looking at him like he was a clown at the circus!"

Myrtle had to ask. "What did Marianne do?"

Lucela rolled her eyes before responding. "She really didn't do nothing. She tried to look straight ahead and act like he wasn't there. After a while she thumped them boys' heads and told them to turn around. At the end of the service she went to the altar and cried and carried on while one of the Church Mother's prayed with her. Truth is, I thank she was just as embarrassed as me."

CHAPTER THREE

Later that year, before the end of summer, Aunt Saxie finally took to her bed. One afternoon, Lucela received a call at the home of the family she worked for. When Mrs. Lofton, Dr. Miller's daughter, handed her the phone with a shaking hand, she knew it was bad news. 'Ceel, Ceel, you there?" It was Aunt Gladys and she spoke with a quiet, hoarse voice that sounded tightened from crying.

"Yes, ma'am, it's me."

"Lucela, Saxie's asking for you. She keeps saying she been talking to Lottie and she got something to say. You better come quickly."

"Yes, ma'am, I'll be there soon as I can."

Lucela hung up the phone then stood immobile, holding the receiver as well as her breath. She was attempting to contain her emotions and somehow felt that if she exhaled, an unrestrained moan would escape. Mrs. Lofton touched her shoulder. She knew that only an emergency would have prompted Gladys to call the home of her niece's employer. The last time she had heard Gladys' voice shaking with such strong emotion was when she had answered the door of her parent's home as a small child. A teenaged Gladys had absent-mindedly ignored the rules of the day and stood on the Miller's front porch obviously distraught, coming to retrieve Saxie when her husband

Jimmy had been killed in an accident at the lumber mill. She'd watched her mother tearfully comfort Saxie when she collapsed in a grief-stricken paralysis once she learned of the death of her husband. Now it was her turn to comfort Lucela.

"Lucela, come on. I'll drive you home. Auntie Saxie is waiting for you. Pray to Jesus. He will give you strength."

Like a robot, Lucela hung up her apron then retrieved her sweater and purse from the kitchen closet. She followed Mrs. Lofton like an obedient child to her late model Buick.

Once she arrived home, Lucela felt as if she had just awoken from a dream. She peered at the bright blue sky and gawked at the crowd of people that had assembled on the porch. Her eyes scanned the crowd for her husband, but her efforts were in vain. *"Where's Abe?"* she wondered. *"Can't somebody get him from the pool hall? I need him."* Lucela felt her knees buckle as she prepared to take the longest walk of her life. For once, she wished Abe would prove himself to be a decent husband by supporting her both physically and emotionally. Her pain brought her back to reality and she silently cursed, something she almost never did. *"Now. This one time, I need HIM. Why can't I depend on him for once? Damn!"*

Aunt Gladys reached out to take her right hand, while Mrs. Lofton let go of her left one. Lucela opened the screen and heard Saxie's weakened voice. "Ceel, is that you baby? Lottie's told me to tell you something and I gotta go because Jimmy's waiting for me."

"Here I am, Auntie." Lucela sat on the bed and clasped one of Saxie's clammy hands between her two. Her aunt's silver-white hair lay around her face like a curled halo and her breath had the sweet smell of a baby's that had just nursed. To Lucela, she looked as if she were becoming younger. The wrinkles and frown lines on her face had vanished and were replaced with a peaceful countenance that glowed with misty dew.

"Lucela, baby, you know I loves you jus' like you was my own. I done lived long and God has blessed me to see you become a fine young woman. I done tol' yo' momma and she say she pleased. She say she been watchin' you, too."

Lucela began to cry at the faint memory of her sweet and beautiful mother. She struggled to maintain her composure so that she could cherish these final moments with Saxie.

"Ceel, she say she want me to tell you somethin'. She say she see yo' heart is heavy but that God is in charge and you gotta believe that. Sometimes we go through hurts and pains, but he always makes thangs turn out right. Like when she left you. She did it because she had to be with Charles. He was too young to take care of hisself and she knew you'd be safe wit' me. Now she wants you to accept that you ain't gon' be a birth momma, but that don't mean you can't be a momma, like I was for you.

Somebody's child out there need love and God gonna give you the baby you need. Jus' might not be the way you want it."

Lucela bent down to kiss her aunt on the cheek. Saxie reached up with her withered, arthritic hand and removed the hairpin that secured her niece's hair. Lucela's loosened bun cascaded down her back and Saxie stroked her locks as if she were a small child. "Lord, girl, why you hide yo' beauty? You such a pretty girl. Always has been, both inside and out. 'Member I used to tell you, *"pretty is as pretty does."* And that you is. Don't fret yo'self over Abe and let him make you bitter and hateful like he is. Jus' be you and stay sweet. Sweet fruit and bitter fruit can't grow from the same tree. One ends up chokin' out the other. Don't let that happen to you baby. You hear me? Stay sweet and let him find a new tree to suck the life out of, even if it means you gotta be by yo'self. At least you'll still be sweet."

Lucela lay on Saxie's sagging bosom and cried uncontrollably. Her aunt's last words had been the salve she needed to mend her broken heart. In those few moments, Saxie's wisdom had given her a new outlook on life, as well as a new attitude towards Abe.

That Saturday, Saxie was laid in her final resting place in the church cemetery plot beside her late husband, Jimmy. Sallie Mae provided a moving rendition of "I'll Fly Away" as the funeral attendants marched behind the hearse that the Miller family had provided as it processed down Main Street. Lucela walked silently, with Abe holding her hand while the odor of sour whiskey seeped from his sweaty pores. Cousin Ruth Anne held her other hand, and solemnly refrained from sucking her thumb the entire day. Aunt Gladys, the last living amongst her siblings, swayed and moaned while Myrtle attempted to restrain her.

After the service, more than a hundred close and distant relatives, friends, acquaintances, and onlookers descended upon Saxie's home. As the dusk of the evening loomed, the crowd drizzled to a few close family members and nosey stragglers. By this time, Abe, who had been sipping all day, had reached a state of drunkenness and began to act so. After calling Myrtle a "used-up whore" he turned towards Lucela. Before he could open his mouth to offer an insult, she opened hers.

"Abraham Lincoln Jessup, I ain't in the mood for your foolishness today. If you plan on opening yo' mouth to say anything ignorant, I suggest you leave this house and go traipsing about in yo' usual whereabouts, where that mess is allowed."

Abe, who had never heard Lucela speak to him in this manner, tried to save face in front of his guests. However, his inebriation caused him to overplay his hand and resulted in Lucela calling his bluff. "What you talkin' bout woman? This here my house. I say what I want, to who I want, and when I want. Don't get sassy wit' me 'cause we got comp'ny. You might get slapped!"

Myrtle stepped in front of Lucela and her oldest son, Clarence, a 6' 4" fourteen year-old, stood beside her. "Cousin Ceel ..." he began, but Lucela had had enough.

19

"What you say? You lowdown, evil, dirty snake! Yo' house? Yo' house! This here ain't yours. Matter fact, ain't nothin' here yours, not even the food you just ate. Now I tolerate a lot of foolishness outta you, Abe, but I done had enough! Of all days, when I just buried my auntie and you done got the fool idea to threaten me in front of my family? I tell you what, if you put yo' damn hands on me, it'll be the last time you put 'em anywhere. And if you feels like you wanna be slappin' somebody aroun' I suggest you go do yo' slappin' where you usually do: out there wit' them whores you run' round wit!"

Clarence stepped in front of Lucela, his bulky frame casting a giant shadow over Abe's small stature. Myrtle wrapped her arms around Lucela, who was sobbing on her shoulder. Myrtle's other son and two daughters stood behind Clarence, in a formation that suggested they were ready for battle.

Abe staggered away from the table; he knew he was outnumbered. Even in a drunken stupor he could see that it wouldn't be a good idea to start a fight with Lucela in front of her family. Especially with Myrtle's two athletic, towering sons present. He crookedly walked out the back screen door and slammed it behind him authoritatively. Then he sat on the back steps and leaned against the post, positioning himself for the night. He'd slept on these porch steps before, even in the rain.

Lucela tearfully retreated to her bedroom. Myrtle and her two younger daughters cleared away the table and washed the few dishes in the sink. Lucela lay on top of her covers, praying silently to God for strength while asking his forgiveness for cursing. Abe wasn't worth not getting into heaven, even if it felt good to act like a sinner for once and put "the fear of God" in him.

During the next few weeks, things in the Jessup household were tense, but quiet. Both enemies had decided to postpone their duel, but they still had their guards up. With the exception of physical intimacy, Lucela continued with her marital duties, but they were performed with indifference. The home remained spotless, bills were paid, and Abe's dinner was always left warming on the stove, awaiting his irregular arrival home. However, Abe noticed that she was rarely available to refill his glass or heap a second serving on his plate, and now dessert was only provided on Sundays. On one occasion, Abe realized that his fried chicken was burned, and no cornbread was provided for his collard greens. In their seven years of marriage, this had never occurred. Lucela was no longer his devoted servant; she was developing a backbone and becoming defiant. This frightened him.

After one week, Lucela returned to work in the Lofton household, among a family that shared her grief. Saxie had practically raised Mrs. Lofton, as well as her father and grandfather. She had chastised the children, counseled them during their "first loves" and consoled them during the loss of their loved ones, including Mrs. Lofton's grandfather, Harold Miller. Although she was "hired help", Saxie was considered a part of the family, and rightfully so since she was a constant, loving presence in their homes. Saxie never missed a birthday, even

21

when the Miller children had approached adulthood. She would often stop by, even in her later years, holding a birthday cake in one hand and her cane in the other. Mrs. Lofton smiled to herself as she recalled the memory of Saxie delivering a cake during the first year of her marriage and her new husband trying to disguise it as one he had purchased for her to cover up the fact that he had forgotten. (As if she wouldn't recognize the confections baked by a woman whose food she had eaten her entire life.) Yes, Auntie Saxie was one of a kind. At that moment Kay Lofton realized why she cared for Lucela so much; she reminded her of Saxie.

CHAPTER FOUR

After about six weeks, Saxie's insurance check arrived. Since her home had been paid for with her late husband's insurance policy, and Saxie did not believe in debt, the entire proceeds were given to Lucela without any restrictions. In addition, Lucela had been listed as the beneficiary on Saxie's savings accounts and was privy to her various stashes of "money pots" that were planted in her garden. Aunt Saxie had left explicit instructions regarding the donations she wished to provide to the church and various family members. Each child in the family, all ten of them who ranged in age from 3- 16, was to be given $1000 on the day they left for college. If they did not choose to continue their studies after high school, Lucela was to give their scholarship to another child that attended Mt. Nebo who was leaving for college that year. In addition, the building fund was to receive $2,000 and Rev. Burnett and his family was to be given a $1,000 "love offering."

During the years, Saxie had accumulated a large savings. She lived a frugal lifestyle, and saved every generous Christmas bonus and monetary gift provided to her during her 50 year tenure with the Miller's. In addition, she supplemented her income by selling pastries and cakes to one of the local restaurants, The Mint Julep, and saved all of these additional earnings. Finally, Saxie had two fully paid life insurance policies that totaled $50,000, one of which had been paid for by Dr. Miller. This was considered a small fortune during the 1960's.

These values had been passed on to Lucela, who also maintained the practice of saving bonuses, maintaining insurance, and supplementing her income with the proceeds she received from The Mint Julep, once she took over when Saxie decided to retire. As she approached the age of 40, Lucela had already acquired a nest egg of almost $20,000. With the addition of her inheritance, this nest egg had grown to a large, golden goose egg that totaled more than $75, 000. Of course, Lucela had taken her aunt's last words to heart and had decided it would be in her best interest to keep the news of her recent inheritance to herself. However, there are no secrets in a small town and gossip always travels much faster than gospel. Within a week, someone at the pool hall who had a relative that worked for the president of the bank asked Abe about his small fortune. However, since it was secondhand news, the facts were incorrect. Luckily, the informant had only been privy to one of Lucela's accounts; otherwise Abe would have likely died from shock. When he was questioned about the funds, Abe immediately sobered up and angrily replied that he had no knowledge of such. While he figured that Lucela stashed away a few pennies for a rainy day, he was not aware that she had amassed a sum of the magnitude his friend described. Marianne, who had been sitting nearby, listened intently. *Twenty-thousand dollars!* That was enough money for her and Abe to buy their own home and a new car! She was sick of the cramped two-room shack she and her children occupied and felt that now was her chance to convince Abe to finally leave his wife and steal her fortune.

Women like Lucela sickened Marianne. They'd never had to suffer at all and always acted as if they were too good to enjoy life. Lucela had grown up in a nice home with enough food and a family that cared about her. Marianne had grown up in a shack just like the one she currently resided in, with her ten brothers and sisters and a single mother who loved alcohol and men more than any of her children. At the age of twelve, Marianne had become pregnant with her first child by one of her mother's boyfriends. When her mother realized who was responsible for the birth of her grandchild, she kicked thirteen year-old Marianne out into the streets in a fit of jealousy with no regard for the survival of her child or the impending birth of her grandchild.

With no place to go, Marianne ran straight to her 30 year-old lover's arms. He put her up for a few months, until his wife caught wind of this new baby and showed up outside Marianne's door with his two teenage daughters. Both of them beat her until she was bloody and swollen, while the wife held her tiny baby as she cooed and burped, indifferent to the situation. Finally, the three of them left, with the promise to return in three days for Round Two. Marianne had no choice but to leave again, this time escaping to the home of Curtis, an older man in the neighborhood, who required her to pay for her keep by sleeping in his bed. Pretty soon, she saw the signs of pregnancy once again and by the next summer gave birth to her second child, a boy she named after his father. Before she had reached the age of eighteen, Marianne was a mother of three children by three different fathers, a regular drinker, and a lover of men--whether they were single or married. Although she didn't realize it, she had already turned into her mother.

Later that evening, as she and Abe lay in her bed, Marianne put her plan into action. "Abe, I know Ceel's auntie just died. I know she left her that big house, but did she also leave some insurance? I'm just askin' cause the boys is growing so fast I can't keep 'em in pants and shoes. Plus, they gettin' to that age when they need they Daddy 'round all the time. I don't want 'em to turn out like Curtis Junior and end up in jail. You promised me you'd leave Ceel and make us a real family. Why don't you do it now while y'all got the money?"

Abe jolted up as if he'd been struck by a lightning bolt. Suddenly he realized that his mistress was no longer a comfort to him, and was beginning to nag him more than his wife. "Woman, why you in my bizness? And what make you think that my money? Ceel's auntie left that to her, not me."

"Well, since y'all married, it is yours. Plus, you know if you her husband you got jus' as much right to go get it out the bank as she do. And ain't nothing she can do 'bout it but cry," Marianne chuckled to herself. She felt a warm feeling inside as she imagined how her life would change once she and Abe became rich. Twenty-thousand dollars would be more than enough to purchase a home, a car, and have money left over! Marianne imagined herself like the rich White women on television, wearing furs and diamonds while she rode in a luxury automobile. People often said she looked like Diahann Carroll, and she imagined how glamorous she'd be wearing expensive gowns and frequenting Hollywood bars and nightclubs and rubbing elbows with the Black elite like she'd seen Carroll doing in "Look" magazine. Her mind wandered off into a dreamy fog, the same one she usually escaped to with the assistance of alcohol in order to avoid her squalid, dissipated existence.

Abe immediately sobered up and his flaming libido flickered out; he decided to leave much earlier than usual. He didn't ever plan on marrying Marianne; she wasn't wife material. She already been ran through and had a house full of children when he met her. Everyone knew that any woman who would sleep with a married man wouldn't be a faithful wife. Plus, Marianne was a drinking woman who kept a nasty house. He'd never live with her. He could barely tolerate her living quarters in the disguise of night, and habitually retreated before daylight. Marianne assumed that he made his early departure out of respect for Lucela, but Abe's real motive was egotistical, not honorable. Abe left during the darkness in order to avoid the veracity of his suspicions regarding the level of slovenliness Marianne regularly subjected herself to.

Once, during their early weeks of their "relationship" Abe was walking home when he felt a scratchy sensation under his hat. After a few steps, he removed his hat to investigate and discovered not one, but THREE cockroaches roaming about on his scalp! Luckily it was so early in the morning that no one was present to observe him, otherwise they might have thought he was a crazed man when they saw him swearing and slapping at his scalp as if it were on fire.

Although Lucela was not as physically desirable to him, Abe prided himself on her level of cleanliness and decorum. Their home was free from any rodents or vermin, and he knew this was due to her exhaustive efforts to maintain a sterile environment. Lucela may have been a respected housekeeper, but her employers would have been amazed to know that she maintained an even higher standard of cleanliness for her own home, even though it was located in a much less affluent area of town. Relocating roaches and vermin to their house would have been easily detectable and a dead giveaway of Abe's philandering. Therefore, he took additional measures to protect himself. Lucela also had additional qualities that made her respectable "wife material"; something Marianne would never be. Besides being a meticulous housekeeper, she was obviously a virgin when he married her, a faithful churchgoer, and an excellent cook.

Anyway, Abe didn't plan on stealing Ceel's money so he could give it to a loose woman like Marianne; he was too self-centered for that. He planned to buy himself something he'd always wanted: a brand new car. He quickened his step in the stillness of the exhausted Saturday night, his mind having formulated a plan of action. If Ceel had any money to spare, it would be spent on him and him alone!

Early Sunday morning, Abe rolled over and kissed Lucela before she rose to fix her coffee before going to church. She

28

opened her eyes, startled. "Hey woman, why you lookin' surprised like 'dat? Who you 'spect to be kissin' you, Harry Belafonte?" Abe laughed and kissed her again, before she could respond.

Lucela felt Abe's lips passionately surround hers, preventing her from speaking. She wanted to scream, *"I'm surprised 'cause you usually ain't home before I go to church, let alone tryin' to kiss me!"* But she held her thoughts and pondered on what would cause Abe to suddenly become such a loving husband. Her mind warned her that he had probably caught wind of her fortune; but her heart fluttered with the anticipation that he had finally decided to change his ways. After a session of passionate lovemaking, Lucela's heart won the battle. She believed that her prayers had finally been answered, especially when Abe asked her if she'd fix him some breakfast before they left for church, something he only did to attend funerals and Easter service.

Once she arrived at service much later than usual, but with Abe beside her, Lucela received an understanding nod from Aunt Gladys and her entourage from the Mother's Board. Each woman thanked God, believing that their prayers had finally been answered regarding Lucela's unstable marriage. During the service, Abe appeared to listen intently to Rev. Burnett, even saying "Amen!" once or twice. During his sermon, the minister spoke of David, and how God had forgiven him for his many transgressions, even when he slept with another man's wife. At the closing of the sermon, Rev. Burnett made his usual appeal to the sinners present who wanted to come forth and change their ways. Lucela almost fainted when she saw her husband walk towards the altar, fall contritely to his knees, and beg God for forgiveness. Finally, her prayers had been answered! Her husband was a changed man! Lucela tried to remain composed, but her emotions were out of control. A strong current of tears flowed down her cheeks as she screamed out, "Hallelujiah!" while the ushers of the church fanned her while they attempted to restrain her in her seat.

Later that evening, after a hearty Sunday dinner and three slices of coconut cake, Abe sat contently on the front porch with Lucela. They each rocked back and forth, talked of the news, goings on in the town, and current events. When darkness fell and the fireflies began to light up the night, Lucela braced herself for Abe's departure to his usual hangout. However, he surprised her by asking, "Ceel, can you fix me another slice of cake and some fresh coffee? I wanna settle my stomach before I go to bed." Lucela jumped up so quickly to oblige him that her rocking chair almost toppled over. Abe's request inferred that he had no intentions of venturing out into the night! When he heard the abrupt "clap" of the screen door slamming behind his bustling wife, Abe smiled contentedly to himself. The old Lucela was back.

When she heard that Abe had joined the church, Marianne thought it was a joke. But when she hadn't felt his presence in her bed in over two months, she knew something was wrong. She'd been hanging on to Abe for almost ten years, even beating out Edna Willis (who finally gave up and moved up North with a serviceman). Now that Abe finally had something to offer, she wasn't about to let him go. She had held out this long, she deserved what was rightfully hers. Besides, she had given Abe something his wife couldn't---children.

CHAPTER FIVE

After about three months, Abe figured the time had come to put his plan into action. He began dropping subtle hints to Lucela about his desire to purchase a car. When they would struggle with sacks of groceries, he would point out the benefits of transportation, but Lucela would laugh and tell him that they wouldn't have so many groceries if he didn't eat as much. However, Abe was persistent. When Lucela would complain about her aching feet after walking home from work, Abe would gently rub them and tell her she was getting too old to be walking on feet she had stood on all day while pointing to newspaper advertisements of cars that would remedy their problem. Once, when they walked to church on windy Sunday, he told her how it was a shame that a woman "dressed as fine as she, had to worry about her hat flying off" before she got to church. Lucela, with her hands clasped tightly over her crown, had to agree with him. A car would have been useful on such a blustery day. Plus, the constant admonishments coupled with compliments had begun to soften her heart. Finally, when Lucela entered the house coughing and soaking wet after walking home during a storm, Abe met her at the door with a towel and told her, "You better stay out that rain, Ceel. Sugar melts." Those sweet words were the straw that broke the camel's back.

Lucela smiled brightly and told him, "Okay Abe. Tomorrow, I want you to go down to that lot and pick us out a car."

The next day, Abe walked Lucela to work then marched proudly down to Foster's Fine Cars. The salesmen peered over their newspapers, saw Abe awaiting service, then returned to their cigarettes and coffee. *"No sense in getting tied up with a nigger who probably didn't have $200 to spend. I'll wait on a **real** customer,"* they thought to themselves. Abe cleared his throat, attempting to draw attention. Finally, a new salesman, inexperienced in reading customers, and too young to be prejudiced when it concerned money, walked up to him and extended his hand. "How ya' doin, sir? I'm Ralph Lovett and I'd be glad to help you."

Abe, finally glad to be receiving the attention he had waited a lifetime for, cleared his throat again and responded, "I'm Abraham Lincoln Jessup. I'd like to buy a car."

When Mr. Lovett began directing him towards the used portion of the car lot, Abe stopped abruptly and stated, "Mr. Lovett, I'd like to purchase a NEW car. Like this." And he pulled a worn, crumpled picture from his pocket, one that he'd been carrying in his wallet for about six months. Although the edges were frayed and the sale price was no longer offered, the salesman could still make out the model: a Buick Electra 225, also known as a "Deuce and a Quarter." Mr. Lovett became excited— his first new car sale! Then he decided to calm himself, until he was sure this customer was serious. "Well, Mr. Jessup, we have only two of that model on the lot. Since it is a little more expensive, we usually order those directly from the factory. Let's take a look and you can see if you like them, otherwise we have some less expensive new cars I can show you.....”

"No sir, I don't need to look at anything else. That's what I want. I'd like a green one, with black on the inside. And I'd like some of them fancy electric windows, you know, that move with the button instead of having to turn 'em."

Lovett was calculating the numbers in his head. "Oh, you mean power windows. Sure."

Abe continued with his speech. He'd rehearsed it a hundred times, in the mirror each morning during his daily shave. He knew he was forgetting something, and cursed himself for acting so nervous just because he was talking to a White man. He regained his composure, "Oh, yeah. And air conditioning. Wife gotta have air conditioning." Abe chuckled at his punchline, and Lovett joined him.

"Sure, Mr. Jessup. Now you know, the options you're asking for will increase the purchase price. In addition, the model you want is not available on the lot at this time. It will have to be ordered. Our policy at Foster's is that a car cannot be ordered until it has been paid for. We don't want to run the risk of a customer making a request, then changing their mind and leaving us with a car we can't sell. You understand."

"Sure," Abe replied.

"Oh boy, he's still not getting the hint. Let me just come out and ask the question," Lovett thought to himself. "Mr. Jessup, the car you're asking for will cost a few thousand dollars, which must be paid in full before I can make the order. Are you prepared to purchase it today?"

Abe cleared his throat and clearly recited the last line of his oft rehearsed speech. "Yessir, I can pay for the car in full. I just need a few minutes to go withdraw the money from my bank. It's only a few blocks away. I got it all saved up, won't be no waiting for a loan." Abe beamed proudly in response to the salesman's surprised expression. Lucela had given him permission to withdraw whatever he needed from her savings account, and she had assured him that there was enough there to purchase any car up to $8,000.

Mr. Lovett recovered his composure and smiled broadly before extending his hand once again. "Well, Mr. Jessup. Let's step into the office and complete this sale."

Three days later, Abe parked in the Lofton's driveway and waited for Lucela to emerge from the back entrance. He was wearing his "Sunday best", and had rode through town with the windows down, even though it was 80 degrees and he had air conditioning. He worried that people might not recognize him if the windows were up; plus he wanted to be free to wave at people as he drove through the town.

Lucela was surprised by his presence and flattered when he jumped out and opened the passenger door for her. "Abe, this sure is beautiful. Why, your car looks better than Mr. and Mrs. Lofton's cars!" Abe laughed and proudly pulled out of the driveway. Lucela continued, "What's all these buttons for? And where the handles to roll up the windows?"

"These them new electronic windows. They don't need no handles. And look, this button here for air conditioning. We can use it when it's real hot outside. A pretty girl like you shouldn't sweat, Ceel." Lucela blushed and beamed with pride. Finally, Abe was happy. Therefore, she was happy.

Later that evening, after a dinner of hamburgers and shakes (Abe didn't want to get out of the car so they ate at a drive-in), Abe asked his wife if she'd mind if he went for a late night ride over to the pool hall, to show the car to his Cousin James. Of course she didn't mind, and he quickly took her home to retire for the evening.

After dropping Lucela off, Abe proudly ventured over to the pool hall. The sun was setting and he moved quickly. He wanted to be sure that enough sunlight remained so that he could still garner attention. Once he pulled into the lot, his cronies that sat and stood lazily on the stoops of the establishment perked up, eagerly trying to determine who was driving such a flashy vehicle in their small town. Abe parked the car, and proudly stepped out. Once his friends recognized him, they swooped down on his car like vultures.

"Man, what you got here?"

"Abe, man, this is one baaaad car!"

"Crip, you the man! You the man! Gimme five, brother!"

Every knob in the vehicle was touched, every electric window was rolled up and down at least three times, and each seat was sat in. The radio was tuned in to five separate stations, all full blast, with Cousin James finally stopping on a fast James Brown song that had a loud bass line. Smitty, the leader of the group and the local hustler, slapped him on the back and told him, "Crip, man, you got a good woman. Better not lose her man, she's got real class."

Suddenly, the party ended as if the record had been scratched. Abe's ego was bruised and he felt insulted. Any other time, he would have let Smitty's comment slide. He was always making snide remarks that were insults disguised as compliments. But today, Abe was feeling himself and had the courage to speak up. "Man, what you mean? What my wife got to do with this? This my car!"

Smitty looked at Abe and let his eyes wander up and down, as if he were sizing up his shortcomings. Then he sucked his teeth in disgust before explaining his remark. "Aw, man. Everybody know yo' wife done come into some money. I been knowing you over ten years and you always been broke. You spend most yo' money on wine and women, and gamble away what's left. Now where you gon' get enough money to buy a car like this? You ain't even got no job!"

Abe's cronies laughed uproariously, the humor of Smitty's comments ignited by their jealousy. Even James cracked a smile. Many of them worked twelve hour days and went home to nagging wives, undisciplined children, and small hovels they considered as residences. For years, they'd watched Abe meander around town, without a care in the world while living off his meager military pension and residing in a nice home. None of the men could understand why he preferred to lay up and make babies with loose women around town, like Marianne, instead of cherishing a clean, subservient, churchgoing, and hardworking wife like Lucela. If she had ever taken the notion to drop Abe, at least three of his friends had secretly decided they would be on her doorstep the next morning. Each one of the maturing men realized that women like Lucela were now valuable, even though many of them had looked past her in their youth because they had been intrigued by women who appeared to be more exciting and sexually inviting at the time: two traits that faded quickly once they were married. As they approached middle age, these men realized that a comfortable home and a good companion were more important to a productive life than a sensual bedroom partner. Smitty silently cursed himself for letting Lucela get away, having been fooled by his wife Bertha's shapely figure and big, apple-shaped bottom---a bottom that now looked like an oversized watermelon and a shape that ballooned to twice its size during the first three years of their twenty year marriage. Now, every time Smitty looked at Abe he felt a renewed sense of jealously and resentment that he couldn't conceal.

Abe felt his face flush with anger. His fingers trembled and he suddenly longed for a drink, something he hadn't tasted in more than six months. Abe's insecurities began to cloud his mind. *"Goddamn Smitty! Always got something to say, just cause he's jealous!"* Suddenly, Abe felt ashamed of his new vehicle because he realized that it didn't really represent him, but diminished his manhood because it actually represented Lucela. At that moment, the hatred and resentment Abe used to feel for his wife returned with a vengeance. The venom from his anger dried his throat and he longed for his old remedy—alcohol. He walked over to the bar and smiled at the woman wiping the counter. "Bessie, get me a drink, the usual. And keep the change." Abe playfully swatted her on her ample backside and held out his payment. She snatched the five dollar bill away from Abe and waddled away with a giggle, covering her toothless smile with her hand. She was glad to see Abe returning to his usual hangout. He was a regular tipper and a good conversationalist who often entertained her with exciting stories of his exploits in other countries during the war. In addition, he had sometimes served as a part-time lover when he became too drunk to stumble home and had to share her bed in the back room of the bar.

Once Abe's drink was placed on the counter, Marianne sauntered over and sat on the stool beside him. She'd been hanging around the bar for most of the day, and was already tipsy. Abe signaled for the bartender again. "Bessie, fix Marianne a drink." The mother of his children stroked his arm lightly and smiled.

Marianne moved her hand from Abe's arm to his thigh. She beamed brightly with excitement at his return. "Hey, Abe. I see you been takin' care of business. Glad to see you back. I sure been missin' you. You gonna take me for a ride in yo' new car?"

CHAPTER SIX

When Abe crept into their bed around five in the morning, Lucela rolled over to greet him and smelled the familiar scent of liquor on his breath. Before she could kiss him, he rolled over and turned his back to her. At that moment, Lucela knew things had changed.

The next morning, Lucela walked to work. She had expected Abe to drive her, but since he had only been home about an hour she decided not to wake him. Her heart was troubled, but she hummed a spiritual to herself as she completed her duties and it appeased her soul. Her day moved quickly and before she had a chance to take a break she realized that it was already time to fix the Lofton children dinner.

Mrs. Lofton and her husband had three children: Bobby, who was sixteen; Susan, who was fourteen (and already boy crazy!); and little Timmy, who was eight. Now that Bobby and Susan were teenagers, Lucela had become used to their mood swings and self-centered attitudes. While she had once been their "second mother", now they hardly regarded her, and often took the liberty of ordering her around when their friends were present. However, little Timmy remained her favorite.

Timmy had always been a sickly child (Aunt Saxie had said it was because Mrs. Lofton had birthed him when she was past her prime) and therefore needed a lot of care and attention on a regular basis. Being the baby of the family, he was expected to be

41

bratty and spoiled. However, nothing could be farther from the truth. Timmy was a thoughtful, shy, and inquisitive little boy. He had clear, bright blue eyes and thick, blond, curly hair that any girl would envy. When he was a toddler, he was often mistaken for a female because of these soft features and his quiet disposition.

Due to his various ailments, Timmy often spent time isolated in his room. As a result, he adjusted to entertaining himself alone and developed interests that could be solitarily enjoyed. Timmy collected butterflies, insects, stamps, coins, and books. He rarely played sports, and had few friends his age. In fact, his closest companions were Lucela and his mother, in that order. Timmy hated when his mass of curls would fall over his eyes and prevent him from seeing clearly as he pored over the many books in his room or closely examined his coin and stamp collections. He would beg Lucela to trim his hair every four weeks, and she would often joke with him that he should sell his beautiful locks to a wigmaker, for they would be sure to fetch top dollar.

Since he was not athletic, Timmy's father rarely interacted with him, and even appeared to dislike him. Mr. Lofton often admonished his wife for making his son "soft" and reserved his parental affections for Bobby and Susan. Susan, being the only girl in the family, basked in this attention and used her status to get anything she wanted; Bobby, being the oldest in the family, actually resented the pressure to achieve and used sports as a refuge to get away from the family. He had hopes of attending college as far away as possible, vowing never to return once he had completed his degree. Although her family could afford to send her to any college she pleased, Susan only aspired to be the wife of George Sampson, the mayor's son, because they were the richest family in town. She barely passed her classes and instead focused obsessively on her appearance, since she felt that would be more important to her future. Every week, Susan was undertaking a new diet, even though she was barely a size four. Susan would consistently make demands about her food to Lucela in her attempts to adhere to her various diet plans, some more outrageous than others, such as the one that had caused her skin to turn orange when she'd decided to eat only carrots for 30 days.

Tonight, Lucela had fixed fried chicken, mashed potatoes, and creamed corn, one of Mr. Lofton's favorite meals. Once the food was placed on the table, Susan began to complain. 'Lucela! You don't remember me telling you not to fix me any fried food? I no longer eat fried foods!"

Lucela, who had been humming to herself, attempted to respond. However, Timmy spoke for her. "Susan, wait a minute!"

"Oh, shut up, you! You're always taking up for her. The both of you make me sick! All that grease breaks my face out and plus, it's fattening! I can't believe you---." Before she could continue, Lucela placed her plate in front of her. Susan had her own serving of baked chicken and a small salad. Suddenly, she felt bad for her outburst. "Oh, wow, Lucela. I'm sorry, I really am. I didn't ask for a salad. How'd you know?"

Lucela turned to her with an admonishing look before giving her a smile. "Last night you said you wanted to eat more salad. Thought it would be better for you. Timmy reminded me that you were no longer eating fried foods when we went to the market today. "

Susan whispered an apology to Timmy. He nodded back an acceptance.

After the two eldest children finished eating and left the table, Timmy began his usual routine of sharing his day with Lucela since he finally had her all to himself. "Lucela, guess what? In class today, we talked about the process of a caterpillar turning into a butterfly. I knew so much about it, that Miss Sims asked me to come up to the front of the class and explain it. It's called metamorphosis and it lasts about a month. Did you know that?"

"No, Sugar, I didn't. You such a smart boy. You read that in one of your books?"

"Yes'm. I did. Plus I knew it because I saw it happen. Remember when I kept that caterpillar in that big jar last year?"

Lucela really didn't, since the boy kept numerous jars of animals and insects on a regular basis. However, she gave an affirmative nod to appease him. "Yes, Sugar. I do."

Timmy slyly tried to change the subject to what he really wanted to focus on. "Lucela, you know what tomorrow is?"

"Hmmm. . . . lemme see. I think it's a special day for a special boy. "

"That's right! And do you know what kind of cake that special boy wants for his birthday?"

"Let me guess, coconut?"

"That's right, because it's his favorite. And do you remember what that special boy wants for his birthday?"

"I think he wants a microscope set. And I think it's on sale at Pelletier's. In fact, I think this special boy showed it to me last Saturday when he and I were in the store. But I think this special boy should remember to eat all his corn and drink all his milk so that he'll be ready for his big day tomorrow. Otherwise, he might not have enough energy to eat any coconut cake or play with his microscope." Lucela walked over to Timmy and tickled him until he giggled.

"Okay, Lucela. I promise to eat all my corn. But can you sprinkle a little more sugar on it for me? It's not sweet enough."

"Sure, baby." Lucela sprinkled a teaspoon of sugar on Timmy's corn. She knew he had a sweet tooth, but didn't mind. She figured that it might fatten him up and help him develop into a strong young man like his brother. "There, baby. Now hurry up. I gotta get home so I can make somebody a birthday cake." She tousled Timmy's blond curls.

He looked up at her and smiled. "Yes'm."

When Lucela arrived home, she noticed the car in the driveway. She had hoped that Abe would be gone, since she was tired and didn't want to fix a full meal. She had planned to warm up some leftover roast beef and make Abe a sandwich. She had already eaten at the Lofton's and wasn't hungry. Plus, she had to complete the task of making Timmy's birthday cake. Three-layer coconut cakes took longer than sheet cakes, and the snow-white frosting required concentration to complete.

Lucela made it a point to fix the children's birthday cakes at her home and arrive with them in the morning. Since they were a "gift" from her, she made them in her own kitchen, where she kept her assortment of special ingredients and felt more comfortable creating her masterpieces. Plus, she didn't want the baking to distract her from her daily duties in the Lofton home. The children always seemed to appreciate these gestures of kindness, since they provided evidence that Lucela genuinely cared for them and did not display her maternal instincts towards them simply due to her job. Also, using her own kitchen instead of the Lofton's kept anyone from questioning whether she was neglecting her work duties.

Since the age of two, each Lofton child had been bestowed with this honor. Lucela laughed to herself when she recalled how diet conscious Susan had eaten a piece of her chocolate birthday cake before leaving for school, then cowered in embarrassment when her father asked her why one piece was missing as she'd prepared to blow her candles out later that evening. She also fondly recalled how Bobby had screamed with delight at the age of six when she'd created a football shaped cake for him. It had taken three tries to get the aluminum pan bent perfectly so that it resembled a football. Myrtle's hearty boys had gladly eaten the first two, laughing at how one looked like a basketball and the other a submarine.

Abe entered the kitchen, interrupting her thoughts. Lucela smelled liquor and knew immediately that he wasn't in a good mood. "Hey, woman. What's for dinner? I ain't ate nothing all day."

Lucela noticed that her usual greeting of a kiss was not provided. "Well, Abe, I was planning on fixing you a sandwich and fries. Give me just a second and—"

"A sandwich? I ain't eatin' no sandwich. I gave up sandwiches when I left the Army. I got a wife, so I oughta be eatin' a hot meal. You been cookin' for them White folks all day, you can't cook for me?"

Lucela sighed then decided to soften her response to avoid an argument. "Abe, I'm tired. It's Little Timmy's birthday tomorrow and I still gotta make his cake. You can eat a sandwich tonight, and tomorrow I'll fix you a nice steak. Okay?"

"Well, it better not be cold. I ain't eatin' no cold food. I got enough of that from Uncle Sam."

"You been out the Army for almost 20 years, and I still gotta hear 'bout it every chance you get," Lucela thought to herself. "Okay, Abe. I'll fix your plate now."

After eating, Abe sat in front of the television, drinking beer. Lucela prepared Timmy's birthday cake and placed it under the cover. Abe turned around when she turned the light out in the kitchen. "You didn't make me no cake?"

"No, Abe. I just made you a cake Sunday. I gotta take this to Timmy tomorrow for his birthday. He's gonna be nine!" Her mind drifted off into a whirlwind of fond memories. "My goodness, I remember when he was born. My baby is growing up---"

Abe turned toward her with a look of disbelief. "Yo baby? That ain't none of yo' baby, Ceel! Hell, you ain't even got no babies! You always messin' over them White children like they yo' own. Them kids gon' grow up and treat you like they don' even know you. You gon' come to visit 'em and they gon' make you go to the back door!" Abe slapped his thigh and laughed at his joke in an evil, contemptuous tone.

Lucela dropped her head in shame. She knew that she was motherless, but hated how her husband always pointed out the fact. "Abe, you ain't gotta carry on like that. Timmy is a sweet little boy. Anyway, he asked me to make him a coconut cake and I'm gonna give him one."

Abe jumped from his seat and began to stomp on the floor with his "good" foot. He looked somewhat comical, like a peg-legged pirate. "Coconut cake! Hell, naw! You ain't fixin' to take no coconut cake outta here! Any coconut cake made in my house is gonna be made for me. I'm the man of this house!"

Lucela tried to calm her husband by making light of the situation. "Abe, don't be ridiculous, stompin' 'round here and makin' a whole heap of racket. You ain't the only person in the world who eats coconut cake. Besides, I just made you a coconut cake on Sunday. I figured you'd have had your fill of it for this week."

Abe knew she was right, and truthfully he had just eaten the last piece from Sunday's cake on yesterday. Basically, he was just fighting this battle because he felt that it was another assault on his diminishing manhood. "Woman, I been eatin' yo coconut cake since the day I met you and I ain't had my fill yet. Ain't no man, White or Black, eatin' nothin' that my wife done cooked in my house and took outta here to him. You hear me?"

Lucela laughed at Abe's childishness. "Abe, I ain't cookin' for no man. Just a little boy who wants a birthday cake. Truthfully, I'm glad he's even lived to see this many birthdays; he's been sick all his life. Now, this here cake ain't nothin' for us to argue about. You bein' silly. I'm tired and I'm goin' to bed." She turned out the kitchen light and quietly walked to her bedroom. The matter had been settled. Or so she thought.

The next morning, Lucela gathered her things and prepared to walk to work. Abe, who had finished drinking the rest of his six-pack of beer after she had went to bed, was snoring loudly from the bedroom. Lucela picked up the cake dome and stepped towards the door. However, as she peered through the cover, something caught her eye. There were two large slices missing from Timmy's cake.

Lucela was so overcome with anger that she felt like she was about to lose control, something that she rarely did. *"How could he be so mean?"* Little Timmy deserved his own birthday cake and a chance to feel special and important on this one day of the year. Lucela knew that he would be disappointed when he saw the cake she had prepared, and he was too young to understand what went wrong.

Lucela placed the cake on the table then threw her hands up in vexation. A prayerful moan welled up in her body and escaped from her lips. "Lord, give me strength. Jesus, GIVE ME STRENGTH!" A few frustrated tears sputtered from her eyelids as she rocked and swayed in an attempt to calm herself.

Immediately, Lucela felt an intense desire to seek revenge against the culprit of this crime. *"That low-down devil! I'm gonna teach him to mess with me!"* Lucela went to the closet and retrieved a pail. She filled it with water and marched back to the bedroom. Abe was snoring loudly, his bottom hunched up like a sleeping infant. *Swoosh!* The current of water doused Abe and caused him to jump up in terror.

50

"What the---?" Lucela stood over Abe, holding the metal container like it was a weapon she was about to throw at his head.

"Woman, are you crazy?"

"Naw, but you are, and I done had enough. " Lucela's voice began to crack with emotion as she struggled to continue her tirade. "It's bad enough that you always got to be so evil to me, Abe, but you got to be cruel to a little boy? A sick little boy at that, that we thought wouldn't even live to see a fifth birthday, let alone his ninth one. All that baby wanted was his own coconut cake. He been talkin' bout it for over two weeks and I planned to make his wish come true this morning. But you ruined it! Like you always ruin everything! I've had enough of your evil ways, Abraham Lincoln Jessup! And so help me, God-----" Lucela became so overcome with emotion that she held her hands up in a plea towards Heaven as a river of tears flowed down her dimpled cheeks. A moan of exasperation escaped from deep within, "Oh, Lord!"

Abe stared at Lucela in astonishment before dropping his head. Now that he had sobered up, he realized the error of his ways. He knew he'd gone too far, but his pride wouldn't allow him to admit it and apologize. Lucela's voice changed. Her tone deepened and when she spoke it held no emotion, as if she were exhausted from running a race and simply wanted to rest. "I'm getting tired of you, Abe, and I'm about to reach a point where I really won't care if you stay or go."

Abe was so stunned he couldn't respond. When he finally opened his mouth to plead his case, he heard the loud slamming of the front door.

At that moment, Abe realized that he had gone too far. The old Ceel was gone and he knew she would never return.

CHAPTER SEVEN

"Good morning, Lucela! "

"Good morning to you, too, nine-year-old! Have a seat. I fixed you something special."

Lucela had decided to leave the partially eaten cake at home and bake another while Timmy was at school. She couldn't bring herself to break his heart by showing up with such a tarnished gift. In order to distract him from asking about the cake, she decided to fix him a special breakfast of waffles with powdered sugar, whipped cream, and strawberries. When she placed his plate in front of him, he gasped in awe. "Dessert for breakfast? Yippee!"

"Now, you hurry up. And don't tell your mama I let you eat whipped cream this early in the morning. Okay, birthday boy?"

"Okay, I promise. But can I have one more? Please?"

Lucela laughed. "My goodness! I guess your appetite is growing, too. Just one more and then you better get on your way to school. We've got a special evening planned for you tonight."

"Are we having hamburgers and French fries?"

"Maybe."

"Maybe? The birthday boy asked for them. The birthday boy also asked for strawberry ice cream and a coconut cake. Will he get that, too?"

"Maybe."

"Maaaaaybeeee?" Both Timmy and Lucela laughed at his silliness.

Lucela walked over and placed another waffle in front of Timmy. He hugged her around her waist and she bent down to kiss him on the cheek, but he turned his head and kissed her on the lips. The kiss was not indecent, but a totally innocent one, full of the affection any child would have for their parent. Lucela walked back over to the sink and wiped her eyes with the corner of her apron. For the first time in her life, she truly knew what it felt like to be a mother.

Later that evening, as she was finishing up in the kitchen after Timmy's birthday celebration, Lucela was startled by the ringing of the Lofton's doorbell. At first, she debated about answering the door, since she was normally gone by this hour. However, she decided to answer it anyway, assuming it was someone with a birthday gift for Timmy. She was shocked when she opened the door to find Abe standing on the porch. "Good evening, Ceel. I came to see if you needed a ride."

"No, I think I'll walk instead. It's been a long day and I think the fresh air will do me some good."

"Well, okay then. Oh, I almost forgot. I brought little Tommy a present."

"You mean Timmy? I'll go get him. In the meantime, why don't you go around back and wait for me to come back downstairs."

Abe grudgingly walked to the back door. He disagreed with the social customs of the town, but didn't want to make trouble for Ceel at her job.

Lucela and Timmy were waiting in the kitchen when Abe arrived at the back door. Timmy opened the screen door for him and extended his hand. "Good evening. You're Mr. Jessup, right?"

"Yes, little buddy, I am. I brought you a little something for your birthday. Catch!" Abe threw the wrapped gift at Timmy, who could easily identify it as a football.

Timmy tried to hide his disappointment and mumbled, "Gee, thanks." Then he walked over to Lucela and kissed her on the cheek before heading upstairs to bed.

Lucela silently wished she had married a more thoughtful man. As often as she talked about Timmy at home, it was obvious Abe hardly ever listened. If he had, he would have known his name was "Timmy" instead of "Tommy" and he would have bought him a more fitting gift. Lucela exited out of the back door and entered the car door Abe held open for her. She sighed loudly and sat back in the seat. By the time Abe started the car, Lucela had already closed her eyes. She'd decided to pretend to be asleep so that she could avoid talking to him. Because she'd worked a long day, he assumed she really was tired and turned on the radio. Except for the sound of Otis Redding's voice, the ride home was silent.

That fall, the Lofton's eldest son Bobby, left for school. He had earned a full scholarship to play at the state college. Mr. Lofton had been so ecstatic about his son freeing him from the burden of paying tuition that he had taken him straight to Foster's Fine Cars and allowed him to pick out any new car he wanted off the lot. Bobby had chosen a fire red sports car that brought him more than his fair share of attention from his friends, admiring females, and law enforcement. Before leaving, he'd already amassed enough tickets to get himself thrown into jail. His saving grace was that the judge was also a cousin of the family, who agreed to let him off if he left for school as soon as possible in order to avoid the risk of him getting any new speeding tickets. Bobby, who had longed to be free from the supervision of his parents, gladly left a month early.

When the day arrived for his departure, the family gathered on the front lawn to give their farewells. Mrs. Lofton held her firstborn in a tight grasp, crying sorrowfully as if he were a soldier being drafted to war. Once she let Bobby out of her embrace, she raced into the house. She was too emotionally fragile to see him drive away. Mr. Lofton smiled proudly and told his oldest son, "Don't worry about your mother. She'll be fine." He then firmly shook his son's hand, passing him a folded hundred dollar bill while conspiratorially winking at him. Afterwards, he quickly turned his head to conceal his own tears. *His first-born son was a chip off the old block!* He hoped Bobby would aspire to paths of greatness he had desired for himself, yet lacked the skills to do so. He had been an average athlete, with above-average desire and minimal sportsmanship skills. However, those only got him so far and thus he was always ranked as 'second-string' or seated on the bench. But not his Bobby! He was the leader of the 'first-string' and his father lived vicariously through him. Kay had ruined his second boy and turned him into a little soft, whiny, pansy. But his oldest son was all his—strong, courageous, and athletic. Everything a father could want in a son. "I'm proud of you son. Do your best, and be the leader you are destined to be. I know you can do it."

Susan, embarrassed at her surge of emotions, tried to look indifferent through tear-stained eyes. She awkwardly hugged her older brother, finally realizing that she was now considered the eldest and would have to accept more responsibility. In her own self-centered way, she felt angry at Bobby for leaving her to deal with the family dynamics alone. She stood back and attempted to nonchalantly stare at the flowers on the front lawn.

Timmy, trying to appear mature, laughed awkwardly when Bobby playfully punched his arm and teased him about growing some muscles so he could help him stay in shape when he returned home next summer. As Bobby turned to walk away, Timmy lost his composure and sobbed uncontrollably. His father

57

immediately admonished him for his immature outburst and told him, "Stop crying like a little girl!" Bobby, who had noticed his father's tears just moments earlier, became enraged at his audacity. He bent down and hugged Timmy tightly, then slipped his hundred dollar bill into Timmy's hand and put his finger to his lips, gesturing for his little brother to keep their secret. Timmy was so surprised he stopped crying immediately. He had never had so much money before and knew he could use it purchasing endless amounts of candy, toys, and other items he desired.

Finally, Bobby hugged Lucela and almost cried himself when she handed him a tin of oatmeal-raisin cookies, his favorite. All at once he felt guilty for all of the times he had treated her in a condescending manner, simply because he felt that it was expected of him as a White young man, even though she had given him nothing but unconditional love his entire life. She rubbed the brown cowlick in the middle of his crown, like she used to when he was a small boy, while he laid his head on her warm breast and clasped her tightly. She knew he was afraid and softly whispered to him, "You go make yo' Mama and Daddy proud. And make me proud, too. You hear me?"

"Yes, ma'am. Bye Ceel-Ceel."

Lucela chuckled as she wiped her moist eyes. She hadn't heard Bobby use his pet name for her in a number of years.

In a flurry of dust so strong that it concealed him, Bobby Lofton sped away like a ghost. Little did the family know that it would be the last time they would see him.

CHAPTER EIGHT

Once Bobby arrived at school, he became a highly respected member of the team and a leader on campus. Being the team's quarterback, he naturally fit into the role. However, his emergence as a campus leader happened by chance.

Bobby's school had recently begun integrating the team. However, this assimilation was in name only. Black players were still not allowed to shower, eat, or room with the others. And their accommodations were definitely not "separate, but equal." Black players were required to room in squalid living quarters below what many of them had lived in at home that were infested with bedbugs, lice, ticks, roaches, mice, rats, and any other vermin imaginable. In addition, they were usually fed the leftover food from the cafeteria, instead of fresh meals like the White members of the team. Finally, their shower and toilet facilities were outside in a makeshift area that was constructed without any consideration for comfort.

One of the Black players on the team, Clarence, was Myrtle's oldest son and Lucela's cousin. On the first day of practice, he and Bobby recognized each other. After the coach ended his opening speech, Bobby walked over to Clarence and extended his hand. "Hey, Buddy. Remember me?" Clarence, entertaining a group of his new friends with his engaging personality, turned around, startled. "You're Lucela's relative, right? I'm Bobby, Bobby Lofton. You used to come with her to work sometimes when we were little." The mumbling and snickers that followed his explanation of his familiarity with Clarence made Bobby realize the rudeness of his mistake. He should have said, *"You're related to Mrs. Jessup, right?"* and therefore avoided inadvertently saying, *"Your cousin was my family's maid and we used to play together when we were little but had to stop when we got older because that's the rule."* Bobby felt his face flush. He hoped the rest of the players didn't turn on him.

Clarence, who towered over everyone in both stature and bulk, had the gentle, easygoing nature of a small child. He rarely involved himself in conflicts and had the demeanor of a peacemaker. Many people in the church said he "had a calling" on his life, meaning he would one day preach. He felt the tension in the group and decided to diffuse it. He knew that it took a lot of courage for Bobby to even approach the group, not just as a White boy but also as the quarterback. He knew that Bobby's motive was purely to embrace all of the members of the team, and at that moment he vowed to help him in this endeavor. "Bobby? Man, you done got a lot bigger since we was kids, but if you ask me, you done slowed down!" He playfully slapped Bobby on the back then turned to the rest of the players. Bobby felt the heat of the angry glares he received from his new teammates. A few of them went so far as to turn their chins up at him in defiance, signaling their disdain at his presence.

Clarence continued trying to ease the noticeable friction. "Lemme tell y'all, this here boy could run so fast when we was kids he used to get burn marks on the bottom of his feet." Bobby

61

motioned his hands in an "aw shucks" motion and smiled awkwardly. The tension in the group lightened as the other players inspected their quarterback more closely. "You know how them other uppity boys gotta wear shoes? Not Bobby. He ran barefoot, and still beat ALL the boys in town--Black or White! I used to tell everyone he was my light-skinned cousin from up North and let him play baseball with us in our neighborhood. Man, I swear he hit a home run every time!" Bobby chuckled at Clarence's exaggeration of his skills. Truthfully, he had only played in Clarence's neighborhood once. He knew Clarence wanted to prove to his friends that Bobby was a real athlete, and not some rich kid who paid for his position. He was grateful for Clarence's pleas on his behalf. Apparently, they worked. The others players laughed and a few even shook his hand. He smiled good-naturedly and heaved a sigh of relief. He knew the respect of the Black players would be crucial to the rest of the players coming together and bonding as a team.

The next day, after practice, the players went to their segregated dining areas. Clarence and Bobby had agreed to get together and practice a few plays prior to retiring for the night. After dinner, Bobby informed his White teammates of his plans and asked if anyone wanted to join him. A few of them snickered and one player, Joey Hudson, remarked that he "didn't want to spend his free time hanging around with niggers." Bobby's face reddened and he retorted, "Well, just remember that one day you might want one of those 'niggers' to block for you. I hope you can get back up again when you end up flat on your back, 'cause if you called me a 'nigger' I wouldn't put myself out to protect you from a blade of grass." With that, he stood up from the table, dusted his hands on his pants, and stomped away angrily.

As the weeks progressed, Bobby and Clarence continued their routine. At first, Bobby and another player, Jimmy Baylor, were the only White players who joined in the recreation. However, as time wore on and the team began to bond during practice and on the field, the group grew to include practically everyone, even Joey Hudson on occasion. Often, when the White players would idly stand by and watch the Black players finishing their meals, they realized the discrepancy that existed between the two groups. Many times, Bobby and his crew would have just finished a hot meal of fried chicken, mashed potatoes, vegetables, rolls and dessert prior to observing that Clarence's group had eaten a meal of hot dogs and leftover grits.

One day, Clarence invited Bobby and Jimmy to his dorm room to help him complete an essay assignment. Both players tried to conceal their awe at the horrid living conditions their friends were subjected to. When Jimmy asked where the bathroom was, Clarence and his three roommates laughed loudly. "Bathroom?" said Willie Watson, "Man, ain't no 'bathroom' in here." Willie pointed to the outhouse out back and handed Jimmy a roll of tissue. "You gotta go, hit the do'."

Clarence chuckled at Willie's attempt to make light of the situation before continuing the conversation. "Man, I ain't seen an outhouse since I went to visit my great-grandpa last summer.

He lives way out in the country on a dirt road. Heck, the town ain't even got a traffic light. Thought a fine school like this would have bathrooms in the dorms. How y'all manage?"

Bobby's face burned with embarrassment. He didn't know how to tell Clarence that his dorm had indoor facilities, as well as other amenities they were apparently lacking such as running water, indoor plumbing, air conditioning, and better sanitation. The team had finally become united and the progress was beginning to show. They had lost only 1 of their 10 games and were slated to compete in the playoffs. He didn't want to create any new tension that might cause irreparable damage. Instead, he decided to pretend that he shared the same predicament. He arched his eyebrows and gave Jimmy the cue to also be quiet. "Man, I don't know. I bet we'd be better off staying at the YMCA. At least we could bathe in the swimming pool!" Everyone laughed at his response.

At that moment, Bobby decided that he would speak with the coach about making some changes. If he expected the whole team to equally give 100% on the field, then the school should equally give them 100% off the field. Fair is fair.

"Lofton, are you crazy? You know what you're asking me to do? The Board of Trustees is not going to agree to spend more money to make things comfortable for a few Black students just because it's 'fair'. Hell, I bet some of them got it better here than they did at home, anyway."

"Well, sir, I doubt that. Thomas McKinnon's dad is a doctor and George Wilson's dad is a dentist. I'm pretty sure that they have indoor plumbing at home, as well as living accommodations that are free of rats and lice. Besides, I have personally visited Clarence's home and can attest to the fact that even he lived in a better environment, and his mother cared for him alone."

Coach Mellon rubbed his chin as if he were deep in thought. It was his second year at the university and he was barely stable in his own employment. He didn't want to 'tip the apple cart' and risk his own financial future. However, he had to admit that since the Black players had been added to the team, their winning record had greatly improved from last year's season. The team was scheduled for the playoffs and considered by some to be a shoo-in for the championship ring. Winning the state victory would guarantee him a job for life.

Mellon had noticed that the crowds at games and the presence of alumni at events had increased dramatically, thus earning more money for the school. He was sure that this could be used as a rationale for improving the living conditions of the Black students. In fact, if the truth of the matter was revealed to the press it could tarnish the image of the university and decrease much of their public support. Besides, these were his students and he did have a responsibility for them. Clarence and Willie were strong leaders both on and off the field and he needed their support if he ever hoped to earn a championship ring. He'd seen their dorm and had to admit that his daddy's horses had better living conditions. Coach Mellon decided to take these concerns to the board and request action.

Within two weeks, the Black players were relocated to another dormitory on campus that was adjacent to where the White players were located. The matter was handled with the explanation that the dorm had to be 'refurbished' before it could be occupied. Since the cafeteria sat between both dormitories, the players were allowed to eat together. This was done for purely economic reasons, since paying two sets of staff to feed one team was an expense that was deemed unnecessary simply to carry out the tenets of segregation. With the school covering the expense of housing the Black players in a better dormitory, the budget manager took measures to cut costs in other areas: one cafeteria staff, one standard meal, and water usage from one locker room. As a result, all restrictions regarding locker rooms, eating, and other activities were lifted due to the additional expenses involved with maintaining accommodations that were 'separate, but equal.'

Bobby had confided in Jimmy of his plans to approach Coach Mellon about the inequities the Black players faced. Once the changes were made, Jimmy told Clarence of the chain of events. When the Black players got wind of Bobby's actions, he'd earned their undying loyalty. One night, Clarence and the other team members gathered outside of Bobby's room and asked him to meet them on the field. "A late night scrimmage? Are you guys crazy? I got a history test tomorrow!"

Clarence pleaded as convincingly as he could. "C'mon, man. Just give us thirty minutes. I got a few new plays I want to show you."

"Alright. Lemme put on a shirt. I'll be down in a minute."

When Bobby arrived on the field, he noticed that all of the players were in the stands. When they saw him approaching, Willie stood up and began clapping. The rest of the players joined in. Bobby was puzzled.

"Guys, what's going on?"

Clarence quieted the group, then cleared his throat as if he were about to make a speech. "Here he is! The man of the hour! Bobby Lofton, the greatest quarterback this team ever has or ever will see!"

"Hurray!" the players responded. Bobby, still puzzled, noticed that Jimmy and another White player, Dave Griffin, were present and cheering for him as well.

"Guys, what's this about? I thought we were gonna scrimmage."

Willie walked over to Bobby, handed him a cup, and placed his hand on his shoulder. "Clarence, man, tell him what this is about."

Clarence waved his hand in the air to quiet the group. "Bobby, man, Jimmy told us what you did, going to speak to Coach and the board and all about getting us better rooms and food to eat. I know you here on scholarship, and you probably could have lost it trying to speak up for us. Man, you really took a stand and we sho' 'preciate it. Now we know that you ain't just bein' cool with us to get what you want on the field, but you really see us as true friends. We jus' wanted to have a toast to you, lettin' you know we 'preciate what you did." Bobby dropped his head in embarrassment, now that his secret was revealed.

Willie lifted his cup and shouted loudly, "To Bobby Lofton, the greatest quarterback that ever lived!"

The rest of the team held their cups in the air. "Hoo-rah!"

Bobby, overcome with emotion, tried to swallow his drink without choking on his emotions. Nervously, he reached up out of habit and rubbed his cowlick with the palm of his sweaty hands. He hadn't set out to be anybody's hero; he just wanted to do what was right.

The next week, Myrtle showed Lucela the letter Clarence had written her which told of Bobby's actions. Lucela, feeling a surge of emotions, felt warm tears spill onto her cheeks. She promised Myrtle to keep the news to herself, since Bobby hadn't written one letter to his family since the first week of school. However, she felt a parental sense of pride. Her boy was making the family proud.

CHAPTER NINE

Later in the year, after football season, Willie and Thomas approached Jimmy and Bobby about their plans for the Christmas Break. Thomas began the conversation. "Hey, guys. We're planning to go down to Birmingham and participate in the 'sit-in' demonstrations. Black people are boycotting the local businesses there until they agree to quit segregating into "White" and "Colored" areas and allow Blacks to work out front instead of just in the kitchens. You know, I've been reading up on some of the teachings of Dr. King and I think he's right. We've got to take a stand to change this country, just like Bobby took a stand to change things here. If we don't, they'll always stay the same, or even get worse."

Jimmy hesitantly responded. He had gotten quite comfortable with the Black team members and somewhat agreed with Willie. However, he knew his mother was expecting him home for Christmas and he didn't want to disappoint her. Truthfully, he was looking forward to her home cooking and all of the attention that would be lavished upon him as the family's first "college boy." He declined their offer. "Sorry fellas, but my Ma will have a fit if I'm not sittin' at the table for Christmas dinner. You understand. Right?"

Willie and Thomas understood. They appreciated Jimmy's friendship and didn't want him to feel ill at ease with his decision. Thomas told him, "Hey, man. We understand. If I had a hot meal waiting for me I might decide to go home, too. Truth is, my old man's new wife can't boil a pot of water without setting a four-alarm fire. Anyway, since Mom's passing Christmas hasn't been the same in our house. My aunt stays near Mobile. I was planning to go to her house for dinner, anyway. She's a much better cook and she's got plenty of room if anyone else wants to come."

Willie, who had no real family to speak of, generally disliked holidays because they usually reminded him of this fact. He was glad to get a home cooked meal anywhere, since he rarely had a place of warmth and refuge. The problem was he and Thomas lacked transportation and were counting on one of their friends to agree to go with them; both Jimmy and Bobby had cars.

Bobby thought about the proposal. He knew that Lucela would be off for the holiday season, so the family meal would likely be catered. Besides, he'd spent many a Christmas with his family and knew the general routine: his father would remain in front of the couch watching football; his sister would complain endlessly about her disappointment at the gifts she received; his little brother would joyously retire to the solitude of his room to play with the toys Santa Claus left for him, and his mother would retire to bed early with one of her 'headaches', probably spurred by his sister's nagging and his father's indifference. Bobby decided to chaperone the group to Birmingham, He'd give his family some excuse about extra mandated practice and explain that he'd eat dinner at the coach's house. His mother would complain, but relent. His father would support his decision by assuming that eating with the coach's family might place Bobby in an advantageous position.

The boys set off on their journey a few days before Christmas. Their plan was to participate in a sit-in that had been scheduled by some of Birmingham's local leaders due to the extra attention the demonstration would bring with the surge of holiday shoppers. Willie, who was rather militant and outspoken, had become active with a student group that was affiliated with Southern Christian Leadership Conference and had heard through the grapevine that the demonstrations would take place. Although the SCLC advocated non-violence, Willie often lost his cool when confronted with the angry, racist mobs. However, he always felt a surge of excitement during the events and felt that he was doing his part to confront the numerous injustices he had already experienced in life, all of which he unfairly attributed to the racist attitudes of his country.

The boys began their long road trip by sharing bits and pieces of their personal history in an effort to bond, at first with effort and eventually through camaraderie.

Willie, always the outspoken one, opened up the conversation. He talked about how he felt growing up in state orphanages and foster care homes after the death of his mother at the age of ten. Having never really known his father, since he had been incarcerated by the time Willie learned to walk, he had no real sense of family and instead idealized his early life in addition to filling in the blanks in his memory with a few embellishments that were clouded by his anger. "Yeah, man. My old man was framed for killing a white man in a store robbery. His friend admitted to doing it, but they gave him life anyway.

71

Everyone said he didn't do it and it was a case of mistaken identity. In St. Louis, the police think that all Black men look alike—whether you're five-foot nine or six-foot seven, high yellow or charcoal black, skinny as a rail or fat as a whale, they'll lock you up and say you did it, no matter what the witness' description says." Thomas and Bobby laughed at his joke about the corrupt police system before he continued.

"My mom always told me he was innocent, but the rest of the family didn't believe her. Used to tell me that he was a 'black ass, no-count nigga' and they'd told her not to marry him in the first place. Used to see us struggling and refuse to put even a dollar in her hand, knowing they could afford it. See, my mom's family was all high yella people and they thought they were better than everyone else in town--used to brag on the fact that they had a lot of White blood in them, even though they were treated just as bad as the rest of the colored. When she married my Pa, they pretty much disowned her. So of course when he got locked away they told her she was getting what she deserved for 'disgracing' the family name. Instead of taking us in, they just watched her struggle, working as a laundry woman and breaking her back. Her hands used to be so swollen and gnarled up that she could barely get herself dressed." Willie's voice cracked and softened before he continued. "I used to get up extra early so I could stop her before she left for work. I'd tell her in my Oliver Twist voice, *'M'Lady, sit down for a minute and take a rest before you start your day.'* Then I'd reach down and tie her shoes for her because I knew she couldn't do it. "

He cleared his throat before continuing. "One winter she got so sick, I think she coughed from November to February. She still got up every morning though, trudging through the snow, picking up and delivering laundry. Once spring came, she still couldn't shake that cough. By the time she went to the doctor, they told her that she had walking pneumonia and had to take a break. Well, this old White lady she worked for, Mrs. Winthrop, had a daughter that was getting married and she wanted my ma to clean and press the napkins and tablecloths for the dinner. Ma had been lying in bed for about three days when she sent her maid for her. My ma told her she was sick and couldn't do it, but she wouldn't take no for an answer. Sent the maid back with a message: 'Betsy, Miz Winthrop says to tell you that if you can't clean her table linens for her girl's wedding then she's gonna put the bad mouth on you so's you never work again.'

Well, my ma crawled out of bed to do that old biddy's laundry. Fact is, it didn't make no difference cause she never did work again anyway. That pneumonia grew stronger and she never washed or ironed another basket of laundry. Died right before Christmas. The rest of her family wouldn't even take me in. State people came by and took me to my grandma's. She opened the door and told that White man through the screen that she 'Wasn't taking in none of them Black-ass Watson's just because her daughter had been fool enough to marry one.' Can you believe that? Spoke to the man like I wasn't even standing there. He looked just as shocked as I was; I mean, the lady didn't even allow us to step a foot inside her door."

Willie laughed softly and shook his head as if he were reliving the moment and still in disbelief. "Man, I think he felt worse than I did. I remember because he wiped his eyes with his handkerchief and shook his head. Then he said to me, 'Hey, kid. You wanna go get some ice cream?' and he took me out for a sundae. Well, after that, it was pretty much foster care and a couple of stints staying with some of my father's folks. Those never turned out too well 'cause I guess they were already too shaky. One of my aunts was cool during the week, but from Friday to Sunday she stayed drunker than Cootie Brown. Another one of my uncles was alright, and I stayed with him until I was about 15; but when he decided to marry his girlfriend he didn't think I'd fit in, especially cause she was always looking at me sideways. Shoot, that didn't help him. She left him before I finished high school for a guy in my class." Willie laughed, a little too loudly, possibly to cover the pain and irony of his story. "So you see, I ain't never really cared for the holidays, especially Christmas. Too many bad memories."

Thomas reached from the back seat and patted Willie on the shoulder. "Man, don't think you're the only one who had it rough. I lost my mother and HAD a father to fall back on, but it didn't make a bit of difference." He went on to talk at length about his resentment towards his extremely young, docile step-mother and the betrayal he felt of his father's marriage a mere two months after his mother's passing. He now looked forward to visiting his Aunt Pearl so that they could reminisce about his mother. "She was a schoolteacher, but man, she could have been a principal. All of the kids respected her and she wasn't mean, just firm. She ran the school for so many years that when the principal retired they asked her to take over, except my dad wouldn't let her do it. Said the job would keep her too busy to take care of us. Never mind that my sister Gloria was already fifteen and I was thirteen. We really could fend for ourselves, but Dad wouldn't have it. If he came home and a hot meal wasn't on the table, he'd hit the roof. Then this idiot turns around and marries a ditz who can't boil an egg, and so he hires a housekeeper! The killer is--she doesn't even work. Do you know she went to high school with Glo? She was a 12th grade cheerleader when my sister was on the squad as a sophomore. Man, I sometimes wonder if he was checking her out back then. Now I got a two-year old brother and a three-year old sister. What a trip!"

After a few hours of sharing family memories and intimate conversations, Bobby's car reached their destination. Aunt Pearl lived in a modest home, with a large porch swing. When she saw the car approaching, she shielded her eyes from the sun in order to peer into the vehicle as it parked along her rarely inhabited road. Since Bobby was driving, Aunt Pearl braced herself for trouble, wondering why a White boy was stopping in her neighborhood. However, those fears were assuaged when Thomas opened the door and abruptly raced to the porch. Pearl stepped to the edge of the steps and greeted each one of the boys with a big, warm hug as if they were ALL relatives. Feeling homesick, Bobby allowed himself to be enveloped in her embrace. While Pearl was also a large woman, unlike Lucela, her body was full and plump. Bobby breathed in her earthy fragrance of lavender and talcum powder as she enclosed him in her arms. For a moment, he felt as if he were a small boy again receiving a hug from his beloved Ceel-Ceel.

"Y'all come in here and set down. Lemme fix you somethin' to eat."

Willie, always the bold one, responded, "Yes, Ma'am! We sho' appreciate it! I ain't had a home-cooked meal in a month of Sundays! Is that fried chicken I smell?"

Pearl laughed. "It sho' is! Got it simmering in some gravy, just waitin' on y'all. Also got some fresh corn, mashed potatoes, black-eyed peas, cabbage, and hot biscuits. I even got a fresh coconut cake on the counter for y'all's dessert tonight."

Thomas gave his aunt another hug. "Auntie, you cooked all this for us? And you remembered to make me some of your hot biscuits! Boy, I sure appreciate it."

Aunt Pearl reached over and pinched one of Thomas' full cheeks as if he was a five-year old. "Well, Honey, anything for you. You my sister's only boy, and you know she's watching me closely so I BETTER take care of you!"

Thomas laughed quietly as his eyes drifted away at the picture of his mother in her college graduation gown that was prominently displayed on the wall. With the exception of their body frames, she and Pearl could have been twins. While Pearl stood at least 5'10", Ruby had been a mere 5'3" in heels and her petite athletic build starkly contrasted her older sister's roundness. Bobby watched Thomas stare at the picture on the wall. "Is that your mom?"

"Yes, that's her. I wasn't born yet. This picture was taken when she graduated from Tuskeegee."

"She was a pretty lady. She got her teaching license there?"

Pearl joined in the conversation. "No, Honey. She got her teaching license from Miles. She got her Master's from Tuskeegee. They wouldn't let her into the University of Alabama, even though she was valedictorian of her high school and a straight "A" student. Gave her an acceptance letter AND a full scholarship, until she showed up for the interview. She must have cried for a week, she was so disappointed. My daddy made a few phone calls and got her admitted to Miles at the last minute. That girl was smart! She was planning to become a doctor, until she met Thomas Senior."

Bobby slightly dropped his head at this shift in the conversation. He regretted the injustices suffered from such a beautiful, talented woman. Inside, he wondered if this disappointment led to her early demise.

Willie, noticing the unease in the room, decided to lighten the mood. "Well, Aunt Pearl, I'm about to eat this tablecloth. Don't mean to be rude, but I haven't eaten a homemade biscuit since I was ten years old. Can we say the grace and eat before my stomach falls out?"

Aunt Pearl laughed. "Yes, Baby. Come on to the table, fellas. Let's bow our heads for the grace."

The meal was filled with lively conversation about current events, local gossip, and family business. Willie and Bobby mostly kept to themselves while Thomas enjoyed his visit with Pearl. They conversed mostly about things that interested only the two of them, such as local events and family business. "You know your cousin Teddy has a son?"

"Teddy? He's barely eighteen!"

"Yep! Had to marry that Blackmon girl before her daddy put some buck-shots in him! He left for the Army last week." She and Thomas giggled at the thought of scrawny Teddy in an Army uniform.

"How's his little sister, Clara?"

"She's grown up into a pretty girl. Remember how she used to look so homely with those large eyes, big teeth and scrawny legs?"

Thomas laughed loudly as he recollected the image. "Yeah, that's why we used to call her 'Buck', cause she looked like a deer.

"Well, Honey, she done turned from a 'buck' into a beautiful 'doe' and I told Big Ted he better keep his shotgun ready! That girl look like she needs to be in somebody's movie picture. Them scraggly legs done firmed up and she got a grown woman shape on her already and ain't nothin' but thirteen years old! She sure done changed from an ugly duckling into a swan!" The two of them laughed loudly at the metamorphosis of Clara, while the other boys sat quietly at the table.

Bobby felt comforted from Aunt Pearl's hospitality and couldn't help but feel a longing for Lucela. He thought about how she, like Pearl, seemed to thrive on comforting others with their warm, gentle hearts. He silently wondered how she was spending her holiday, and whether she was lonely or surrounded by loved ones.

The boys retired for the night and were soundly asleep within minutes. They awoke the next morning to the distinctive smell of sugar-cured ham. After washing and preparing for breakfast, they stared in awe at the feast prepared for them. The platter of ham was surrounded by two stacks of pancakes, warm syrup, a dish of butter, fluffy eggs, grits, freshly squeezed juice, cold milk, and a pot of coffee. Bobby felt right at home.

After breakfast, Aunt Pearl provided the boys with a large box of goodies that apparently had been prepared while they were sleeping during the night. The night before, Thomas had begged his aunt for a few dozen chocolate chip cookies.

"Well, I'll see," Aunt Pearl had told him. "You sure are getting spoiled. You already ate three slices of coconut cake. What if these two boys don't like chocolate chip cookies? What are they gonna eat?"

"Aw, Auntie Pearl I'll share. I promise!"

"Boy, quit your lying! I can't count how many times Glo used to complain about you eating all the cookies and leaving her the crumbs!" Thomas laughed before she continued. "Willie, are chocolate chip cookies your favorite, too? I don't want y'all fightin' over the crumbs; y'all got a long ride ahead!"

"No, ma'am. Peanut butter cookies are my favorite."

She turned towards Bobby who was sitting by himself in the corner. "Bobby, boy you always this quiet?"

Bobby, remembering his manners, cleared his throat before honestly replying, "Yes, ma'am."

Aunt Pearl chuckled and said, "Well, I don't know how you get along with my nephew. He talks more than a parrot! Son, what kind of cookies you like?"

"Well, I'll take anything. But my favorite is oatmeal raisin."

"Well! See Thomas? If I try to bake cookies I'll have to do a lot of work. Won't get any sleep tonight. When you boys stop back through after Christmas, I'll have a tin waiting for each of you."

Thomas protested and pouted like a spoiled child, but Bobby shrugged his shoulders and continued munching on his second slice of coconut cake. He hadn't expected this much hospitality in the first place, so Pearl's kind gestures so far were genuinely appreciated. He had to admit though, her cake wasn't as good as Lucela's, but it was a fitting substitute.

The next morning, Aunt Pearl refused to allow them to continue their travels without a basket of food. "Fellas, I put some fried chicken, ham sandwiches, potato salad, sliced bread, and punch in this here box. Should last you for a couple of days."

Thomas searched through the box and found a warm tin. "Aunt Pearl, you made the cookies? Thanks!" He grabbed her in an affectionate hug.

"There's a tin in there for each one of you. I don't want any confusion among you boys."

Willie pulled the lid off his tin and immediately smelled peanut butter. "Aunt Pearl! You made cookies for each one of us?"

Pearl laughed and waved her hands at Willie modestly. "Aw, Honey, it wasn't nothing. I stayed up a little late, but that's okay. It's not every day I get to see my favorite nephew."

Willie couldn't resist his opportunity to be a jokester. "I thought you said he was your only nephew?"

Pearl laughed. "He is, but. . ."

Willie interjected with the punchline. "Well, see, he's only the favorite because he's competing with himself!'

Bobby opened his tin and the scent of cinnamon tinged his senses. Aunt Pearl had taken note when he'd told her that oatmeal raisin cookies were his favorite. He was deeply touched at the kindness of his host, who had been a complete stranger to him less than twenty-four hours earlier. He was amazed at her ability to extend such a genuine love for someone who most likely reminded her of those who had shown her so much hate in her long life. He wanted to respond with words, but found himself too emotional to form a coherent thought. Instead, he lightly touched her shoulder and mumbled, "Thanks, very much, ma'am. I appreciated your hospitality."

Willie left Aunt Pearl with a big, familiar hug as if he were a member of the family. This affectionate display was a stark contrast from his usual guarded demeanor. Then he and Bobby proceeded to load the car to allow Thomas and his aunt to have their last few moments alone.

Bobby struggled to fit the box of food into the backseat. "Man, she fixed us enough food to feed an army," he jokingly remarked.

Bobby thought she was merely being hospitable, until Willie explained her real intentions, a thought that had never crossed his mind. "Man, she knows we can't stop and get anything to eat or even use the bathroom. We gotta have plenty of food and supplies in order to be safe."

Before Bobby could respond, Thomas jumped into the backseat, his eyes slightly teary. He wiped them on his sleeve, adjusted his glasses and said, "Okay, fellas. Let's go take a stand for freedom!"

CHAPTER TEN

During the brief ride, the boys pumped themselves up with bravado to mask the anxiety they were feeling. Willie, the most militant and vocal of the trio, opened up the conversation by explaining that he had no fear in risking his life to take a stand, because he really felt that he had little to live for. "You know Thomas, spending the night at Auntie Pearl's really made me realize that unlike you, all I have in this world is me, and me alone. Man, I had to catch myself. When I hugged her, it really took me back to favorite foster mother, my last foster mother, Mama Jenkins."

Bobby glanced over at Willie. He rubbed his large hand across his face, his eyes clouding over with the recollection of another painful segment of his life. "Man, I had so many foster mamas; some of 'em were okay, and some were just mean! I had one that used to wrap a belt around the handle of the refrigerator and link it to the stove handle so that I couldn't open either one without her permission. If she caught me, she took this same belt and beat me with it until my black-ass turned blue! When I couldn't take it anymore, I ran away and escaped to my uncle's house and I swore I'd never go back again. But after he kicked me out, I had nowhere else to go so I ended up back in that system."

"A damn shame," Thomas interjected sympathetically.

Bobby, not really knowing what to say, stared intently ahead and silently regretted the callousness in which he had regarded his own familial stability.

"So anyway, I really considered lying about my age and joining the Army, just to have a place to eat and lay my head. But one of the coaches at my school told me he knew a lady at his church that he could talk to and ask her to take me in. She had been a foster mother years ago, but had given it up once the children she'd cared for had grown up. He let me stay with him for a couple of weeks until he could convince her to call the agency and let them know she wanted to keep me.

Man, I was so scared, but I trusted the coach 'cause I figured he would look out for me since I was important to the team. He did. Man, that lady was so sweet. She wadn't no more than 5 feet , and she was about as wide as she was tall." Willie chuckled before continuing. "Mama J was always smiling, and always singing some church song, especially when she was waddling around in the kitchen cooking. That's how I'd know it was time to get up. She was my alarm clock. When I'd hear her singing one of those old time hymns while she was making her coffee, I knew it was time to get up. She had such a pretty voice.

She was a little older than my other foster mothers, but she was really nice to me. Every day, she cooked big meals, just for me—anything I wanted. I couldn't leave out the door for a game without her handing me a bag of fried chicken and a bunch of cookies for me and my friends to eat on the bus. I didn't even have to do no chores, except cut the grass. Even when I offered to, she shooed me away and told me that I was a growing boy and needed to save my energy for the football field.

She was more like a grandma than a foster mother. Every Saturday, she would clean and press my clothes—she even ironed my underwear! And every Sunday she made a huge meal and whatever dessert I asked for: banana pudding, lemon meringue pie, caramel cake, anything! Man, I was living the life." Willie smiled to himself before his face dropped into its usual sour visage.

"Just like my mama, Mama J started getting sick around Thanksgiving. Used to get these headaches that kept her in the bed. I'd come home from school and not smell any food and know that she'd been lying down all day, 'cause nothing kept her from cooking. I'd go in there and take her a cold rag for her head and rub her swollen feet like I used to do for my mom." Willie softened his tone and slowed his speech, imitating Mama Jenkins. "She'd say, 'Thank you, Son. You're such a sweet boy. Got me feelin' better already. In a little bit, I'll cook you some dinner. Can't have my boy 'round her hungry.' Sometimes, she'd get up and cook, but after a while she couldn't even do that. I'd go in and try to heat up some stew and make a little cornbread. She'd fuss over the food like I'd just made a five course meal. 'Look at my little Chocolate Drop! Tryna make cornbread. Got it light and fluffy, too, with a whole lot of butter. Just like I like it!' She would never mention that I burned it half the time, or teased me when it didn't rise and sat on that plate like a rock. Guess she didn't want to hurt my feelings." The trio laughed at Willie's last comment before he continued.

"Well anyway, she didn't get better. Got so sick that she had to go to the hospital right before Christmas. On New Year's Eve, she passed on. I was miserable. I felt like I was burying my mama all over again. Guess that's why I hate the holidays. I always lose someone I love around this time of year."

Bobby looked over at Willie, who was struggling to maintain his composure. "Hey, Man. What happened after that?"

"Well, since I'd turned eighteen in December, all I had to do was sign a few papers to get out of foster care, even though I wasn't through with high school. Since I had already gotten a scholarship, my coach agreed to help me out and he let me stay with his family for the rest of the school year. "

Bobby remained quiet. As someone who had always had a sense of family, being without a loved one was an idea he couldn't fathom. From the backseat, Thomas echoed his thoughts. "Man, I know I complain about my dad and all, but at least he's around. I couldn't even imagine being all alone and on my own before I finished high school. I just couldn't. I don't know how you did it, but you made it to college. I don't know if I could have done the same."

Thomas went on. "I know I talk about my dad, but I guess I sometimes focus on the bad things because I'm still sore at him about losing my mom. After listening to you, I see I'm not the only kid who's lost a mom and I guess I should be glad I have my dad left. He's not that bad, a little strict, but he's a really cool guy sometimes. Like, I remember when my mom didn't want me to join the football team when I was young because she was scared I'd get hurt. He convinced her to let me play and never missed a game, no matter what he was doing. And when we were kids, Glo and I really were quite spoiled. Every new toy that came out we had it. Christmas was a big deal. We used to have so many toys they wouldn't all fit under the tree and so they'd have to pile them up on the sofa!" Thomas paused then continued, "Listening to you made me realize that I took a lot for granted. I mean, I haven't even talked to my dad in four or five months and he's the one paying my tuition. I wasn't even gonna call him, but I think I will when we get to Birmingham and wish him a 'Merry Christmas' and chat with him for a while."

Bobby chimed in, "Yeah, Man, I agree. I think I'll call my folks, too."

CHAPTER ELEVEN

When the crew arrived in Birmingham, they were in awe at the number of other college students that had also decided to spend their holidays protesting. "Man, I thought this was gonna be a small, local event. Looks like the word got around. There must be at least 200 people here. If we do go to jail, we'll have plenty of company."

"*Jail?*" The idea had never crossed Bobby's mind. But when he thought about the experiences of his friends and their families, he realized that he was willing to be locked up if it would bring about some kind of change. He pulled the car to a stop in front of a local gas station that was adjacent to the local city square.

Thomas spotted a pay phone and rushed out of the back seat. "Gonna call my Pops and let him know I'm here. He'll probably be mad, but at least he'll know I thought enough to call."

"Well, Fellas, I gotta go. Now!" Bobby quickly headed towards the bathroom then slowed his pace when he realized the sign above it said *"Whites Only"*. Struggling to control his bladder, he returned to his car and filled Willie in.

Willie laughed. "Man, you been driving for the longest. This ain't no time to be righteous. Go pee. I mean, for real Bobby, I will refuse to sit next to you at the counter all day if you're gonna be smelling like piss. And, when we get back to school I will tell EVERYBODY that you pee'd your pants!"

Bobby playfully threw a jab at Willie before walking back towards the facility. Willie perched himself on the hood of the car so that he could maintain a view of his two friends as he did a little 'girl watching' to occupy his restless mind. When Bobby walked back to the car, he shook his head at his outgoing friend, who was waving and smiling at all of the attractive females that walked by.

After a few minutes, Thomas returned to car, visibly upset. "Man, that didn't go so well."

"What happened?" Bobby asked.

"Well, after we got all of the pleasantries out of the way, I decided to explain where I'd be spending my holidays. Before I could get a word in, that tramp my dad married started going on and on about how she's been watching the news and I need to *stay away from those marches and all that foolishness before I get myself killed!'* So of course, my dad has to put his two-cents in and the conversation just takes a turn for the worse. "

Thomas cleared his throat before continuing. "I mean, we'd started off apologizing and promising to meet up and catch up on things, but then he starts yelling about how he's not paying tuition for me to run around down South protesting with 'King and the rest of them fools'. Starts going in on him and some of the others, saying that their just using us as pawns in their scheme, that all of them have received their education and have nothing to lose."

Willie stared in disbelief. "Your Pops said that?"

Thomas wiped his sweaty face before throwing both of his hands up in exasperation. "Can you imagine that? My dad, who I always respected for working hard and being an educated man, telling me to 'leave it alone' and back down from trying to change things. He had the nerve to say, *'That nigga King FINISHED Morehouse before he was your age. You think he ain't smart enough to manipulate everybody else into doing his dirty work?'*

Thomas began to animatedly move his hands, emphasizing his words. "Man, I couldn't hold it anymore. I told him, if he doesn't want to help me finish college then I'll do it myself. I'm a grown man, and I don't need him running my life like he tried to run my Ma's. Always tried to control her and kept her from achieving any of her dreams before she left here. She could've been a great doctor, or principal, or scientist, but he held her back. And now she's gone with nothing to show for it, except me and Glo. Well, that did it. He started hollering so much, I couldn't even understand a word he was saying. So I just hung up. To hell with him."

Bobby stood there in shock. He couldn't imagine having a conversation of this nature with his father. "Thomas, you didn't mean that, and I'm sure he didn't mean a lot of what he said. You guys just need some time to cool off."

Willie agreed. "Yeah, man. Give him a call tonight, once things blow over. I mean, you guys haven't talked in months. Maybe this conversation was just too heavy right now. You dig?"

"Yeah, maybe you're right. I'll call him later, once my head clears. But I gotta be honest, I meant every word I said. And I'm not taking it back." Thomas emphatically pounded his fist into his hand.

Once again, Willie lightened the mood. He altered his voice and did a dead-pan imitation of Dr. Martin Luther King. "Alright, Buddy. We're here to be non-violent. Un-ball that fist, young man, before you get us into trouble! We're trying to make it into the Promised Land, and we can't get there with anger in our hearts. Can I get an Amen?"

Bobby, struggling to control his laughter, answered loudly, "Amen!"

The trio erupted in a fit of joviality that diffused the tension and anxiety they were all feeling.

After chatting with other college students (and Willie arranging for a late night date with a young lady named Marsha), freshening up, and snacking on the provisions Aunt Pearl had given them, the teammates decided to head over to the

Woolworth's and complete a shift at the counter. Just as they were about to leave, Bobby realized that he had gotten so caught up in the whirlwind of activity that he had forgotten to make his phone call. "Hey, fellas! Hold on. I forgot to use the phone."

Willie pointed out the window before responding. "Man, you're not gonna use that phone anytime soon. Look at the line."

All three of them stared in the direction of the phone booth. The line stretched for almost a block. Bobby realized he would definitely have to wait.

Bobby shrugged before stuffing his hands in his pockets and preparing for their brief walk to the store. "Oh, well. I guess I'll try again before bed."

As they approached the Woolworth's, the boys noticed a small group assembled a few feet from the entrance. About twenty teenagers were standing in a huddle, listening intently to the man who appeared to be the leader of the demonstration. He was about average height, of a slender, yet muscular build, and wore a clean shaven face and well-groomed haircut. He was dressed impeccably, in a suit and tie, and held a Bible in his right hand. Willie recognized him and pulled Thomas and Bobby along and the trio joined the huddle. "That's Rev. Shuttlesworth," he whispered to his friends. "He's our leader." The man nodded at the boys to acknowledge their presence, before continuing his speech.

"We are NOT here to fight, but we are here to take a stand using NON-VIOLENCE! No matter what the aggressor does, we cannot repay him or her with our anger because this is exactly what they expect. They call us beasts! They say we are less human than them! We will NOT prove them true by acting that way! I know some of you feel that it's a high price to pay, but I hope you know that you are not here just for you. You are here for your children, and your children's children, so that THEY will never have to face the injustices which have slapped you in the face for so long. You are here for the maids, and porters, and others who CAN'T be here because their jobs and livelihoods have been threatened and they have to mask their pain in silence in order to feed their children and care for their families. "

His words were met with various vocal and emotional affirmatives from audience members, both male and female, including Willie.

"Amen!"

"Preach On!"

"Tell it, Brother!" Willie shouted.

"Please, young people. Make no mistake in feeling that you are the only ones laying down your lives for this cause. They blew up my house while me and my family were inside. Then, these same folks beat me and left me for dead and stabbed my wife. But God protected us and we're still here. That didn't stop them, they kept beating me and bombing me, but God has STILL kept me safe; because he has a work for me to do!"

The crowd erupted in applause before he continued. "And I'm gonna do it, until the day I die!"

Bobby joined in the applause as his courage grew. *"This man has survived all these times, trying to take a stand. I'm definitely brave enough to do my part today. Sitting at a lunch counter is nothing compared to what he's been through."*

Rev. Shuttlesworth continued his directive. "Now, I know some of you are feeling nervous, but all we ask is that you swallow your fear and remain calm at all times. No matter what happens, remain calm and without emotion. If someone calls you a name, remember, it's just a word. It's not what you're called, it's what you answer to. And if you react, you're answering to the name. If someone throws something at you, or spits on you, think about King Jesus. They spit on him and nailed him on the Cross, and he STILL said, *'Father, forgive them, cause they know not what they do.'* He recognized that those folks were ignorant and so they were acting ignorant because that's all they knew. You're gonna face off with these same types of folks. They ignorant; so they gonna act ignorant. But you know better; so act better."

A young assistant emerged with a clipboard and instructions. He was a very fair complexioned Negro, one that would require a second glance to confirm his ethnicity, with green eyes and sandy hair. He wore a bow-tie and vest with a starched white shirt, and maintained a posture of importance, despite his small stature. He adjusted his gold-rimmed glasses before speaking. "Okay, we need ten people, preferably some Whites and some females for our next shift. We need to show the media that this issue is not just about Negro men, but our whole nation."

The crew looked around and realized that besides Bobby, there were only two other Whites, both female. The short, bespectacled assistant pointed at Bobby. "You! Come give me your name. You're sitting in the next shift."

Bobby puffed out his chest with false bravado and proceeded to the front of the line. Willie and Thomas followed. "Hey, my man," Willie stated, "we're going in on the next shift, too."

The young man paused, and peered at Willie authoritatively, his pencil held in mid-air as if he were offended at the interruption of his duties. Willie responded with an even icier glare that shifted the position of power, his tall stature placing a huge shadow over the clipboard that blocked the assistant's view. The young man let out a sigh of resignation. "Okay, fellas. Give me your names. The next shift starts in five minutes."

CHAPTER TWELVE

The team stood in semi-formation outside the restaurant, waiting for the boy with the clipboard to give them the signal. While standing, they engaged in small talk to quell their excitement.

Besides Willie, Thomas, and Bobby, the incoming team consisted of one of the White females, two Black females named Mary and Kate, and four other Black males. While they were waiting to enter, Willie had engaged in small talk with the females, and learned that all three were students at a girls' college from up North. Kate was a senior, Mary was a junior, and their Caucasian friend was a freshman.

Kate was the most talkative of the group, and she volunteered information regarding the other two. She was taller than most females, about six feet, and had the slim, but shapely build of an athlete. Her creamy complexion glistened in the sun, and Bobby was surprised to notice that she had both bright red hair and freckles, two traits that he had always thought were exclusive to Whites. Since he didn't want to stare, he diverted his attention to Mary. She was a strikingly beautiful girl, with flawless, deep, dark skin, about the color of a licorice stick. Her high cheekbones were accented by her sharply slanted eyes that made him wonder if she had an Oriental heritage. Her thick hair cascaded in long waves near the middle of her back. She stood about 5' 8", standing eye to eye with Thomas, and possessed a thick, curvy figure that even Jayne Mansfield would envy. While

Bobby wasn't attracted to her, he completely understood why both Willie and Thomas were. Poor Kate seemed to sense her exclusion from their interests and appeared to continue monopolizing the conversation in order to receive attention.

Kate animatedly moved her hands and turned her face towards Willie, attempting to break the mesmerizing spell Mary had apparently cast on him. "Yes, we're from the North. We've come here to try and help our brothers and sisters in the South. Mary here was scared, and so was she, but I convinced these two that this would be a perfect way spend our holiday. I mean, we'll remember this for the rest of our lives, you know what I mean? I mean, it sure beats shopping and being materialistic and self-centered, you know? I think it's best to give back when you can. Don't you agree?"

Willie, apparently still distracted by Mary, was at a loss of words for the first time ever in his life. He and Mary's eyes were locked in an unseen embrace, the magnetic attraction between them obvious to any onlooker. He shook his head as if he were waking from a dream and responded to Kate. "What? Oh, I'm sorry. I didn't hear the last part of what you said."

Thomas, now realizing that he had lost the duel, turned towards Kate and looked upwards towards her face. "I think you ladies are doing a good thing. I wish more women would stand up for themselves and take the initiative to make changes in this world. Sometimes we men need intelligent, strong women to push us to take a stand."

Kate, who was proud to finally be acknowledged, smiled down at Thomas before replying, "Thanks." The two of them proceeded to engage in a deep conversation about the teachings of Gandhi and his impact on the movement. Standing idly by, Bobby decided to be polite and introduce himself to their reserved friend.

Bobby extended his hand towards the young lady. "Hello, I'm Bobby Lofton."

The young lady shook her long blonde hair out of her eyes before giving him a timid smile. She shyly took his hand in a weak grasp and responded in a low whisper, "Hi. I'm Carol. Nice to meet you."

Before the two of them could begin a conversation, they were loudly interrupted by the young assistant. "Brothers and Sisters, let's prepare for our shift. Remember, non-violence is the key to our movement. We Shall Overcome!"

Once he opened the door, the group entered the restaurant area of the store in a single file line. As the incoming students walked in, the individuals they were relieving tiredly shuffled out; some wearing the wide-eyed expressions of soldiers who had just encountered the deadly horrors of war.

Bobby gasped in amazement at the condition of some of the students. Some had been doused with flour; some were covered in ketchup and other condiments; some were even wearing an unknown substance that he recognized after they passed by due to its awful stench. His mind was clouded with thoughts of anger and disbelief. *"These people are crazy! Who would do that do another human being?"*

In less than a minute, although it felt like an eternity, each member of the team was seated. The counter was severely unkempt, with flour, trash, and condiments littering the entire area. *"Lucela would have never tolerated this filth in our kitchen,"* Bobby thought, all the while wondering why he was thinking of her and not his family at this time. As soon as the question left his mind it was immediately replaced with the answer. *"Lucela's really the only Black person I know well. She's so much older than Thomas and Willie. I wonder what she's endured during her life. I feel ashamed that I never thought or cared to ask until now."*

Once everyone was seated, Willie, the self-appointed leader of the group, spoke first. "We'd like some service, Ma'am."

The plump White Lady stood with her arms folded across her ample, sagging breasts. The sweat of the day had plastered the brown wisps of her hair to her forehead like scraggly spider legs. She wiped away the beads of perspiration with one of her pudgy hands before giving him a response. "Looka here! I'm 'bout tired of ya'll Northern Nigras! Cuttin' into my tips 'cause ya takin' up spaces for my payin' customers. I ain't made two licks all day and I got kids to feed!"

She wiped her soggy hands on her apron before continuing, her voice rising continuously throughout her tirade. "I'm sick of sayin' it, 'cause I know ya already know the rules; If ya want service, ya can't sit at this counter. I don't give a damn if ya sit here 'til the rooster crows, I ain't givin' ya no service!"

One of the local onlookers walked up to the counter. "These folks givin' you any trouble, Maybelle?"

Maybelle, the waitress, walked over to the man. "Yeah, Sonny. They takin' up my seats and keepin' me from getting' tips. I ain't made a plumb nickel all day!"

The man sauntered towards the group. He had a short, stocky build, and wore jeans and a plain white t-shirt that were smudged with sweat and dirt. Although he appeared to consider himself White, his complexion was extremely dark and about the same shade as the clipboard-wielding assistant's. His thick, jet-black hair stood up in pointed spikes due to the high humidity, and gave him the appearance of a mischievous imp. He looked down the line at the students with an evil scowl, locking eyes with Willie. "Looks like we got us a Martin Luther Coon here, thinkin' he can bring his black ass in here and get some service like a respectable White man. We ain't gonna serve you, Boy! So you might as well take your crew and head on home before you bite off more than you can chew."

Willie's jaw tightened. Bobby held his breath, hoping that Willie wouldn't fall for the bait. Willie began to sweat profusely and his Adam's Apple bulged when he took a long swallow, but he remained silent.

Sensing that Willie would not respond, Sonny moved on down the line with his insults, seeking a weaker victim. His eyes rested on Carol and Bobby. "Why, look at what we have here. Two nigger lovers! Y'all must not be from aroun' here 'cause this here ain't tolerated! Whites and Nigras don't mix!"

Sonny walked over to Bobby and peered into his face, standing less than an inch away from him. "You from 'round here, Boy? Are you?"

Bobby refused to answer and continued to look straight ahead. Sonny continued, barking loudly into Bobby's ear, like a rabid dog. "Ya hear me, Boy? Or do you Northern boys lose ya hearin' from hangin' 'round too many niggers?"

Bobby remained focused on maintaining his composure, fixing his eyes on the large clock behind the counter. He studied the second hand as it crept around its face, moving slowly, like it belonged to a decrepit invalid. *"Tick... Tock.... Tick...Tock."* One of Sonny's accomplices decided to egg him on. "I don't think he hears you, Sonny. I think he done started lovin' the niggers so much he can't hear us good White people anymore."

Sonny, not to be outdone, decided to continue to assert his perceived authority. "Maybelle, lemme have some of them coffee grounds. If this here boy wants to be a nigger, I say we make him one."

Maybelle handed Sonny the basket of grounds hesitantly. "What ya gonna do, Sonny?"

Sonny replied, "You'll see."

Sonny grabbed the basket and walked back over to Bobby. Willie locked eyes with Bobby before quickly looking away, feeling somewhat responsible for causing the situation, since it was originally his idea to attend the protest. As Bobby stared stoically ahead, Sonny dumped the entire container of grounds over his head. "Now, you Black, too. You wanted to be a nigger, so now's you is one. How's that feel?"

Carol dropped her head and began to cry, and Thomas' chest began to puff with anger. Bobby, although humiliated, remained composed. He decided to calm himself by thinking of his family and loved ones and pretending he was in another place. He thought of his father, and how he'd probably criticize him for not fighting back like a man. He thought of his mother and how she'd probably intervene on his behalf in order to protect him. He thought of Lucela and wondered what she'd think of him sitting here with his new friends, after never sitting with her at his own dinner table because of the same rules he was now protesting. He suddenly wished he could go back to his family's kitchen for just a moment and tell her, *"You sit down. I'm gonna fix your plate and then eat with you.*" He tried to comfort himself by softly singing a gospel song she had taught him as a small child.

"This little light of mine, I'm gonna let it shine.

This little light of mine, I'm gonna let it shine.

This little light of mine, I'm gonna let it shine.

Let it shine, let it shine, let it shine."

Sonny began to laugh loudly, but Maybelle looked away from the group and began to wipe the already gleaming glass behind the counter, as if to distance herself from the situation. She had no problem with mistreating the Blacks, but knew that mistreating an upper-class White could lead to trouble.

In a deep bass, Willie joined in, as well as another male in the group. Carol stopped sobbing and also joined in, singing in a barely audible whisper. Sonny, who was still not finished wreaking havoc, continued down the line. He stopped at Mary.

"My, my! Fellas, we got us some sweet brown sugar!"

Sonny's two friends walked towards him, all giving Mary inappropriate looks. One replied, "Sonny, let's be gentlemen." He then placed his hand on his crotch. "How 'bout we take this sweet thing here to get something to eat where she can get some real good service?" All three of them laughed loudly before his friend continued, "I see she's got a friend. Let's see if she's a natural redhead." The group laughed even louder at this comment, and Sonny stepped closer to Mary.

"Say, girl. You and yo' friend wanna take a ride? We promise to be gentlemens and treat y'all to a real nice time."

Mary remained completely still, like a store mannequin. Her ample chest had no rhythm; to an observer, it appeared that she wasn't even breathing. Sonny stepped closer, placing his tongue inside of her ear and licking her from her lobe to her neck. Although her breathing never increased, a single tear rolled down her cheek, like a raindrop on the face of a statue.

Thomas, who was seated next to Mary, lost his composure. He jumped from his seat and slammed Sonny on the floor before quickly punching his comedic friend in the gut and hitting the other friend with a chop to the throat. In less than three seconds, all three of the men were out of commission. Willie jumped up, chastising Thomas. "Man, are you crazy? You're about to get us all killed!"

Before Thomas could reply, Maybelle interrupted the conversation. "I'm callin' the law! Y'all comin' in here and tearin' up the place! I'm callin' the law!"

Thomas stood as if he were in a trance, rubbing his hands across his face as if he were wrestling with his conflicting emotions. Willie grabbed Bobby by the back of the shirt and grasped Thomas' shoulder. "Come one, guys! Let's hit the road before the law comes!"

The boys raced towards Bobby's car, jumped in, and sped out of town.

CHAPTER THIRTEEN

The boys raced out of town, each of them feeling their throats choke with anxiety and fear. None spoke a word for quite some time, until they had left the area and were on the outskirts of town. Finally, when they began to see country roads and mile markers, they breathed a sigh of relief. Thomas broke the silence.

"Hey, fellas. I'm real sorry about what happened back there. I guess I just let my anger get the best of me."

Willie, still angry, didn't respond. Bobby, however, was forgiving. "Aw man, it's okay. We understand." He looked at Willie for affirmation. Willie nodded in agreement, but was still too angry to speak.

After they approached the next mile marker, Thomas noticed the flashing lights approaching. "Hey man, pull over. I think a police car is coming."

Bobby, unaware that the car was approaching to capture them, leisurely sauntered over to allow the car to pass. When the car came closer and stopped behind them, each boy felt his stomach tighten.

The first officer to emerge from the vehicle was the driver. He was a young, skinny man with a huge Adam's apple that bulged from his throat. His partner slowly emerged from the passenger side of the vehicle. He resembled the stereotypical

Southern police sheriff: fat, balding, and smoking a cigar. He readjusted his tight pants and allowed his oversized girth to drop and cover his belt buckle.

Bobby rolled down his window and removed his wallet. He had received enough speeding tickets to know the routine very well. Although the deputy approached the driver's side of the car first, the sheriff was the first to speak from the passenger's side. Before speaking, he peered into the vehicle and adjusted his mirror sunglasses. "Well, where are you fellas headin' to so quickly?" He removed his cigar from his mouth and blew a cloud of foul smoke into the vehicle while staring intently at Willie's steely glare.

Bobby nervously removed his driver's license. He handed it across Willie to the portly officer. "Here's my license, officer. Is there a problem?"

The officer laughed loudly and eventually his deputy joined in, wearing a look of unease which revealed that he was somewhat unsure of what was so humorous.

"Bertie, he wants to know what the problem is. I guess these Northern nigga-lovers don't know how we do things around here."

His sidekick laughed. Willie, Thomas and Bobby shifted uncomfortably in their seats.

"Well, you see here boy, we got rules in the South. Not only was you speedin', but you also violatin' our transportation laws. You see, Whites and niggers can't ride together in the front seat. These two niggers should be in the back TOGETHER. Y'all ridin' up here all comfy like y'all friends." The deputy looked at Bobby. "These yo' friends, boy?"

Bobby didn't know how to respond. If he said "no" then he'd have to endure the wrath of his friends. During their trip, he'd formed a strong bond with them and totally changed his racial attitude. If he said "yes" then he'd have to endure the wrath of the officers. He wasn't sure what that would entail, but deep down Bobby really believed that it didn't matter how he responded, he would have to deal with negative consequences either way.

Bobby's face reddened. He took a deep breath before saying in a low voice, "Yes."

The sheriff reddened and removed his glasses. He removed a handkerchief from under his gut and wiped his dripping forehead. "Lemme get this straight, boy. You tellin' me that these two niggas is yo' friends?"

"Yessir," Bobby replied, a little louder this time.

The skinny deputy seemed to have gathered his courage and interjected a response, "Why don't y'all get out of the car. We need to make sure you ain't transportin' no weapons across state lines."

The boys emerged from the vehicle uneasily. The two officers searched the vehicle, tearing open bags and suitcases in utter disregard. Finally, the sheriff located the large box of food from Aunt Pearl. He removed a chicken leg and a cookie and began munching alternately on both of them.

The sheriff's voice took a grave tone. He dropped the chicken bone on the dusty ground. "You boys ain't from 'round here. So y'all must be part of that group of rabble-rousers that been keepin' up trouble in the city."

None of the boys responded.

He removed another cookie from the tin and took a large bite. "We got a report about a group of boys, two Black and one White, makin' a big scene at the diner. Y'all fit the description. Said them boys was makin' trouble, tryna integrate the diner and have Whites and Nigras served together."

The deputy interjected, "An' that ain't gonna happen down here!"

The sheriff laughed. "You got that right! Bertie, let's show these Northern boys what happens when they come down South causing trouble." He removed his gun from his holster.

Thomas, realizing they were going to die, began to plead. "Please, sir, my father, I can call him right now. He'll pay you, anything you want. Please sir! Please!"

Bertie said, "Oh, looka here sheriff, we got one of them rich niggas, tryna buy themselves a chance to be White. Well guess what, boy? It ain't gonna happen!"

The sheriff laughed again. "Boy, there ain't enough money in the state of Alabama to stop me from putting a bullet in your ass! Get down on your knees, all of you!"

Thomas dropped to his knees, his hands covering his tearful face. Bobby lowered himself, his head hung in despair. Willie refused to lower himself to the ground. He figured that he was going to die anyway, so he might as well die like a man. The sheriff approached Willie and hit him on the side of the head with the butt of his gun. Once Willie's limp body fell to the ground, the sheriff placed two shots in his back. Willie lay wheezing loudly, like an unattended tea kettle, struggling to survive.

Thomas crumpled over in emotional pain, sobbing uncontrollably and making him almost oblivious to the round of shots he received in his chest. Bobby looked around and saw both of his friends lying in a crumpled heap. Thomas lay backwards with his glasses broken and a trail of blood spreading across his shirt; Willie, no longer wheezing, laying on his side with his eyes open and unfocused. A thick pool of blood was forming between the two of them, the liquids mixing like a dark, purple river. The sheriff laughed again and dropped the ashes from his cigar on Willie's bloody back. "Okay, Bertie, your turn. Show this Nigga-lover how we do them in Alabama. He don't get a body shot, he gets a shot to the head. After we're finished with him, were gonna set this fancy car on fire and send them on an early trip to Hell!"

Bobby looked into Bertie's eyes, searching for compassion. Bertie, who had never shot anyone before, looked away. It was one thing to shoot a nigger, but he couldn't imagine shooting a White person. "Hoyt, I don't know, I mean, he's a White boy—"

Hoyt bellowed at him, "He's not a White boy! He's a Nigger-Lover! He's just like a Nigger! Shoot him!

Bobby realized that his fate was sealed. He began to sing softly, thinking of his family, his friends, and Lucela and how he would give anything to turn back time and do things differently. Bertie unsteadily removed his gun from his holster. Bobby began to sing softly, his voice struggling to remain controlled as he anticipated the bullet that would end his life.

"This little light of mine, I'm gonna let it shine.

This little light of mine, I'm gonna let it shine.

This little light of mine, I'm gonna let it----"

Bobby's voice was silenced by the single shot to his temple. His body fell to the ground in the purple river between his two friends, adding fresh blood to the stream of death.

CHAPTER FOURTEEN

The boys had set off for Birmingham on December 18th . On December 25th, the family's Christmas dinner was interrupted by a knock at the door. Sheriff Coleman removed his hat before giving Robert, Sr. the news: Bobby's red sports car had been found on the side of a road outside of Birmingham. After the local law enforcement's investigation, a report was given that covered up his murder and gave a less accusatory explanation. According to the Alabama Sheriff, it appeared Bobby had crashed from speeding and the car had burst into flames. (In actuality, after each murdered boy was thrown back into the vehicle, it was doused with gasoline and set afire.) As a result, the Lofton family was unable to have an open casket at the funeral.

Given his recent run-ins with local law enforcement, this explanation seemed plausible. Kay Lofton collapsed with grief. Robert, Sr. fell to his knees. Susan screamed hysterically. Little Timmy vomited up his recently eaten dinner.

A few states away, Aunt Pearl sat at her table, waiting for the boys to come partake of the feast she had prepared for them. Suddenly, the phone rang. She heard a garbled voice and finally realized that it belonged to Thomas Senior. "Pearl, Tommy's gone. The boy done got himself killed, trying to be a hero down there in Alabama."

"Lawd! Have mercy, Jesus! Mercy!" Pearl dropped the phone instantly, her hand burning as if fire were pulsating from it.

A low scream emerged from deep in her large belly, a painful place that had been opened once before when Thomas told her she had lost her beloved sister.

The Lofton's did not know that their son had participated in a Sit-In demonstration in Alabama. Unbeknownst to them, the boys' pictures had been taken by various media outlets during the event. One prominent photo featured Bobby standing beside Fred Shuttlesworth while he gave a statement to the local media regarding his stance on Civil Rights. This photo was later featured in a national magazine.

Word had spread throughout the Colored grapevine of the boys being chased by an angry mob of local Whites and being forced to leave town. Once they were outside the city limits and away from the prying eyes of the media, local Blacks correctly assumed that they were murdered by for trying to "stir up trouble", an atrocious act that they had seen occur time and time again.

Weeks later, when Bobby's photo appeared in Life Magazine, the true facts began to surface. However, with little cooperation from the local Alabama law enforcement, the Lofton's faced a nearly impossible bureaucratic cover-up. Punishment for Bobby, Willie and Thomas' lives was never granted. The Lofton family never recovered from this cruel injustice. Robert, Sr. sought refuge in the bottle, Susan sought refuge in the surging 'Hippie' movement, and Timmy sought refuge in Lucela. Kay Lofton sought refuge within herself, but her body betrayed her. Within a few months, cancer had ravaged her entire being and sent her to be with her eldest son.

Prior to Mrs. Lofton's passing, the team won the state championship. With Bobby, Willie, and Thomas gone, the team practiced with renewed vigor and vowed to earn a ring in their honor. Later, when the real reason for their passing surfaced, the remaining teammates became even closer. Even Joey Hudson had a change of attitude, having seen how untamed racism could result in the loss of three, precious young lives. A team with such a strong bond was unstoppable, both on and off the field. Clarence assumed the role of quarterback and the team won their first championship, beating their opponent 28 to 3.

The stands were packed, and ironically, the families of the players sat integrated, much to the puzzlement of their foes. The players' attitudes seemed to have influenced their parents, and the seating of families seemed to be a trivial matter in the grand scheme of things. The united goal of cheering the team to victory was their primary focus. Besides, each family was especially grateful that their child's life had been spared.

Lucela attended the game with Myrtle's family. Clarence's sixteen year-old brother, Craig, and his two younger sisters, Minnie Sue and Mabel Jean waved banners and cheered wildly for their older brother. Mr. Lofton, Susan, and Timmy sat nearby in the stands. Mrs. Lofton had already taken ill and was bedridden. She remained at home with her nurse, watching the game on local television while holding a picture of Bobby in his football uniform next to her bosom.

Robert, Sr. tried to maintain his composure; the wounds of his son's death were still fresh and this was the first game he had attended since his son's position was vacated. The flask of whiskey in his pocket kept his insides warm and provided a small comfort to his chilled heart. His hands shook as he took a quick swallow, thinking of his impending loss of the love his life, Kay. She had been the picture of perfect health before losing Bobby. He knew that cancer wasn't killing her, but the bitterness of grief that he also felt on a daily basis. Kay had never been a drinker, taking only a sip of champagne on New Year's for good luck. It was one of the many qualities he had always admired about his wife: her angelic nature. Now he wished she had been a little less saintly. Then she could have embraced the bottle like he did and walked the long and winding road towards death, instead of taking a shortcut.

Once Timmy spotted Lucela, he immediately perched himself close beside her. He had changed so much during the last few months, becoming even more reclusive than he previously was. He spoke very little, hardly laughed, and spent hours at his mother's bedside or as close to Lucela as possible. He knew that his mother was leaving him soon. Even though he was saddened, as a child who had faced death on more than one occasion during his young life, he understood her reasons far better than anyone. If his mother left, he still had Lucela to care for him. However, Bobby had no one and needed her more. His biggest fear was that his mother's passing would leave him solely in the care of his father. He knew that his father secretly wished that it had been him he had lost instead of Bobby, his pride and joy.

Once word spread among the Black residents of the reasons behind Bobby's demise, he became a local hero, often elevated to a mythical, martyr status. The facts surrounding the case were repeated so much that they took on a life of their own. One popular story was that Bobby had fought off two policemen, broke the neck of a police dog with his bare hands, and sped off at 200 miles per hour before being killed. Bobby's high school retired his jersey and placed it along with a plaque in the school's trophy case. Mt. Nebo held a special memorial service for Bobby, and planted a rose bush in his honor.

Lucela's words to Bobby did come true; he made not only his family proud, but the entire town's residents, both Black and White.

Two weeks after the game, each player was presented with their championship ring. Coach Mellon choked up when he noticed that three extra rings remained after each player received their memento. Clarence boldly stepped forward and cleared his throat. "Uh, Coach, sir, I'd like to know if it'd be alright for me to be trusted with the care of Bobby's ring. My auntie's gonna come get me this weekend and take me over to his family. We kinda grew up together, and his Mama ain't doin' too well. We thought this might brighten her spirits a little."

Coach Mellon was grateful to have been relieved of this task. "Thanks, son. Please wish the family well for me."

That Saturday afternoon, Clarence arrived at the Lofton home. Robert, Sr. saw him approaching the back door and hurriedly opened the front screen. "Clarence, come on in. What brings you this way?"

Clarence extended his moist hand before entering the home. Mr. Lofton shook it vigorously then patted him on the back. "Good afternoon, Mr. Lofton. Uh, is Mrs. Lofton here? The team sent me with something I'd like to present to y'all."

Robert, Sr.'s throat tightened and he longed for a swallow of warm whiskey to loosen his vocal chords. "She, uh, she hasn't been doing too well. You see, uh..."

"Yes, sir. I know. Lucela being my cousin and all, she told me a little about her condition. I thought, sir, that maybe this might brighten her up a little. The fellas wanted me to present her with Bobby's championship ring. Would that be alright, sir?"

"Well, uh, yea, son. I guess so. Lemme see if she's feeling up to it. Have a seat."

Truthfully, Kay Lofton had heard the entire conversation. Timmy sat beside her, softly brushing her hair to relieve her aggravated scalp.

"Timmy, put the brush away for now, dear, and hand me my glass of water. My throat's a little dry." Kay took a long sip before licking her chapped lips. Immediately, she became self-conscious of her normally immaculate appearance. She longed for a bit of lipstick to make herself more "presentable" for the approaching company. Kay sat up in bed and smoothed her gown just as Robert entered the room.

Robert looked relieved to see Kay alert and upright. She normally spent her days lying in the bed, often crying silently. Robert was often puzzled as to whether his wife's tears were a result of pain that was physical or emotional in nature. 'Honey, Clarence, Lucela's relative, is here to speak with you. You feeling up to it?"

"Sure, Rob. I'm feeling pretty good today."

Robert returned a few minutes later with Clarence timidly clutching his baseball cap in his hand. He waved at Timmy before approaching the bed. "Hello, Mrs. Lofton. How ya feelin' today?"

"Why, Clarence. I'm feeling alright. How's your mama and grandma doing?"

"Mrs. Kay they doin' just fine. My granny said to tell you "hey" and extend my best wishes for your recovery."

"Please tell her I said "thank you" Clarence. What brings you by today? I know you've got plenty of other things you could be doing on a sunny Saturday like this than visiting me."

Clarence immediately felt his throat swell, as if a frog was blocking his windpipe. He swallowed and inhaled deeply in an attempt to clear his airway. "Well, uh, Mrs. Lofton, the team thought it'd be fittin' if I took the privilege of presenting you and Mr. Lofton with Bobby's championship ring." He reached into his pocket and removed a black velvet box that was adorned with a gold imprint of the state flag. Robert stood stoically against the wall, as if he were using it to prevent him from collapsing. Timmy looked on in awe while silently stroking his mother's hand. Kay managed to remain composed, even though her eyes began to fill with water.

Clarence continued his mission. "Even though Bobby wasn't with us at that final game, we felt him with us on the field. You know, we would have never won these rings if it weren't for your son. He's the one that brought us together." Clarence went on to explain how Bobby had orchestrated the changes on campus, fighting for all of his teammates to be treated fairly. "Mr. Lofton, sir, I hope you don't mind me saying this: you raised a fine son. I know that a lot of boys wouldn't have taken a stand like Bobby did. My grandma always says that good men learn to be good men by watching their fathers. I never had a father around, so I never had a "good man" to watch. I'm glad I had a chance to know a good man like Bobby. Even though he was young, he taught me a lot about what it means to be a real man."

121

Robert wiped his eyes with his handkerchief. He never knew his son had been such a fine example of manhood, something he knew he couldn't take sole credit for. Although he wasn't a robe-wearing Klansman, he often displayed discriminatory attitudes and dropped racial slurs in the presence of his children. He liked some Blacks, like Lucela, but he felt that the races got along better when they were separated. Truthfully, Bobby's behavior toward his teammates was a result of Kay's influence, not his. His reddened eyes were the result of the guilt he felt by accepting Clarence's compliment.

Clarence opened the box in front of Mrs. Lofton. The brilliance of the gold ring brightened the room like a ray of sunshine. "The coach was going to mail the ring, but I felt it would be better if y'all received it personally." Clarence removed the ring from the box, dropped to his knee, and prepared to place it on Mrs. Lofton's small finger. "May I?"

"Yes," Mrs. Lofton responded. Clarence placed the ring on her tiny finger then clasped both of his large hands around her small palm. He stood up, his bulk blocking the sunlight in the room.

Mrs. Lofton held up her hand and inspected it closely. *"Her Bobby! The town hero, the team leader."* She'd gladly take it all back to hold him once more in her arms. Kay held the ring close to her caving chest and caressed it. She wiped her tears and called to Clarence before he left the room. "Clarence?"

"Yes, ma'am?"

"Thank you, son. I appreciate you taking the time to bring this to me. You were right. It brought me joy to receive this precious gift personally. Please tell Coach Mellon and the team that I said "thank you" for thinking of our family."

"Mrs. Lofton, you're welcome."

Kay wore Bobby's ring for three days before he told her to come to him. She decided to comply on the morning of that year's Good Friday. When Reverend Warner preached her eulogy he remarked that only a woman as angelic as Kay Lofton would be allowed to leave this Earth on the same day as Christ Jesus.

CHAPTER FIFTEEN

The loss of two family members in less than six months was too much for the Lofton's to bear. Susan, who was already emotionally fragile, began to distance herself from her group of friends during her mother's illness. She decided that she didn't want to become the mayor's wife, but instead wanted to detach herself as far from her community as possible. She began hanging out with a rag-tag, racially diverse group of individuals that often indulged in various vices that included mind-altering drugs and irresponsible sex. Two weeks prior to her mother's passing, she realized that she was pregnant with a child that had been fathered by a boy she had met at a house party. Frightened, she wished that she could discuss the matter with her mother, even though she knew her news might negatively affect Kay's health. Although she and the boy were practically strangers, she knew enough about him to locate him if she needed to, since he was a friend of a friend. She hadn't contacted him yet because she wasn't sure what she wanted to do or what her options were.

Susan figured herself to be about two months along, and wondered if she could somehow avoid the shame she would bring on her family with this pregnancy. They had already endured enough this year, and she didn't want to be the cause of any more turmoil. Her father was becoming more and more fragile, and she knew this would break his heart. He would be dismayed to know she was no longer a virgin. He still called her his "little angel" and hated for her to mention boys, let alone date them. He even grilled each boy that came to take her out as if he were cross-examining them in court, even though he'd known most of them all of their lives and was usually a friend of their parents. Perhaps she could ask around and get the number of that old lady on the Colored side of town, Mrs. Delacroix, who knew how to "fix" things like this for girls who wanted to end their pregnancies.

One afternoon, Susan summoned the courage to discuss her dilemma with Kay. She waited until Timmy had momentarily left her side to go to the bathroom and hurriedly sat in his chair beside the bed, moving in a definite, quick motion like someone sneaking into a movie theater seat without paying. Kay looked up, startled to see her there. Susan immediately felt guilty when she saw her mother's surprised face. The presence of her only daughter should have been a regular occurrence, not an unusual one.

"Hey, Mom. How ya' doin?" Susan felt stupid at her forced attempt at casual conversation--another indicator of her usual absence. She clasped her hands tightly, until they reddened and became moist, then reached out and clasped one of her mother's frail hands between them.

Kay recognized her daughter's rare gesture of affection. Even in her illness, she still took a moment to encourage her. "Susan, I'm a little tired. But I am glad to see you. I know you've been very busy with your school work. Timmy's told me all about the studying you've been doing for your science class. I heard you've become a member of the Botany Club. How are things?"

125

"Botany Club?....Oh, yeah! Botany Club. Yeah, Mother, I have been busy. That's why I wanted to take some time for you." Susan figured that Timmy must have told a few "fibs" to cover for her and give Kay a legitimate explanation that explained why she rarely visited with her. Truthfully, Susan honestly didn't feel she was strong enough to watch her mother suffer. She'd already lost her brother and felt like the acknowledgement of more grief was an intrusion on her young life. Perhaps if she avoided reality it would begin to change to her liking. So far, this hadn't worked, but her young mind was not mature enough to realize that magic realities and "happily ever after" only existed in fairy tales.

They sat for about an hour, making small talk while watching an episode of Bonanza. (Timmy peeked in, gave her a timid smile and mentioned that he had some cataloguing to do for one of his collections before retreating to the sanctity of his room.) She'd even made her mother laugh when she commented about how she thought Little Joe looked like a younger version of her father and asked if that was why Kay had married him. Kay giggled like a schoolgirl when she told Susan that she did indeed see the resemblance and that her father was even better looking than Michael Landon when they were courting as teens. She went on to share how she had proudly wore his letterman's jacket in high school and his varsity pin, just to aggravate the other girls who had their eye on him. Susan was surprised to see a slight blush in her mother's hollowed cheeks, as she spoke of her first and only love.

As her mother began to tire, Susan regretted that their memorable interlude would soon end. She couldn't figure out how to reveal her secret, so she decided to keep it to herself instead of ruining the moment. Before she rose to leave, Kay reached out and touched her on the cheek. Her voice had begun to weaken and she spoke with a raspy whisper. "Susan, I hope that you will one day realize that you are stronger than you think you are. People often think that they have to be loud in order to show their strength, but that is not really true. You can be strong in your own, quiet way. And you can handle anything you face in life when you look to God to give you strength. Remember the scripture, *'I can do all things through Christ that strengthens me.'* Susie, you CAN handle anything you face in life." Kay moved her hand from Susan's wet cheek to her noticeably protruding stomach. "Anything."

"She knows! Mother knows!" Susan began to sob uncontrollably at the realization of Kay's discernment, her final gesture of motherly love. Loose tops and sweaters had fooled the rarely sober Robert, Sr., but Kay had known all along from her deathbed.

"Susie, don't fret yourself, thinking that you've hurt me. I feel so blessed to know that part of me will live on through you when I am gone. I am sure that you will do the right thing." She chuckled to herself. "You'd be surprised to know how many of your friends were born four or five months after their parents were married. Love sometimes breeds life. That's how we keep living on."

127

Susan's flow of tears increased from the spurring of two different emotions, joy and pain. She felt joyful at the fact that her mother understood her problem and did not demonize her for her wrongdoing. However, she felt pain at the fact that she was deceiving those she loved. She would never marry the father of her child because it was not an option. First of all, Susan's child was not the result of lovemaking, but simply sex with an acquaintance. Secondly, the father was Colored.

Two weeks after Kay's passing, Susan packed up and escaped during the night. She had met a new "friend" who was planning to hitchhike to California and join some friends who were living in a commune and part of "The Hippie Movement." He had no problem with her current situation and told her he believed that *"all things happen according to the cosmos and love should be freely given among all of God's children."* She wasn't sure exactly what that meant, but it sounded like a better option than shaming her family within their small community by having a mixed-race child out of wedlock.

Susan left a note to her father, simply telling him not to worry, that she had left to "find herself." Robert, Sr. fell to his knees when he read the words, not knowing the real reason why Susan had left. One benefit of alcoholism was oblivion to even the most obvious. Timmy, on the other hand, had seen it coming. He immediately noticed Susan's increased distance once Kay had finally passed. He was saddened, but somehow understood her reason for wanting to escape their household; something he was too young to do. Lucela had also seen the signs months prior, but

128

for the same reason as Kay. As the laundress and custodian of the family, she noted that Susan's monthly visit had been absent for about three months. Plus, Susan had always detested bacon. However, she had lately eaten it on a daily basis. She said a quiet prayer for Susan before she retired to bed that night. "God, bless that child. Help her find her own in this big world."

Before she left her family, Kay made preparations for each and every one of them. When Timmy and Susan would leave for school, she would dictate instructions to Lucela from her bed. "Lucela, once I am taken to the hospital, please proceed with the instructions I have given you. Because of your duties, no one will question you and things will take place as I desire. Robert has not recovered from losing Bobby and he will not be of much help when I leave. I know that you are aware of where my fine jewelry is, please take it and keep it in a safe place until Susan is settled. I would like for her to have my great-grandmother's pearls when she is married. I would also like for my friend, Norma Myers, to have my diamond brooch. She has been my best friend since childhood and has always admired it. I know that Robert's sister, Earlene, will try to take it. That's why I want you to write all of this down. I will initial each page when you are finished to prove that these are indeed my wishes. Also, I'd like for my mink stole to go to Gladys. She'd picked it out for me one year and told Robert to give it to me as a Christmas gift. Saxie had wanted me to have a fox, but Gladys said she thought I'd prefer mink. She was right." Kay chuckled. "Fox makes me think of the times when Grandpa and Daddy would go hunting. Like coon and rabbit. Nothing I'd want to wear on my shoulders after I'd seen its carcass hanging on the back of a truck."

Lucela wrote until an entire tablet was completely full, detailing specific items such as china, linens, and other family heirlooms. Once she had completed her task, Kay instructed her to take the notebook home and hide it for safekeeping. "Lucela, there's one last thing. I don't want you to write it down, because I'm not sure how people in the family would feel about it." She paused and cleared her parched throat before proceeding. "Timmy has always been close to you, and loved you like a mother. I know it, he knows it, even Robert knows it. It doesn't bother me, because children can never have too much love. But he and his father have never been close and I know that his health will begin to fail again if he is left to be raised in this house. Robert loves him, but he just doesn't UNDERSTAND him like he should. They're too different, and I would hate for Robert to be burdened with trying to parent him. Lucela, when I die, promise me that you will finish raising my son. I want him to grow up to be a healthy young man. He won't be able to do it in this house."

"Yes, Mrs. Kay. I promise to look after your boy. You have my word." Lucela wasn't sure how she would do it, and dreaded discussing the topic with Abe or Mr. Lofton. She figured that she would leave it in God's hands. True to form, God handled things for her.

CHAPTER SIXTEEN

Two months after Kay's death, the stillness of the home began to sink in. Most friends and family had begun to visit less frequently and the loss of Bobby, Kay and now Susan had become more evident in the once crowded home. The whiskey bottle had become Robert's sole comfort, since he could no longer share his thoughts with anyone. Even in her sickness, Kay had still provided him with a listening ear and the routine of work had kept his mind occupied. Now that he had empty days and restless nights, the distance between Robert and Timmy became more obvious. Timmy would often retire to his room, occupying his mind with insects, books, and his imaginary friends.

June 8th was too much for Robert to handle. It would have been Bobby's 19th birthday and the hardship of the situation was too cumbersome for him to bear without the assistance of his friend Jack Daniels. Once he had reached the last drops of the bottle, the full extent of Robert's grief and rage consumed him. His protégé' was gone, as well as the love of his life. What else did he have to live for?

When he retired to his cold, lonely bed each night, the ache in his heart was unbearable. He missed Kay's voice, her soft skin, her smell, her touch. When she was living he had been ashamed to admit the fact that she wasn't the only virgin on their wedding night. She'd always spoke as if she assumed he had been experienced, like most twenty-one year old men. Truthfully, he'd loved Kay since he was sixteen and had never even kissed another girl, even when she patted away his roaming hands in her attempts to remain chaste. Now that she was gone, he'd lost count at the number of available women who had approached him, most of whom had been Kay's friends. He'd been too embarrassed to respond, not knowing how or even if he wanted to touch another woman since it would not be a fitting substitute for his beloved Kay.

He reminisced about when Bobby was born, how proud he'd been when the doctor informed him that he had sired a son—and a healthy one at that: nine pounds, seven ounces! How proud he was when Bobby first picked up a football and showed real talent. How proud he was when Bobby scored the winning touchdown in junior high and took the team to a championship. How proud he was when Bobby was interviewed in the local paper and had even made the news. His family had called from all over the state, proud of the Lofton tradition of athleticism that allowed him to hold his head high in a town that was ruled by the wealth and prestige of his wife's side of the family. Bobby, his pride, was gone and the emptiness could not be filled by women, liquor, or money. He felt angry at God for taking everything he loved away from him and leaving him with a pathetic reminder of the weaker side of himself—sickly, scrawny Timmy. The "accidental" child that had popped up when Kay thought she was going through the change and he was beginning to ache and stiffen with middle age. He cried out to God, "Why? Why? Why did you do this to me? Why did you curse me like Job? I hate you! Do you hear me? Damn it, I hate you!" When God did not call his bluff by striking him down or changing his body into a pillar of salt, he became even more enraged. He threw the bottle at the wall and the brown shards of glass scattered about the room like sharp bits of topaz. Now fully consumed by his anger, he marched down the hall and kicked in the door on Timmy's room. The boy shivered in his bed with fright, clutching his mother's brush under the covers. "Look at you, you little sissy! Why are you holding your mother's brush? You pansy!" Robert shook Timmy like a rag doll before slapping him repeatedly across the face.

Timmy couldn't explain that he wasn't fond of women's things for unnatural reasons, he simply wanted to hold it because the blond strands within the bristles still contained her smell—a scent he found comforting. However, the terror of his father's ranting and raving made him mute. He struggled to retain control of his bladder, knowing that if he soiled his sheets it could be the death of him.

Robert stared at his son, the last pitiful remnant of his once solid, stable family. He had never struck his child and the stinging sensation of his palm brought him back from the blurred reality of his inebriation. He rubbed his hands over his balding head as the tears moistened his already sweaty face. Saliva escaped from his lips as he sobbed and blubbered like an infant before asking Timmy, "Why did it have to be Bobby? Why couldn't it have been you? Why couldn't you have died instead of Bobby?"

Timmy's bright blue eyes finally blinked him back from the edge of terror. A large tear traveled over the reddened palm print

133

that remained on his cheek. An onlooker would have thought the tear was due to Timmy being slapped or the explosive comments his father was making. Truthfully, Timmy was crying out of pity for his father. He had accepted that his father preferred his brother and sister instead of him many years ago. However, he realized at that moment that although his father had presented himself as the "head of the family" he was really its weakest link. He hated to see him implode out of grief.

Once Robert had passed out in a drunken stupor, Timmy made his escape. He packed his clothes, boxed up his collections, and called the town's only taxicab service. He might have been only 10, but he had the intelligence of a grown man. When the driver arrived, he seemed puzzled until Timmy explained that his father had left town for business and made arrangements for him to stay the weekend with the family's housekeeper. Although Lucela lived on the "Colored" side of town, she lived in what would be considered the upper class area and so the driver felt comfortable dropping him off.

Lucela was about to retire to bed when she heard a timid knocking at the door. At first, she thought it was Abe then realized that the door was unlocked and only a stranger would choose to summon her in this way. She softly called out, "Who is it?"

"Lucela, it's me. Timmy. I've come to stay with you."

Lucela opened the door and Timmy thrust himself into her arms. He buried his head into her bosom and unleashed a current of tears. His soul was immediately comforted by her signature scent of rosewater and talcum powder. He inhaled deeply and tightened his embrace. Lucela gasped slightly at the increased clamp on her midriff, then stroked his soft curls and gently rubbed his shoulders. Timmy's muffled sobs echoed throughout the entryway of his new home. Lucela continued to stroke his shaking body and the severity of his sobs decreased. "There, there, Sugar. It's alright now. Everythang's gonna be alright."

Long after Timmy had went to bed, the man of the house voiced his opinion on the matter. "Ceel, what that little Lofton boy doin' in my house?" Abe had arrived home slightly before sunrise and discovered Timmy in the guest room. He'd entered the bedroom and shook Lucela awake.

Lucela rubbed her eyes and squinted at Abe before responding. "He's staying here. From now on."

"The hell he is! Ceel, naw! Now looka here..."

Lucela sighed and turned over so that her back was facing Abe. She was finished discussing the matter and silently hoped that Abe would say, *"It's me or him"* so she could tell him that she was choosing *"him"* and end the argument. She released a loud sigh before responding. "Abe, this matter ain't up for discussion. I gave Mrs. Kay my word and I ain't takin' it back. That boy came over here in the middle of the night like a vagabond and I ain't puttin' him in the street. Now, I done put up with a lot from you over the years and had to endure a lot of open shame because

135

you haven't respected me as your wife. You made some foolish decisions, but I dealt with them and so now I guess you need to do the same. This here ain't your decision to make; it's mine and I done made it. Had you been here during the night like the man of the house instead of layin' up God knows where, then we might have had some time to discuss this. But that time has gone and this is how it's gonna be."

Abe tried to stutter a response, but was greeted by Lucela's resumed snoring. He stomped off to the basement and slept on the old cot while he listened to the radio. He sadly realized that he had never really been the "man of the house" and thus acted so childish and irresponsible for this reason.

CHAPTER SEVENTEEN

Lucela continued to undertake her duties in the Lofton home. By this time, Mr. Lofton had retreated into the downward descent of full alcoholism and required care on a daily basis. He rarely left the home, choosing to eat, sleep, and of course drink, on the couch in front of the television. He would spend hours watching sports, yelling and screaming at the players and coaches as if he were present on the field. Timmy chose to avoid visiting the home, and on rare occasions when he did Robert would stare at him as if he were a stranger that had intruded into his world of solitude.

Each day, Lucela prepared a basic meal that could be eaten at Mr. Lofton's leisure, such as sandwiches or fried chicken, since he rarely had an appetite. Robert rarely ventured through the house, therefore only a few rooms required cleaning. In order to encourage Robert to consistently wash and change, she would lay out a fresh outfit for him on a daily basis, since she knew he was too incapacitated to do so. Lucela and Kay had often spoken of Robert's condition, with Kay surmising that he would not live much longer after her departure. Lucela began to believe that Kay was correct in her assumption. Robert was becoming so dependent on alcohol that he was losing control of his bodily functions. On more than one occasion Lucela had noticed that his pants were damp from the waist down due to his lack of bladder control.

Unlike Robert, Timmy seemed to adjust to the changes in his life with the naive gallantry of childhood that exists due to the lack of experience. Lucela's three-bedroom home provided him with the space and seclusion he desired, as well as new, unfamiliar surroundings that his inquisitive mind yearned to explore. The cellar of the home contained numerous, empty shelves that Saxie had built to house her preserves and jellies. Timmy had eagerly cleared away the large cobwebs that covered them and filled the spaces with multiple jars of dead and living specimens of nature.

Still angry about the situation, Abe often arrived home intoxicated and unruly. However, Timmy had learned to deal with Robert and applied these same skills to Abe. Once he heard the screen door slam, he would immediately retreat to his room. If he had no option of retreating, then Timmy made sure that he remained in the presence of Lucela for protection. One difference worked to Timmy's advantage. Unlike Robert, Abe rarely arrived home until the wee hours of the night. It was not uncommon for Timmy to observe him only once or twice per week, even though they resided in the same living quarters.

Despite the circumstances that led to the situation, Lucela felt a small surge of happiness at the chance to finally become a mother. Timmy was constantly bestowed with toys, trinkets, pastries, and nourishing meals that were created to his liking. The two of them spent numerous hours in their usual sanctuary--the kitchen. Timmy would share and discuss the details of his collections while Lucela kneaded breads, frosted cakes, and braised meats. He would greet her each day with a chirpy "Good morning, Mama Ceel," and retire for bed each night with a good night kiss on her cheek. Now that she was being provided with the love from Timmy's affections, Abe's indifference was no longer noticed and his reluctant touches were no longer desired. For the first time in many years, Lucela felt complete.

Abe, of course, felt the sting of his competition and realized that he was slowly being dethroned. He would often bicker and attempt to engage his wife in verbal altercations regarding small, trivial matters that he attributed to the changes made now that Timmy lived in the home. One night, Abe sat down to eat supper and made a feeble attempt at stirring up trouble.

"Ceel, why you make this stew without okra? You know I like okra!"

Lucela placed a large, warm, buttered piece of cornbread beside his bowl. "I'm sorry, Abe. I didn't think you'd notice. Timmy doesn't like okra so I used peas instead. "

Abe hungrily ate the stew while he continued his tirade. "Oh, so now the "Master of the House" gets to dictate the menu? I'm in charge here, and any changes that get made should be discussed with me!"

Lucela absently washed the dinner dishes while conversing with her husband. "Well, Abe, you weren't here and I didn't think it was a big deal. Next time, I'll make sure to cook you a pot with okra, okay?" She knew that Abe was grasping for straws and just wanted to fuss. She was tired and wanted him to finish eating so that she could finish cleaning the kitchen and retire to bed.

Abe continued to gobble, hollering a response while his mouth was full of food. Crumbs flew from his mouth and landed on the spotless, gleaming Formica table. "Humph! Don't you think that's a little expensive, making two pots of food just to please some child? Groceries is high and we ain't got the money to be spending like that. Children should be seen and not heard. Let that boy eat what you give him or starve!" Abe pounded his fist on the table for emphasis, as more crumbs spewed from his half-open mouth.

Lucela chuckled to herself. In their almost twenty years of marriage, Abe had never, ever purchased one item of food he ate. The expenses of the house didn't concern him, which was probably a blessing in disguise since he normally drank or gambled most of his pension check away. Lucela decided to use sugar instead of salt to soothe his bruised ego. "You're right, honey. I'll just tell Timmy to pick out the okra next time. By the way, I'm going to the market tomorrow. You want a couple of t-bone steaks for dinner?"

Abe, still seething, pounded on the table before responding. "Oh, so you planning on buying THREE t-bones? That boy in there gotta eat his share!"

Lucela sighed before responding. "Oh, no honey. The steaks is for you. That young'un ain't gonna want no steak. I'll let him finish off the rest of this stew with a cheese sandwich."

Abe stood up from the table and authoritatively hitched up his pants around his slim waist before limping away. He called over his shoulder, "Well, alright then. T-bone's will be fine. Long as you ain't tryin' to fix me no sandwich. I gave up mess hall grub long ago."

Lucela walked over to the table to retrieve Abe's empty dishes and utensils. The laughter she had struggled to contain erupted in response to his retreating footsteps. For a minute she wondered who was really the little boy in their house-- Abe or Timmy?

As time passed, Timmy thrived under Lucela's physical and emotional nourishment. He grew in stature and filled out so that he was no longer considered small for his age. At the age of twelve, he could look Abe in the eye without lifting his head and his muscles had begun to develop. Although he still liked collecting items and enjoying nature, his exposure to Lucela's social circle had caused his interests to shift. He enjoyed attending church services at Mt. Nebo and amazed everyone when he joined the choir with his outstanding singing voice. At first, Rev. Burnett was reluctant to accept this little blond-haired boy within the sea of brown faces. He had no personal issue with Timmy, but feared that his presence might stir up trouble within the community. But he had a definite change of heart when Timmy

141

brought the house down with his rendition of "The Old Rugged Cross" on Easter Sunday, a solo he dedicated to the memory of his mother.

Timmy had always known that he could sing, soothing a sickly Kay with the songs of her favorite artists such as Perry Como and Pat Boone. However, he had always been too shy to share this skill with the rest of his family, thinking it would be considered as another unmanly trait that would cause his father to continue labeling him as a "pansy." Timmy knew that he wasn't a sissy like his father said. He was sure of this fact because he strongly liked girls and honestly preferred Colored ones. In fact, he had even kissed Martha DuBois at the annual church picnic when they took a walk in the woods.

Due to the strong bond that existed between the Miller/Lofton family and Lucela's, Timmy was accepted as a member of the group with open arms. Clarence, who was approaching graduation from the state college, became a surrogate big brother to Timmy and pushed him to engage in sports. He initially encouraged Timmy to practice catching and throwing the football through flattery; he told him that he had the same "quarterback hands" that Bobby once had.

"Quarterbacks need large hands so that they can grip the ball easy. They also gotta have skillful fingers so they can throw and hit their targets." Clarence held his hand up and placed Timmy's hand in front of it. At the age of twelve, Timmy's hand was almost as large as Clarence's. "Look here. You ain't even hit yo' growth spell and you already got large hands. And all that time you spend holding them microscopes and using them pins and needles done taught you how to use your fingers to handle tiny things and trained your eyes to focus on a target. Now drop your hands to your side. See how your fingers reach down to just about your knees? That means the rest of you gotta grow taller so your knuckles aren't scraping the ground like a caveman. Boy, once you catch up with your hands you gonna be taller than your Daddy-- maybe even taller than Bobby was."

Timmy beamed with pride at the thought of towering over his father, looking down at him and feeling powerful. *"I doubt he'll call me a pansy then,"* he thought. *"I'll show him that I'm a REAL man!"*

Clarence affectionately slapped Timmy on the back before continuing. "Right now you already taller than Uncle Abe. But heck, so was I when I was your age." Clarence's tone softened. He could see Timmy's expression change when Abe's name was mentioned. "If he ever start with you, just stand your ground. He's mean as a snake, but he ain't nothin' but a big coward. He just tries to use his mouth to make himself seem big, but trust me, he ain't gon' do nothin'." He laughed to himself when he recalled watching Abe cower in fear when he stood over him in his teens, intervening to protect his mother and Lucela. Clarence tossed the ball to Timmy. "C'mon boy, lemme see you use them hands."

CHAPTER EIGHTEEN

As the years passed and seasons changed, life in the small town remained the same. Timmy began to blossom physically and socially and became more acclimated to his surroundings. As a result, the unfamiliar became familiar to him and he became more "Jessup" and less "Lofton." When it was time for him to enter high school, Timmy asked Lucela if he could attend Jefferson High School instead of Bobby and Susan's alma mater, Monroe High. Seeing the surprised look on her face, Timmy tried to explain. "Mama Ceel, I know there won't be too many other White kids there, but I think I'll feel more comfortable going to school with Harvey, Jr., Minnie Sue, Martha and the other kids from the church. Besides, Jefferson's just two blocks away. I don't want to trouble Uncle Abe with taking me way over to Monroe every day."

Abe, who had been listening from the living room while he read the paper, smiled to himself at Timmy's consideration of his time. For once, he and Timmy were on the same side. He knew that getting Timmy to school would be his responsibility and thus interrupt his nighttime creeping and daytime sleeping. He decided to voice his agreement, much to Lucela's surprise. "Ceel, the boy got a point. He always with the kids in the neighborhood, why should we change it now just cause he goin' to high school? If he wanna go to old raggedy Jefferson, let him."

Timmy smiled after hearing Abe plead on his behalf. Lucela, feeling outnumbered, gave in. "Okay, Sugar. We'll go down there Monday and take care of everything."

To everyone's surprise, Robert, Sr. had held on longer than anticipated. He had shriveled away to a shell of himself, but had managed to survive on the fuel of his bitterness. In order for Timmy to attend Jefferson, Lucela would need his consent. She approached him with the issue that Monday, while Timmy sat listening in the Lofton's kitchen. "Mr. Lofton, Timmy has decided that he wants to go to Jefferson. He seems to have his mind made up, but I told him that I wouldn't feel right doing it without your consent."

Robert appeared to be startled and struggled for a response. His normal existence involved days and nights of solely internal conversations. He shook his head as if he were trying to awake from a coma. "Lucela, what's that you said?" Lucela explained again, more slowly while Robert nodded his head in response. Timmy entered the room and stood beside her, standing past six feet. Robert was taken aback and rubbed his eyes while he attempted to recognize his own son. "*Is this that little scrawny boy that had run out of here a few years ago?*" Except for the blond curls atop his head, Robert saw no resemblance to his youngest son. He thought that his ears were also betraying him when he heard the deep, baritone voice escape from the body that used to house the nasally whine of Kay's little pansy.

"Dad, I'd like to attend Jefferson. It's just two blocks from Lucela's and all my friends go there. Besides, Clarence is the new football coach and he promised me a shot at being the next quarterback. He's been working with me, and I think I can handle it."

Quarterback? High school? When did this boy grow up? Robert cleared his throat and tried to quiet the voices in his head. "Well, uh, Bob-I mean, uh, Timmy if you want to play football, I guess it's okay." Robert wiped his sweaty forehead then chuckled to himself. "Boy, since when did you start playing football? I thought you'd be in charge of the butterfly catching club!" Robert laughed uproariously then quieted himself. He didn't want Timmy to be offended at his comments. "I mean, uh, when you was little I couldn't get you to pick up a ball. You were always catching birds and butterflies and stuff."

Timmy stiffened before responding. "Well, I still do that. And I am a member of the Botany Club. But I realize that I like sports, too. I even play basketball. I'm just a better football player."

His boy was going to be the next high school football star! Now, he finally had a reason to live. Robert stiffened and pushed away his morning screwdriver. Lucela noticed and silently thanked God for an answered prayer. Timmy, thinking it was simply orange juice, failed to see the significance. "Well, if you're going to be the quarterback, then I guess it's okay. It might be better for you to go to Jefferson anyway; if you go to Monroe, you might face some stiff competition for that spot." Robert stood up and proudly slapped Timmy on the back. "My boy's going to be quarterback! The Lofton name rises again! I can't wait for the season to start!"

Timmy laughed inwardly at his father's remarks. For one, he knew that Jefferson's athletic roster was far more talented than Monroe's; he faced much stiffer competition for the role of quarterback at the Colored high school. These facts didn't deter him because he was ready to face the challenge. The real reason he wanted to attend Jefferson instead of Monroe was to avoid the constant comparisons to Bobby, in case he didn't measure up to his older brother's standards. But he had to admit that he was elated to see his father finally taking some interest in him, even if it was due to football. Perhaps this could be one reason for his father to stop or at least lessen his drinking. The alcohol had taken a toll on him during the years and he was beginning to resemble a man 20 years his senior. "Well, Dad, can't wait to see you in the stands. You'll be there, right?"

"Of course, Son. Wouldn't miss it for the world. Isn't that right, Lucela?"

CHAPTER NINETEEN

True to his word, Robert, Sr. attended each and every game. He wasn't always completely sober, but he wasn't falling down drunk. Now that he had a source of joy in his life, Robert decreased his dependence on alcohol. He began working again and interacting with friends and family. He still missed Kay, but realized that it was possible to live his life without female companionship.

Although he was old and rusty, he and Timmy began to spend time throwing the football and discussing team plays. Every Saturday afternoon, Timmy walked over and watched the *Wide World of Sports* with his father while Lucela prepared a filling lunch for the two of them. Watching Robert's appetite for food increase, while his appetite for alcohol decreased, was thrilling for Lucela. She encouraged him to eat heartily by fixing his favorite foods such as barbeque ribs, beef brisket, cornbread, collard greens, and potato salad. Each week she left him with at least four dozen chocolate chip cookies to munch on while he watched his Sunday sports. Within less than a year, Robert had practically given up alcohol and gained more than fifty pounds. On anyone else, the weight increase might have appeared unhealthy. However, Robert had previously appeared so malnourished that the additional weight made him appear to look "normal."

Now that Timmy was making a name for himself in the community, Abe once again felt dejected. Instead of feeling some sense of fatherly pride for the child, Abe's personal demons arose

148

and filled him with an intense jealousy. To make matters worse, Timmy was such a good-natured and likeable child that when people wanted to ridicule him they had a hard time doing so without feeling extremely guilty. Everyone in the town, Black or White, liked Timmy. He could venture into any area on the Colored side of town because not only was he the high school quarterback, but he was also the "cousin" of Clarence Smalls, the football coach and a respected minister at Mt. Nebo. In addition, he was also the little brother of Bobby Lofton, the local hero who had sacrificed his life by taking a stand for Civil Rights. Although he chose to hang with and attend school with the Black students, Timmy also garnered a certain level of respect among the Whites due to the status of his mother's family and the fond memories of his older brother. Finally, Timmy was an extremely handsome young man that did not possess an ounce of conceit. This fact made him even more likeable.

When Abe hung around the pool hall, his ears burned with jealousy each time he heard the mention of Timmy's name. "Hey, Crip! That boy of yours sure played a heck of a game last week. Man, Monroe ain't lost to Jefferson in ten years!"

"Yeah, you see that boy throw? Man, I remember when his brother used to play for Monroe. He was a good player, too, but I think this kid is even better."

Smitty, aware of Abe's feigned indifference to the conversation, spit a stream of tobacco juice before he chose to aggravate him even more. "Yeah, Crip! You must've really been a proud papa, seein' all three of yo' boys on the field. Why didn't one of them twins catch that White boy's pass and run for a touchdown? I get 'em mixed up, cause they look just alike. Which one of you and Marianne's boys made that catch?"

Marianne perked up when she heard her name. She silently sat at the bar, waiting for Abe to at least ACKNOWLEDGE his paternity. She'd diminished her hopes of ever taking Abe from Lucela, especially after he let his wife move that White boy in without ever contributing more than a few pennies for her two.

Abe paused and placed his pool stick on the edge of the table. He'd had more than a few drinks and this liquid courage moved him across the floor towards Smitty. "Hey, man. Why you always gotta be startin' wit' me? I don't know which one of them boys made the catch and truthfully, I don't give a damn! Them ain't none of my kids nohow. Y'all know how Marianne is; them kids could belong to anyone of us in this room. Now don't be tryna call me out and spread no lies about me. I got me a wife and I ain't fathered no bastards wit' Marianne!"

Marianne had had all she could take. It was bad enough that Abe wouldn't help her feed those two, strapping boys; but she had to draw the line when he chose to shame her in front of everyone. She'd shared her lonely bed with no one but Abe for more than 15 years, in vain. Her heart was bruising her chest from grief and she felt her breath coming in short spasms, as if she were being choked. She struggled to maintain her composure as she looked at her reflection in the mirror behind the bar, feeling like she were trying to recognize a stranger. The face peering back at her looked as if it belonged to someone else, someone she instinctively felt she should be familiar with, but struggled to recognize. Marianne squinted then felt her eyes fill with tears when she finally realized who was peering back at her. The image pointed at her and threw her head back and cackled in laughter, and Marianne finally realized she was the victim of a cruel joke. As her insides burned from shame, the laughter of her mother echoed in her head. *"Ha, ha, Miss High and Mighty, you always thought you'd be something better than me. Lookin' at all those magazines and movie pictures and thankin' you'd be one of them rich White ladies in Hollywood. Talkin' bout how you gon' get a husband. Men don't marry women like us, cuz' we hoes! Hoes! Yo' little ass was hoeing right under my roof, thas' why I put you in them streets, hopin' you'd learn yo' lesson early. But yo' dumb ass didn't and you jus' kept on hoeing, givin' it away like a damn fool for FREE! Didn't have no sense. Least yo' sisters wised up and went down to New Orleans and worked in a real sportin' house. But you? You stayed your dumb ass here and wasted away, jus' like I did. I told you! I told you--you wasn't gonna be shit! You was gonna end up just like me! Look at yo'self, girl! You JUST LIKE ME!"* Marianne heard her mother end her insult with one last, loud, high-pitched witchy cackle. The echo of her laughter deafened her alcohol-induced fog, and she struggled to escape back to reality as if she were pushing her head up from under water and straining to gather oxygen. At that moment, Marianne realized that she'd become the person she despised the most: her mother. She wondered if she'd die alone and never having been married, just like her.

Before Smitty could respond, Marianne rose from her usual barstool and staggered over to Abe. She placed a hand on her skinny hip and shook a long, scarlet polished fingernail in her slanderer's face. "Abraham Lincoln Jessup, I know you ain't gonna stand here in front of everyone and say them ain't yo' boys. Bad enough I had to give 'em my granddaddy's last name cause you refused to upset yo' precious Ceel, but you got the nerve to say you didn't make 'em? I'll be damn! I'm fit to be tied 'cause I done seen all. Even yo' damn wife got enough sense to keep her distance 'cause she know them two boys is the spit of you! Here I done made do with the scraps you done gave me for more than 15 years, while you parade around town with your uppity wife and her little White boy in yo' fancy car and livin' in yo' big, fine house! I been waitin', hopin', hell, even prayin' that you'd get some sense and come make us a real family, but I see I done fooled myself all along. And you got the nerve to call me a whore? When you know good and well you lay up with me six or seven days out of every week!"

Marianne looked around the room at the various men's faces. Some of them dropped their heads out of pity when she met their gaze. True, she may have been loose with many of them before meeting Abe, but after mothering his children she had changed her ways. "Ain't a man in here can say he slept with me since I got wit' you Abe. Not a one! But I know for a fact that Bessie and some of these others can't say the same about you."

152

Marianne stomped back to her table, grabbed her purse, and stepped towards the exit. All movement in the establishment had ceased, with some pausing out of respect and some due to curiosity.

Once Marianne reached the door, she halted and turned towards Abe. Her voice cracked on a ragged sob and a single tear dropped from her bloodshot, drooping eyes. "From here on, we through. No dealin's anymore, period. I done wasted enough time on you, and I see now it ain't done me no good! Probably let a good man pass me by while I was waitin' for you to come to your senses." She stepped out into to the fresh evening, leaving at a much earlier time than usual. The screen door slammed behind her, briefly interrupting the deadened silence in the room.

Abe, feeling embarrassed, shrugged his shoulders and took a swig of his now warm drink. Smitty, having purposely caused the disintegration, smiled to himself before adding insult to injury. "Bessie, fix me another one. Oh, and bring yo' lover man here another beer. He's lookin' a little down in the dumps." The entire pool hall erupted into fits of laughter, with the exception of Abe, who responded with a soured expression. Before he could reply, Smitty continued to mock him. "Don't worry Abe. It's on me. We all know you ain't got no job."

Abe had taken enough. He threw his pool stick down on the ground and walked towards the door. Before leaving, he called over his shoulder. "Smitty, you can go straight to hell."

Smitty had to have the last word. "I will Abe. All I gotta do is follow you there. Looks like already on the path that leads to it." Abe slammed the screen door in response to the continued laughter at his expense.

Smitty shook his head in pity. As much as he despised his overweight and lazy wife, he respected her enough to avoid openly shaming her in front of the community. All five of his children belonged to the two of them. He didn't have any outside children and all of his offspring bore his last name. As far as he was concerned, Abe was an idiot that had no self-respect.

CHAPTER TWENTY

Marianne remained true to her word, much to Abe's dismay. His withered ego missed her consistent adoration and he began to feel rejected and unloved. Lucela, having become used to his constant disinterest, had adjusted her lifestyle so that it did not include her husband's affection or attention. Since Abe was rarely home until the early morning hours, she and Timmy had built a life together that did not require his presence.

Now that he was present, Abe began to feel his intrusion on their space. He would often complain or bicker when either of them insisted on watching shows that did not interest him, or engaged in conversations about topics that he was ignorant of.

"See, Mama Ceel, the Viceroy butterfly has an extra stripe here. The Monarch doesn't." Timmy, sitting in his usual spot at the kitchen table, pointed to a picture in one of his many books. Lucela, drying a dish, looked over his shoulder. "That's how you can tell them apart. People get them mixed up all the time, but it's really easy to tell the difference."

Abe, in a sour mood, attempted to start an argument. "Humph! You always readin' bout bugs in them books. Why you wastin' yo' time lookin' at pictures when all you gotta do is go out in them fields and look at some of them boll weevils and earworms? Butterflies don't do nothing' but look pretty. Them pests can take out a whole field of crops!"

Timmy's face reddened and Lucela tried to maintain peace. "Abe, leave this boy alone. He talkin' to me, not you. Anyway, he ain't tryin' to catch no rashes scoutin' through these fields." She rubbed Timmy's head affectionately, "Sugar, you so smart. You don't need to be out in no fields. You oughta go to school to be one of them people that wear them white coats and hold them little, tiny glasses-- what you call 'em? "

Timmy laughed. "You mean test tubes? You want me to be a scientist, Ma? I don't know. I think I'd get bored having to stay in a laboratory all the time."

Abe grunted loudly, signaling his boredom with the conversation. Lucela and Timmy passed a knowing smile between themselves before she attempted to bring him back to the conversation. "Well, Sugar, you sure are smart enough to do it. I bet you could get a job with the government, maybe even the military and help them mix up some chemicals to make some of those bombs they use on them foreigners. What's those bombs y'all used in the war, Abe?"

As usual, Abe's ears perked up when the war was mentioned. His eyes brightened and he turned toward what he believed to be a rapt audience, to occupy them with stories of his younger days, some true and some fantasy. "We dropped 'tomic bombs on them Japs! Yessir, we went in there with force! Thas' when they gave up, 'cause they knew we had 'em." Abe paused, rubbed his chin, and begin embellishing his faded memories. "I remember when it went down. They were comin' at us, and

156

shooting overhead. We was armed and ready! I was loading the plane to get ready for battle, and one of those Tuskegee Airmen told me, "Make sure I'm packed tight, soldier, 'cause I'm gonna drop a shitload of gas on them Japanese!" Lucela and Timmy laughed, as if on cue, and went back to their previous activities. Abe dreamily smiled to himself before returning to his favorite television show, Hogan's Heroes.

In actuality, Abe had only been promoted to Private First Class, a rank which required him to assist with the janitorial duties of the unit since Colored soldiers weren't allowed in combat. The Tuskegee Airmen were a selected group of pilots that operated under the supervision of the Air Division, a unit Abe was not even assigned to. As a result, he had never even met any of the Tuskegee Airmen nor fought in any battle. In fact, he hadn't received his injury saving the lives of fellow soldiers in Germany; he'd actually injured his leg while sweeping the mess hall when one of the drunken White officers had accidentally fired his weapon in anger when Joe Louis defeated Billy Conn and took his heavyweight boxing title. In order to avoid embarrassment, the Army had provided Abe with a disability pension and a bus ticket home.

Exaggerating the facts of his exploits made Abe feel extremely important among his peers; they weren't hard to impress. Few of the people he spoke with had never left the state, let alone the country. He had told these entertaining stories so often that he believed them to be true. But after a while, his audience would lose interest and divert their attention to more constructive activities.

After his humiliating skirmish, Abe lost complete interest in the pool hall. He'd returned once, but felt self-conscious as if everyone there could see through his façade of bravado. Marianne was seated on her usual stool, but had her arms around Fred Carson, one of his Cousin James' friends. Fred was a large, hulking man of limited intelligence. He worked at the local lumber mill with James, Smitty, and the rest of the crew. He was also about ten years younger than Abe, a widower with a young daughter.

Once Marianne noticed his presence, she purposely tried to attract his attention. Running her long nails along her date's biceps, she slyly peeked at Abe to see if he was staring. To her delight, he was. "Oh, Fred! You got such BIG muscles, look like your arms 'bout to bust through that shirt. Where'd you say you was takin' me again, in your fancy NEW car? To the drive-in? I hope the back seat has PLENTY of room!"

Fred, feeling like the "big man on campus" responded to her open invitation to intimacy. "Oh, I got enough room for us, baby! Don't you worry yo' pretty little self!" Marianne giggled like a school girl while Fred rubbed on her exposed thigh. Abe turned away, feeling like a spoiled child who was watching a playmate pick up a toy he'd discarded. Now that someone else found Marianne appealing, he felt a twinge of jealousy.

Since Abe's late night activities had ceased, he searched for other activities to fill his time. Previously, he attended Jefferson's football games periodically. Now, he became a consistent presence in the stands on Friday nights. Although he'd never admit it, losing Marianne was hurtful, and he soothed his pain in whiskey. Sitting in the night air, the golden liquid warmed his heart and provided him with the self-assurance he lacked. Prior to the changing of Abe's leisure activities, Lucela, Myrtle, and Robert, Sr. had established such a solid a routine that he now felt like an interloper. Lucela supplied the snacks, whether it was fried chicken, hot dogs, fish sandwiches, or lunchmeat. Myrtle provided the beverages, whether it was soda, coffee, or the occasional hot cocoa. Robert provided a comforting presence for the ladies as they reminisced about their joined families.

Since the twins, Johnnie and Ronnie, also played on the team, Marianne was present at most games. Sometimes her daughter came with her; lately Fred came with her and brought his young daughter. She purposely kept her distance from Lucela and her family, not due to fear, but out of a basic respect for her boys. A confrontation in the stands would bring attention to the fact that they were her bastard offspring, a fact she regretted as she matured into the middle years of womanhood. She knew she wasn't the best mother to her sons, but as she aged she realized that they did not deserve to endure further embarrassment due to her mistakes.

The twins were good boys, handsome, and well-liked. This even surprised Marianne since she knew she'd put little effort into

159

raising them. True, she kept them fed and clothed as best she could, but they were usually left to fend for themselves. However, her parental neglect had actually led to the development of their talent. With few toys available, the youngsters had occupied their time by running and playing outside. By adolescence, they had become such skilled athletes that even the coach was trying to assist them with obtaining scholarships to attend college. *"My boys are going to college!"* Marianne proudly thought. She had dropped out of school in the 6th grade when she became pregnant with her daughter Janey, and never imagined higher education in any of her children's future. She had pinned her hopes on them joining the military, working at the mill, or finding employment at the local Colored hospital. Growing up, she only stressed one thing to her boys: never turn to a life of crime and end up in jail like their brother Curtis.

As they matriculated, the twins and Timmy had perfected their performance on the field so well that by the eleventh grade they were unstoppable. When they beat Monroe and emerged as a contender for the state championship, the Jefferson High School fans went wild! The celebration also had a racial undertone, since the Colored high school had beat the White one and earned the chance to represent the city at the state game. The game was won by a "Hail Mary" pass that was caught by Johnnie during the last 40 seconds of the game. Timmy had actually intended for the pass to be caught by Ronnie, but he had been blocked by Monroe's cornerback. Johnnie, urged by an internal sense that his brother would need his assistance, was already rapidly running to his aid. Before Ronnie was tackled, Johnnie had already jumped in front of him and recovered the ball. He ran the last 35 yards to take the team to victory.

Afterwards, Timmy and Ronnie tackled Johnnie in a bear hug and carried him off of the field on their broad shoulders while the rest of the team celebrated in ecstatic jubilation. Abe sobered up in the thunderous applause when he felt a lump forming in his throat. Just as Smitty said, "all three of his boys" were in the spotlight. The problem was, since he had ignored them for so long, any attempt at congratulating them would seem insincere. He watched Lucela, wiping her moist eyes like a mother hen while Robert, Sr. clasped her around the shoulder in a semi-embrace. A few aisles away, Marianne jumped up and down ecstatically while Fred tried to restrain her by engulfing her small frame in his gigantic arms. Within this circle of celebration, Abe felt like he had crashed a party. Having consumed a whole pint of whiskey, his clouded mind conjured up a plan to increase his low self-esteem.

As the teams assembled on the field for the formal announcement of the playoff champions, Abe meandered out of the stands and ventured onto the grass. Timmy, Ronnie, and Johnnie were at the center of the group, holding the tattered football that had led them to victory. Clarence, the team's coach, attempted to control his emotions as he complimented the team on their hard work and solicited the spectators' support at the championship game. Abe stood on the sidelines, expectantly waiting for his opportunity to make his presence known. Clarence, overcome with emotion, handed Timmy the microphone. After a brief pause, Timmy began his heartfelt, diplomatic speech. "First of all, I'd like to give a special thanks to the Monroe High School football team for making us work hard and dig deep within to see what we, as a team, were made of. I'd like to say that I feel proud to have beaten a team that was coached by a legacy of our town, Coach Randolph Bybee, who I learned a lot from as a young boy when he coached my brother, Bobby Lofton." At the mentioning of Bobby, each and every spectator, Black and White, responded with thunderous applause. "I would like to give a special thanks to two people who are very special to me. Lucela Jessup, for always loving and caring for me…" (Abe held his breath in anticipation.) "…and Coach Clarence Smalls who encouraged me to pick up a football." At this point, Timmy held the ball in the air towards his family in the stands. "Finally, I'd like to present this ball to my father, Robert Lofton, Sr. Dad, I appreciate your love and support." Robert, Sr. waved at Timmy proudly, then took a handkerchief from his pocket and wiped his tearful eyes.

Abe, feeling dejected, began to listen to the voices inside his head. *"That little bastard didn't even mention you! After living in your house all these years, you didn't even get a "thank you." Well, that's jus' fine. You got yo'own "real" sons to be proud of. Thas' yo' blood in their veins. Whatever talent they got, they got from you. Go over there and let them know they won 'cause you gave 'em those skills."* As if on command, Abe limped over to his illegitimate sons in their moment of glory. Both boys were being smothered with slaps on the back and handshakes by players, coaches, and fans. Looking up, Johnnie's face hardened when he

162

saw a vision of himself in 30 years shuffling towards him. He stiffened and nudged his womb mate.

Although they did not formally acknowledge Abe, both boys were well aware of who he was. Since their infancy he had been a constant presence in their home, usually at awkward hours. On more than one occasion he had entered the kitchen while they were sitting at the table eating breakfast, shirtless, peering through their bare refrigerator and barking orders like he was the man of the house. He would rarely greet them, treating them like intruders in their own home, not even caring to learn their names or differentiate between the two. Usually, he just called them "boy" and used the name as a reference for whichever of the two was closest to him.

"Boy, go get me a beer."

"Boy, where yo' mama at?"

"Boy, quit puttin' yo' dirty hands on my clean car!"

Besides the crooked walk, the resemblance between Abe and his offspring was uncanny. A complete stranger would acknowledge the children's paternity; too bad their father refused to. Marianne and Fred, who were walking towards the team, stopped when they saw Abe approaching. He walked over to Ronnie and extended his hand. Ronnie grudgingly shook it.

"Good catch you made there. Team wouldn't have won without you. I gotta tell you, I felt real proud watchin' y'all in the stands. Saw that Jessup blood in you, runnin' and takin' charge on the field."

Ronnie pulled his hand back, indignantly. "Mister, you're wrong on two counts. First of all, I got tackled. My brother made the catch. Second, I ain't a Jessup. My last name's Clark."

The voices told Abe that he had suffered enough humiliation for one night. They told him to assert his authority and take a stand. "Now looka here, jus' cause y'all won a big game ain't no reason to act uppity. I guess I shoulda known better, seein' how y'all's Mama probably ain't taught y'all no manners or respect for yo' elders. She ain't never been much of a woman, so y'all might as well acknowledge that whatever good you got came from me!"

Ronnie, the temperamental one, lost control and lunged at Abe. "What did you say about my Mama? You sorry, old nigga, I oughta---" Luckily, Johnnie restrained him. Abe, feeling braver since his opponent was being held, continued to insult Marianne.

"Thas' why I ain't never claim y'all. Yo' Mama bein' so no count, I figured y'all wouldn't turn out to be much. But I see that the "good blood" came through anyway. If you wadn't my boys, you'd probably be jailbirds like yo' brother." Abe turned to walk away, unaware that Fred and Marianne were standing behind him. Marianne struggled to remain composed, not wanting to

164

draw any more attention; a few people in the crowd had become aware of the conflict and stopped to see how it would be resolved. Ronnie continued to shout insults at Abe, while Johnnie held him protectively. Fred saw his chance to step up and prove his love. Before Abe could utter another word, he punched him squarely in the jaw. Since Abe was already inebriated, he fell to the ground, unconscious. Ronnie ended his tirade and went to comfort his weeping mother. The few onlookers laughed in amusement before walking away in search of more excitement.

Clarence, being a true Christian, helped Abe to his feet in order to avoid further embarrassment for his family. Abe groggily pulled away, staggering across the field while cursing under his breath. Clarence shook his head before admonishing him. "Uncle Abe, you gettin' too old to be carryin' on like this."

Two weeks later, Jefferson lost the championship game. Their opponent, Eisenhower High School, barely eked out a win of 24-21. The boys felt defeated, but Clarence told them to hold their heads high. Most of the players were underclassmen that still had one year left in their high school careers. The games were also closely watched by coaches and scouts from the state colleges; Timmy, Johnnie, and Ronnie's outstanding performances did not go unnoticed.

CHAPTER TWENTY-ONE

The next summer, Lucela was greeted at the Lofton home by an unfamiliar face. When she entered the kitchen, a small girl was seated at the table nibbling on a strip of burnt bacon. Lucela placed her sweater in the closet and walked towards the sink. The small child turned towards her, smiled, and said, "Hi."

Something about the child looked eerily familiar. She had a full head of loose, black curls and a light brown complexion, the color of heavily creamed coffee. Her large eyes were so bright and heavily lashed that they captured all attention given to her face, like the Hollywood starlet Bette Davis. Although she appeared to be about the age of three or four, she had the mature mannerisms of a woman of royalty. She daintily nibbled on her meat before dabbing at the corners of her mouth with a napkin, and extended her pinky while she sipped her warm milk from a china cup. Lucela pondered about why she felt as if she KNEW this child, even though she was a complete stranger. Just before she solved the mystery, the missing piece of the puzzle walked into the kitchen.

"Good morning, Ceel-Ceel."

Lucela turned around then held her hand to her breast in shock. She thought she'd seen a ghost. Besides gaining a few pounds and wearing the face of womanhood, the girl looked exactly the same. Her eyes immediately filled with tears and her throat felt as if it had locked on her words. After gasping a few times, she was finally able to speak. "Susan, is that you?"

Susan walked over to Lucela and warmly embraced her. "Yes, ma'am. It's me. I see you've met Bobbie Kay."

Lucela turned back toward the child. Bobbie Kay gave her a slight wave then said, "Mommy, who is this?"

Susan replied, "This is the lady who helped raise me. I've told you about her. Her name is Miss Lucela."

Bobbie Kay's face softened, and she looked at Lucela with welcoming eyes as if she were a stranger she had been longing to meet. She wiped her hands on her napkin, got up from her seat, smoothed her flowered dress, walked over to Lucela, and formally extended her hand. "Hello, I'm Bobbie Kay Lofton. I'm very pleased to meet you."

Lucela was touched by the child's maturity and demeanor which were well beyond her years. "Well, I'll be! I'm pleased to meet you, too Little Miss Bobbie Kay." She shook the child's hand then in a mocking formal tone said, "If I may ask, how old are you?"

"Why, I'm four years old. I'll be five September 12th. Mommy says I'll be able to go to school soon. I can't wait. I already know how to write my name and all my colors and numbers. I can even read, can't I Mommy?"

"Yes, baby. You sure can. Maybe you can read to Miss Lucela while we're here." She turned to Lucela and laughed, "That will give me a break. She tries to read EVERYTHING! Have to watch her, since some things in the newspaper aren't fit for a child. She asked me yesterday how to pronounce "Vietnam" because she saw it in a headline!"

Lucela hugged Susan again while Bobbie Kay returned to her seat. "I'm so glad you're home, Susie. You're gonna do your Daddy a world of good being here."

Susan, feeling uneasy, stepped back and shifted her feet. "You really think so? He seemed glad to see me, but not thrilled when he saw my daughter." She paused, as if lost in thought. "That's why it took me so long to return home. I didn't want to bring any shame on the family. I sometimes thought it'd be better if Daddy thought I was dead, too."

Lucela shook her head emphatically before replying. "Nonsense! Nonsense! Girl, you just gotta give him some time. He's missed you. He'll come around. Your Daddy has changed a lot in the past few years." She walked over to Susan and tightly squeezed her hand. "Just give him some time, baby. Jus' a little time." She sniffled and wiped away a tear, then lifted Susan's head that was drooping from indignity. "Susie, you give him some time and that girl will be the 'apple of his eye' just like you used to be. Your Daddy got some old ways, heck, all of us do. But deep down, he got love for his family and no matter how it happened, that there girl is his family."

Robert, sitting at the foot of his bed in the next room, listened to Lucela's remarks. He held his face in his hands, frustrated and at war with his emotions. As much as he hated to admit it, he knew Lucela was right. When the two of them had arrived on his doorstep in the dead of night, he was startled when Susan uncovered the sleeping child she held in her arms. As strongly as he believed the races should not genetically mix, he also was grateful that his prodigal daughter had returned home. At his age, he didn't want to suffer through the loss of another loved one. If Susan's returning to his life meant he had to accept his grandchild, Robert knew he would do so, even if it was reluctantly.

Lucela, excited about having Susan home, immediately began showing her love in her usual way—through food. "Well, I see Miss Bobbie Kay has eaten her breakfast. Susie, you want something this morning?"

"Well, I don't want to trouble you. Usually, I just drink a cup of coffee. We traveled here by bus and it was a long ride. Bobbie Kay didn't get any dinner, so she woke up very early and extremely hungry this morning. I tried to fix her something quick, just to satisfy her until I could get my bearings, but I was so tired I burned it. You know, I have never cared for bacon, but this girl loves it! She'd eat it every day if I let her."

Bobbie Kay, who had finished her meager breakfast, cleared her dishes and gently placed them in the sink. Lucela, who had seen her ears perk up when breakfast was mentioned, decided to let her choose the menu. "Bobbie Kay, would you like me to fix you something to eat? I know you'd probably like some eggs or maybe some pancakes to go with that bacon you've just eaten."

Bobbie Kay's eyes brightened and her face warmed with a smile. "I'd love some pancakes! Mommy doesn't know how to make them so I only get them when we go to the diner where she works on Saturdays. And I'd love some eggs, sunny side up, with a couple more pieces of bacon." She walked closer to Lucela, lowered her voice and whispered, "Mommy doesn't cook much, Miss Lucela, because we eat at her job; and when she does she sometimes burns things. I don't really like burnt bacon, but this morning I was REALLY hungry!"

Lucela winked at her then the two of them laughed, as if they were sharing a secret. Susan, who was within earshot, felt her face redden. Lucela said loudly, for her benefit, "Well, I'm sure your Mama probably doesn't feel like cookin' much, after bein' on her feet and servin' food all day. But as smart as you are I can see she takes good care of you. You're a very lucky girl to have her as a Mommy."

Bobbie Kay, feeling contrite, immediately began to defend Susan. "Oh, she's a great mommy! She always reads to me and we go to the library every Thursday and Saturday when she doesn't have to go to work. She also draws really pretty pictures and we have a lot of plants and flowers in our apartment. Did you know my Mommy got a ribbon at the fair because she grew the biggest rose? It was so pretty and...."

"Bobbie Kay, you're gonna talk Lucela's ear off. She can't fix you a good breakfast if she can't concentrate." Susan patted the seat beside her. "Why don't you come over here and sit by Mommy and read the funny papers?"

Bobbie Kay abruptly stopped her speech and slowly walked over to her seat, as if she were punished. Once she was seated, she laid her head on Susan's shoulder. Susan leaned down and planted a gentle kiss on her forehead. Bobbie Kay's long face brightened again into a smile.

At that moment, Robert, Sr. walked into the kitchen. He tried to alter his expression, but couldn't help showing his disapproval at his daughter embracing her slightly darker complexioned child. In a flash, Susan noticed his sour expression. She shook her shoulder so that Bobbie Kay would sit erect.

"Good morning, Mr. Lofton. I'm 'bout to fix breakfast. How do you want your eggs today?"

Robert grunted before sitting at the head of the table. Lucela placed a fresh cup of coffee in front of him. "Sunny side up."

Bobbie Kay, unable to remain non-communicative, pounced on the opportunity to converse. "I like my eggs sunny side up, too. I also like bacon. Do you like bacon?"

Robert, slightly startled, struggled to respond. "Yeah."

Bobbie Kay's large eyes brightened and she pursed her lips as if in thought then she placed her tiny hand on Robert's. "Are you a friend of my Mommy's, like Miss Lucela? I hope so. We don't have a lot of friends in California, just Miss Marilyn and Mr. Harold. I'm Bobbie Kay Lofton and I'm four years old. I'll be five in September. What's your name?"

Robert, feeling uneasy, stared at the child with an open mouth like a deaf mute. This child reminded him so much of Kay that it seemed surreal. She shared the same bright eyes, delicate features, curly hair, and dainty mannerisms. If Kay had been slightly browned, this child would have been her twin. Thoughts swirled in his head, of confusion, of love, of puzzlement. If his calculations were right, Susan had left because she was pregnant. Maybe if she had stayed he would not have lost so many years to bitterness, unaccounted for years that only the bottle could answer for." *Life is so short and loved ones are so valuable,"* Robert thought. God had given him a second chance at mending his relationship with Timmy and now he was granting him a chance to reconnect with Susan. Robert's old feelings of prejudice seemed insignificant when he thought of losing his daughter. Even though he wasn't happy about having a Colored grandchild, he was grateful to have a grandchild at all. He took a deep breath before answering.

"No, I'm not a friend of your mother's." Susan's face clouded, and Lucela paused in her movements, both anticipating his rejection. Robert continued, "I'm her father. So, if you're her little girl, I guess that makes me YOUR grandfather. I'm Robert Lofton, Senior. Wish I could have met when you were a baby, but I sure am glad to meet you now."

Bobbie Kay extended her hand for a formal handshake. "I'm very pleased to meet you, Mr. Lofton." Robert shook it gently then pulled her toward him in an embrace. Both Lucela and Susan looked on approvingly through blurred, teary eyes.

CHAPTER TWENTY-TWO

Bobbie Kay, who had never experienced familial relationships, became readily acclimated to life in the Lofton home. She was a lively, precocious child who enjoyed countless hours of conversations with Robert, Sr. and Lucela.

While eating at the table, she would talk incessantly, barely allowing Lucela to get a word in. "Miss Ceel-Ceel, why don't eggs taste like chicken? Didn't you say eggs came from chickens? If they're the same, why do they taste so different? And why do we eat eggs for breakfast and chicken for dinner?"

Robert was also subjected to her wonderment and observations. "Grand-Pop, why can't we get a phone like Dick Tracy and talk with our watches instead of having to use the one plugged in the wall? If I had one, I could talk to you when Lucela takes me to the park. I wanted to let you hear me scream when Timmy pushed me on the swings. And I saw a blue bird I wanted to tell you about. I forgot about it by the time I got home, especially since Mommy made me take a bath and go straight to bed after dinner."

"Because, Sweetie Pie, Dick Tracy's a comic strip. There's no such thing as a phone you can take outside and walk around with. For the life of me I can't see a reason why anybody would want to do that anyway. I can barely stand answering the one plugged in the wall, I wouldn't want to have to answer one all day long. Plus, you'd talk my ear off, Ladybug and make me go deaf!"

"No, I wouldn't Grand-Pop, because then you wouldn't be able to hear me." The child paused, as if deep in thought. "Grand-Pop, can you really talk somebody's ears off? Because if you can, I bet Walter Cronkite's done it. He talks through the television to everybody every night!"

Robert, Sr. laughed at his granddaughter's sense of logic; her presence brightened his day. Susan had discussed the two of them making a departure for California within the next week and he dreaded their absence. He decided to discuss the matter with her after dinner.

Once the family had eaten a filling meal of baked chicken and dressing, Robert conducted his usual routine with Bobbie Kay. Every evening, two books were read: one by Bobbie Kay and the other by Robert. She loved "The Cat in the Hat" and giggled loudly when Robert disguised his voice to sound like a cat. After kissing Bobbie Kay goodnight, Robert walked to Susan's door and quietly knocked.

"Susan, may I come in?"

A startled Susan replied, "Sure, Dad."

Robert stepped into the room and stood beside her bed, wringing his hands nervously. "Sue, I'd like to talk to you."

"Okay, Dad."

"Well, uh, I know you're planning to leave soon. I know you've been on vacation for a while and probably miss all of your friends in California."

"Naw, not really. Bobbie Kay and I stay mostly to ourselves. It's just that we're used to it. And plus, people don't really stare at us there."

"Stare at you? Who?"

"Come on, Dad. You know how people look at us here, since I'm White and Bobbie Kay's not. That's why I left in the first place. I didn't want to embarrass you or the family. I know how you feel about things like this, but I hope you understand that she's my child and I love her just like you and Mom loved me."

"Well, Sue, I might have felt that way about things before, but that little girl belongs to me, too. I love her because she's my granddaughter, but to be honest with you, she's such a sweet girl that I really think I'd love her just as much if she wasn't. I know that when you guys were young I may have said things, and I may have felt differently. But a lot has changed since then. First of all, I learned that in this world, loved ones are more valuable than gold. Secondly, I learned that people are people, not colors. You know who took care of me for years, even when I was so drunk I wet my pants and could barely feed myself? Lucela. You know who took your brother in and cared for him like he was her own? Lucela. You know who spent time with your brother and brought us back together through football? Clarence. They stood by this family when everyone turned away, even my folks. As far as I'm concerned, color really doesn't matter anymore. Just people. But you and Bobbie Kay are more than that to me, you're family. You, Timmy, and Bobbie Kay are all I have left in this world. I've already lost so much time with you. I'd hate to lose more years with you during the rest of my time here on Earth."

Susan was still reluctant, not due to her father, but out of fear of them being accepted in the town. "Well, Dad, I've got a job and an apartment and...."

"I'll give you a bus or plane ticket to go get the rest of your things if you need to. But you don't need to worry about an apartment, you can stay here for as long as you like. This is your home. Besides, Bobbie Kay has already made plans for us. I'm supposed to read her "The Wizard of Oz" before bed each night and that's going to take at least two months, with her stopping me every few pages with a million questions. . . then we're reading "Charlotte's Web." She's got our reading planned until at least Thanksgiving." Robert chuckled to himself, wondering if his highly intelligent granddaughter hadn't purposely orchestrated the whole thing. "Sue Bee, what do you say?"

Truthfully, Susan had left very few items in their cramped studio apartment. She had already left her extra key with her friend Marilyn that lived across the hall with instructions to provide her plants with a loving home and to either keep or sell her couch and bed for her own personal gain. In addition, she had already told her boss that she might not return if her fictional "sick relative" did not recover soon. Before leaving, she had secretly hoped that Robert would allow them to remain. As she matured, the once unscholarly Susan had realized that she did have a desire for higher education; she had planned to attend college and study to become a horticulturist. With her family's support with caring for Bobbie Kay this might be a possibility.

"Sure, Dad. We'll stay. Thanks for welcoming us back into your home."

Before he retired to bed that night, Robert, Sr. did something he had not done in many years; he knelt beside his bed and extended a prayer of thanks to God, and to Kay whom he now believed to be his guardian angel.

The beginning of a new school year was highly anticipated in the Lofton household. With the exception of Robert, every member of the family was embarking on a new and exciting educational journey. Bobbie Kay eagerly looked forward to her first day of Kindergarten. She'd persuaded Robert into purchasing every school supply imaginable, even a protractor that she would not be able to use until at least the fifth grade. Timmy, being a senior, had mixed emotions. As much as he wanted to complete high school, he dreaded leaving the comfort of his family when he attended college the next year. Susan, through a few connections her father still had, managed to gain acceptance at the local community college. Now in her twenties, she felt much "older" than the typical teenage freshman. However, she knew that her maturity could prove to be an advantage. Late night drinking, wild fraternity parties, and social sorority activities would never distract her; for the first time in her life she was solely focused on academics.

Susan decided to enroll Bobbie Kay in the local Colored school, even though Robert objected. He felt that Hill Elementary lacked many of the modern amenities of Fillmore Elementary, the alma mater of his children. Plus, Fillmore was five blocks closer. However, Susan rationally explained her decision. "Dad, Fillmore might have a better building, heck it might even be a better school. But is it a better school for Bobbie Kay? I don't want her to 'stick out' and have to deal with people treating her funny. She's a bright girl, but she's very sensitive and highly perceptive. She can tell when she's being slighted and she doesn't like it. Making friends is hard enough for all kids; I don't want to make it any worse for her. If she goes to Hill, no one will really notice that she's different and she can concentrate on learning. Plus, Lucela says she'll walk her to school and pick her up for me. Most of the kids will probably think she's her aunt or grandmother and things will be much smoother."

"So, you're gonna fool everyone into thinking she's Colored? That's not right."

"Dad, she is Colored. Yes, she's my daughter, but in this world she's also Colored. I've accepted it and so should you."

"Well, I'm her grandfather, too. Are you saying I can't walk her to school if I feel like it?"

Susan laughed. "Dad, it would probably be best if you didn't do that. I don't want to make things difficult for her. She knows who we are, and she loves us just the same. I just don't want the outside world to mistreat her."

Robert, feeling insulted at being denied the right to express his love for his granddaughter, fumed with anger. He had promised Bobbie Kay that HE would escort her to school for her first day and take her for ice cream when HE picked her up that afternoon. His face reddened and he indignantly replied, "Well, she's my grandbaby, damn it, and if she wants me to walk her to school I'm gonna do it and I don't care who has a problem with it. And if she comes home saying somebody does, they're gonna hear it from me. That girl's a Lofton! We're not yellow-bellied and we don't back down from anybody!"

Susan chuckled to herself, amused at the irony of the situation. Three months ago her father was reluctant to hug her daughter due to her race, now he was willing to start a war because of it. "Dad, you never cease to amaze me. I'll let you and Lucela work it out however you see fit. Okay?"

Robert exhaled as if he were releasing steam. He pulled a handkerchief from his back pocket and wiped the angry beads of sweat from his brow. Susan bent down and kissed him on the cheek before returning her gardening, to signal their truce.

Robert felt his skin cool down from her touch. "All right, Sue Bee."

Lucela, who had been dusting in the living room, smiled to herself. As far as she was concerned, the matter was resolved. If Robert wanted to walk her to school, that's how it would be. She was amazed at how much Mr. Lofton had changed over the years. "Miss Kay," she whispered, "you must be talking to that man in his sleep."

That Monday, Bobbie Kay leaped happily from the porch and excitedly grabbed her grandfather's hand. Lucela watched them from the window, the child skipping along and the elder man walking proudly beside her. When they reached the school, Robert bent down and Bobbie Kay finished their routine by kissing him on the cheek. She then whispered in his ear, "I'll meet you right here, Grand-Pop, at noon. I promise to be a good girl just like you said. Bye-bye!"

Robert stood upright and waved to Bobbie Kay as she raced up the steps. When she reached the top of the stairs, Bobbie Kay hollered back, "Grand-Pop, which one are you going to choose today, vanilla or chocolate?"

Robert shielded his eyes from the morning sun and located his granddaughter among the crowd of children before he responded, "Chocolate, Sweetie Pie, chocolate."

CHAPTER TWENTY-THREE

Bobbie Kay took to school like a fish in water. She loved to learn, but she also loved to socialize as well. Robert continued his routine of walking her to school each morning, and although they received a few curious stares, the child was never ill treated. On one occasion, Miss Collins, a matronly teacher who was approaching retirement, made a snide remark within earshot of Bobbie Kay. "Who is THAT? He certainly doesn't belong around here. I hope he's not out there trying to stir up trouble!"

The child, in her innocence, quickly responded before the other teachers could intervene. She tapped Miss Collins on her plump arm and tugged at her sleeve. The woman looked down at the child indignantly, as if she were insulted by her touch. Bobbie Kay pointed out the window at Robert. "Are you talking about him? That man is my grandfather, Robert Lofton, Sr." The adult onlookers chuckled to themselves. Bobbie Kay, ever the social one and always polite, formally extended her small hand. Miss Collins reluctantly grasped it. "My name is Bobbie Kay Lofton. I am very pleased to make your acquaintance." She then curtsied, smiled, and skipped away towards her class.

Miss Lawrence, one of the few teachers present who was not intimidated by Miss Collins, laughed then said, "What a polite little girl. I wish more adults were like that."

In his final year of high school, Timmy once again led Jefferson to the state finals. However, this time the team successfully won the championship. The town was in an uproar, with all residents proud of the recognition, black and white. Clarence, holding back tears of joy, congratulated his team and gave a special thanks to its leader, Timmy Lofton.

Each member of the team received a trophy and a medal for winning the championship. Timmy, now standing 6'4", reached down and pinned his medal on his much shorter father before handing the trophy to Lucela. Robert, overcome with emotion, wiped his reddened face. Lucela, sobbing uncontrollably, hugged Timmy so strongly that he almost lost his breath. Abe stood by, stoically, smelling of sour whiskey and cigarettes.

Susan rubbed Timmy's head affectionately, and Bobbie Kay tugged on his arm. "Timmy, do I get something, too?" she anxiously asked. Timmy reached down and picked up his niece as the news reporters' cameras flashed. He kissed her on the cheek, then removed his sweaty jersey and draped it over her shoulders. Bobbie Kay jumped down, almost stumbling in the garment that almost covered her shoes. Always the "ham" she smiled and waved proudly for the cameras, bright eyes, curly pigtails and all. She made the local newspaper under the headline "Young Fan of Jefferson." The reporters had made the assumption that she was simply a fan and not a relative of Timmy's. Robert bristled with anger when he realized the error; Susan simply shrugged her shoulders and let the matter rest. It wasn't the first time Bobbie Kay had been misidentified as someone else's child and probably wouldn't be the last.

That Sunday, Abe awoke to the smell of country ham, red eye gravy, grits, and buttered biscuits. After completing his morning constitution, he groggily staggered to the kitchen table. Lucela was pouring Timmy another glass of fresh-squeezed orange juice. His trophy was gleaming from the center of the fireplace mantel, in the spot where Abe's Army medal had been before it was moved to the left. The trophy's large presence loomed and glistened in the morning sun, making Abe's small medal appear dusty and tarnished. He bristled with bitterness.

Lucela greeted him warmly, "Good morning Abe. Let me get your coffee."

Abe, feeling dejected, decided to assert his position as the center of the household. He had just seen his wife pour out the last of the orange juice and knew that she would have to undertake the grueling task of squeezing more if he requested some. Even though he rarely drank juice, he chose to be ornery. "I don't want any coffee. I'd like some orange juice. "

"Oh, well, honey, that'll take a minute. I just squeezed enough for Timmy, since me and you usually drink coffee. Sure you don't want coffee?"

Abe folded his arms across his chest defiantly, like a two-year old. "Dammit, woman! Can't a man have a glass of juice in his own house if he wants to?" He pounded on the table for emphasis and the dishes clinked. Timmy put his fork down and stared at him angrily. Abe tightened his face and frowned back, trying to stake his claim.

Lucela sensed the tension between them and decided to lower her voice and decrease the friction. She picked up the cup of coffee she had placed beside her husband's plate and rose from the table. "Abe, don't curse on a Sunday. I'll get your juice. Timmy, hurry up and finish. You know you're singing a solo today. I pressed your suit. Why don't you wear that nice blue tie that Susan and Bobbie Kay bought you? That'll tickle Sugar Pie to death!"

Timmy, aware of his signal to retreat, softened his face and replied with a quiet, "Yes, ma'am."

"Abe, you comin' to church with us today?"

"Hell, naw. I'm too tired. Anyway, how am I gonna get ready in time if I ain't even had breakfast?"

Lucela shook her head at Abe's childishness. Timmy rose from the table and placed his dishes in the sink. He stepped over to Lucela, who was busily squeezing pulp from the oranges while humming a gospel spiritual, and kissed her gently on the cheek. His lips came away wet. He turned towards Abe and scowled at him before exiting the kitchen.

. . . .

CHAPTER TWENTY-FOUR

Later that day, Marianne timidly approached Lucela after service. "Um, excuse me, Sister Jessup? You got a minute?" Lucela turned, startled that Marianne approached her. For the life of her, she could not figure out what Marianne's motive would be to speak with her, so her face held a guarded look. Myrtle, who had been speaking with an acquaintance a few pews away, abruptly ended her conversation and moved in Lucela's direction.

Lucela attempted to place a strained smile on her visage. "Why, uh, yes, I suppose so." Myrtle stood guard beside her and shot Marianne a look of warning.

"Well, uh, Sister Jessup, I heard you announce this mornin' about the scholarship from yo' late Auntie Saxie, God rest her soul."

"Amen," Lucela and Myrtle responded in unison at the memory of their dear departed.

"Well, anyway, I'm sure you know my two boys, Ronnie and Johnnie, they play with yo' boy Timmy?"

"Yes...."

"They usually here with me on Sundays, but they went fishin' wit' my husband, Fred, today. Well, the thing is, my boys have worked real hard and gotten themselves some scholarships

186

to Bethune-Cookman. They both been promised spots on the football team, but the coach says he can only give a full scholarship to one of the boys. Johnnie got a full scholarship to Morehouse, but the boys think that's too far from each other and they really don't want to be separated. . . Truth is, I think they'll do better if they go to school together."

Lucela and Myrtle nodded in understanding. Marianne continued. "I, I just want them to do SOMETHING with themselves, as long as they stay outta trouble. Once they get outta school, ain't gon' be too much for them to do in this town. Anyway, I'm sure y'all know I ain't got no money to send 'em off to school. So I was thinkin' that if one of 'em got yo' auntie's scholarship then they could go to school together. "

Marianne paused, as if she were searching for the right words. She wrung her hands anxiously before continuing. "I know we ain't never been friends, Mrs. Jessup, and I know you might have some ill feelin's towards me and thas' jus' fine. In my younger days I did a lot of bad things. I was so full of the Devil. Took me a little longer to get myself together, but I thank God for savin' my soul. " Marianne looked contritely at the ground before taking a deep breath and continuing her plea.

"I ain't askin' you to consider helpin' me, cause I know I ain't got no right to. But I got one son, an older one, been in jail for more than fifteen years, and I don't want to lose another 'cause they got caught up in some foolishness. Mrs. Jessup, I'm askin' on behalf of my boys. They good kids and they got a future.

187

They'll be the first ones in my family to ever go to college."
Marianne shook her head in amazement. "The first ones ever!
Sometimes I can't even believe it." Her voice wandered off, as if
she were talking to herself. ". . . hadda drop out in elementary,
when I got put out. . . didn't think I'd make it. . .a mama at
thirteen. . . but look at God!" She raised her hand towards heaven
in praise, wiped her moist eyes, and placed a hand on Lucela's
shoulder before continuing. "I know I can't repay you, but I'd be
willin' to put a little somethin' in your hand, every week, soon as
I'm able."

Lucela interjected, "That won't be necessary. The
scholarship is a gift. My aunt left it so some of the young people in
this church would have a chance to get an education."

Marianne lowered her voice to a whisper. "Well, what I'm
tryna say is, I'd sure 'preciate it if you'd consider givin' 'em the
scholarship. I know my boys will make you proud." Marianne's
young stepdaughter observed her uneasiness and shyly walked
over to her and clasped her moist hand for comfort.

Lucela and Myrtle looked at each other in amazement
before Lucela responded. "Well, Sister, uh, uh—"

Marianne proudly interjected with her new last name.
"Carson."

"Yes, Carson. Well, uh, Sister Carson, I will certainly think
about it. We usually make the announcement on Easter Sunday. "

Marianne smiled brightly, satisfied that Lucela would at least consider her request. "Why, thank you. Thanks so much!"

Myrtle, still surly, sourly replied, "Well, Easter's more than a month away, Sister Carson. We got more than yo' boy applying for the scholarship. Just 'cause you ask don't mean it's guaranteed."

Marianne's bright smile dimmed slightly. "Well, I'm jus' gonna pray and believe God for a miracle. Thank you for givin' me a moment, Sister Jessup." She then embraced a startled Lucela before exclaiming, "Praise the Lord!"

As Marianne walked away, Myrtle turned to Lucela and said, "Girl, you a saint. Ain't no way I'd ever even SPEAK to my husband's ho, let alone hug her!"

CHAPTER TWENTY-FIVE

Once the men in her family had returned from their fishing trip, Marianne informed them that she had asked Lucela about the scholarship. Ronnie, who constantly harbored resentment towards Abe, lost his cool. "Ma, how could you go beggin' that man's wife for money to send us to school? Ain't you got no pride? I'm sure she already hates us enough and you just gave her one more reason to look down on us!"

Johnnie, who was more easygoing, tried to rationalize with him. "Ron, don't be angry with Mama. She's just trying to help. And you wrong about Mrs. Jessup. She's always been nice to us, sending extra chicken and ham sandwiches with Timmy for us when we take road trips. You can't blame her because she got a jack-ass for a husband. Besides, if we don't get a scholarship, we're gonna be separated. Do you want that?"

Ronnie calmed down and thought more rationally. His brother was right. Mrs. Jessup had always been kind to them, even when they were kids. As much as he hated to admit it, his resemblance to Abe was so strong that she obviously knew he was their biological father. Yet she'd never frowned at them when they came to her home to speak with Timmy or when she saw them at any school functions. In fact, he couldn't even recall her ever having a harsh word for their mother, who he knew had slept with Abe for many years before marrying Fred.

Ronnie thought about his options if he didn't choose to attend college. His older sister, Janey, had promised to talk to the family she worked for and see if he could get a position as yardman. His older brother, Paul, had told him he's try to get him a job at the mill. Paul made pretty good money, enough to adequately support his wife and their twin daughters, Darla and Carla. They lived in a decent house across town, and drove a decent car. However, Ronnie knew he wanted more out of life. Paul had told him that being educated would be the key to ensuring he could live comfortably.

Since Abe was practically non-existent, and their eldest brother Curtis was incarcerated, Paul fulfilled the role of "father figure" for the boys. However, Paul rarely came around Marianne's. The boys usually visited with him when they sought him out for guidance, or a little extra cash for necessities or pocket change. Unlike Ronnie and Johnnie, who had a chance to experience Marianne's softening of her wild and wanton ways, Paul still held a strong resentment towards his mother for her lack of maternal skills and abundance of neglect during his childhood. These reasons motivated him to provide some level of support to his younger brothers, hoping to decrease the negative influence Marianne's lifestyle might have on them. In his youth, he had also sought out a male for guidance in his dysfunctional family through his Uncle Barabbas, also known as "Boo."

Uncle Boo had served in the military, attended two years of college at Tougaloo, and worked at the local mill. He never graduated because he had returned home from college to take care of his two youngest siblings when his mother passed from liver failure. Boo was Marianne's oldest brother and the only one of her siblings to amount to something "decent", having never been arrested, incarcerated, addicted, or abusive. Many people in the community attributed this to the fact that he was raised by his paternal grandmother in Mississippi for the first ten years of his life. After her passing, Boo was sent to live with a mother he had never known that resided in a heathenish environment his devoutly Christian grandmother had tried to protect him from. Having adopted a different view of life and a Christian value system by this time, Boo had already established goals and aspirations for his future. Since he arrived late on the scene, he had been spared the abuse inflicted by his mother as well as missed out on the camaraderie established among his siblings from being victimized. For these reasons, his brothers and sisters always regarded him as an outsider. They mimicked his accent, his intelligence, and his skin tone (he was much lighter than them). In fact, he earned his nickname because his brothers said he was "white as a ghost" and would taunt him by saying "Boo!" whenever he came into the room.

Boo soon realized that the influence of his mother had already diminished the futures of his younger siblings, and no matter how hard he tried to influence them, the damage had already been done. He returned to Mississippi at the age of sixteen and lived with a paternal relative to finish his remaining years of high school before enrolling in college. He would have remained there and probably never returned except for his heartstrings being tugged when he was called on the assist with his youngest siblings. None of his other brothers or sisters were willing to take them in, and they were about to be sent to a state orphanage. Boo, having known the feeling of family abandonment, did not want his younger brother and sister to have to endure the same. When he reconnected with his nephew, Boo saw it as a second chance to make a family connection. Since Paul, like his siblings, never had a relationship with his father, Boo was grateful to have been chosen to fill the role.

Although he knew the boys believed that he made a decent living, Paul constantly impressed on them the importance of education. Having only completed high school, he always regretted choosing to earn a paycheck instead of sacrificing a few years of his youth to invest in himself as his Uncle Boo had told him to do. He had always promised him he would enroll in college when "the time was right", but the time never came. When Boo had passed away, Paul grieved with regret at having never kept his promise to his uncle who had constantly stressed to him the importance of uplifting the family's name.

Paul had worked at the mill for almost 20 years, but knew that if it were to ever close, he would have to face the impossible task of finding employment that would compensate him at the level he was used to due to his lack of education. There had been rumors of the mill possibly closing for the past two years; Paul just prayed and hoped that it would be delayed for at least five more years until he could retire. He realized that he could in some way keep his uncle's promise by helping his younger brothers finish college. His mother had called his wife, Laurie, and informed her that although both of his brothers had received scholarships, they did not receive them to attend the same college. He realized that his mother had called when she was aware Paul would be at work, hoping that she could convince Laurie to carry the message to him and plead on her behalf. After a filling dinner of his favorite meal of smothered chicken and rice, creamed corn and buttered rolls, Laurie broached the subject carefully as if she had been pondering on it all day.

"Paul, honey, your mother called. She wanted to talk to us about helping the twins with college. Anyway, she and Fred have saved about $250. She just needs about $250 more to send the boys off to school and pay for their housing. She's been looking for some day work to help her earn enough to keep them there and Fred is hoping to get some overtime." Laurie noticed that Paul's brow began to furrow, a sure sign he was becoming agitated. His wife began to chatter nervously in an attempt to ease his uncomfortable disposition. She waved her tiny manicured hands in the air animatedly before placing them on the table. "She's so proud of them! She kept raving about how these would be the first members of the family to attend college since Uncle Boo. She regrets dropping out so early, and she really appreciates you setting such a fine example for them by finishing high school. She thinks so highly of you, Paul. She's always talking about what a great father and husband you are."

"Yeah, Laurie, I know. Glad she's finally decided to take an interest and decide to be a mother to me. Took her long enough."

194

Paul's beautiful wife turned to face him and shook her sandy brown locks admonishingly. "Paul, how long you gonna be mad? Your mama's changed a lot in the past few years. She goes to church EVERY Sunday, and she's settled down with Fred. She's a wonderful grandmother to the girls. She took them to the movies last weekend and even baked them some cookies the other day." Laurie's voice softened before she continued. "Paul, your mother and I have become very close. She's shared with me that she realizes she wasn't much of a mother to you, and she wishes she could do it all over. She knows that she can't, but she says that's why she tries so hard with the girls and Fred's daughter. She considers this to be her second chance. Now I know you used to talk to Uncle Boo a lot. I'm sure he told you some of the same things your mother has told me; your grandmother shouldn't have been allowed to raise a cat, let alone eleven children. Now I'm not making excuses, but women learn to be mothers from *their* mothers just like men learn to be daddies from *their* daddies. You can't learn it in a book."

Paul dropped his head with conviction. He knew his wife was right. He just couldn't swallow his anger or his pride long enough to establish a relationship with Marianne. He began to lose control of his emotions and his face became hot and sweaty.

Laurie got up from her seat and walked over to her husband. She loved him dearly and recognized that in spite of it all, he was a good man that was simply dealing with a lot of unresolved issues. "Paul, you are a wonderful father to the girls. But you learned to be a good father from your uncle. Your mother

195

didn't have anyone around to tell her how to be a good parent; her own mother put her out at thirteen after she was raped by one of the many men she let roam through the house. Thirteen! Paul, the girls just turned twelve. Can you even imagine one of them living on their own in the streets with a newborn baby? Now, I'm not saying your mother was right in everything she did, but I am saying that you can't fault her completely. Besides, you are only hurting yourself when you try to hurt her. All that anger and pain, Honey, you need to let it go."

Paul turned his head abruptly so that his wife of thirteen years wouldn't see him cry for the second time in his adult life. In their entire marriage, he had only cried once before, when his dear Uncle Boo passed. However, Laurie hadn't seen it because he'd locked himself in the bathroom and drowned out the sound of his racking sobs by filling the tub with water. Paul pulled away from his wife, wiped his sweaty forehead on the cuff of his sleeve, and quickly traipsed up the stairs towards the bathroom. Before he opened the bathroom door he struggled to maintain his composure and hollered in a strained voice down to his wife, "Call my mother and tell her you'll bring her the other $250 on Saturday. I'll go by the bank and bring it home to you tomorrow." Then Paul shut the door and turned on the water. By the time the tub was full, he had finished crying.

CHAPTER TWENTY-SIX

The sun's early rays crept into Robert's bedroom like an intruder. Each year, he dreaded Easter Sunday, since it always reminded him of losing Kay. He turned on his side and placed a pillow over his head to shield him from nature's alarm clock. His thoughts were soon interrupted by the excited voice of his granddaughter, who ran abruptly into the room in her pink robe and bunny slippers. "Grand-Pop! Are you going to come to church with us? Mama Ceel already ironed a shirt for you and she came over this morning to fix us a special breakfast. Timmy's going to sing a special solo. Mommy's going, but I told her I want you to come too. I want you to hear my Easter speech." Robert pretended that he didn't hear Bobbie Kay, hoping she'd believe that he was asleep and leave quietly. True to her Lofton nature, her determination and stubbornness wouldn't allow her to lose the battle. Bobbie Kay pounced on the bed and removed the pillow from Robert's face. Robert kept his eyes closed. "Grand-Pop. Grand-Pop!" He continued to ignore her. Bobbie Kay used her tiny fingers to lift both of his eyelids, then jumped back when he peered back at her. "Grand-Pop, are you going to come to church with us? Pleeeeease? I want you to hear my Easter speech."

Robert rubbed his now irritated eyes and sat up. "Well. . . I don't know Sweetie Pie. I, I..."

"Mama Ceel is fixing us breakfast—pancakes AND waffles! With strawberries, bananas, and whipped cream. I know you

197

don't go to church, but can you go this one time? I want you to see my speech. Timmy's going to sing, too. Mommy's going. She said for me not to ask you, but I snuck up here to ask you before she wakes up, so don't tell on me, okay?" Bobbie Kay placed a finger to her lips in a "shh" motion to signal their secret. "Mommy said Easter makes you sad. She said it used to make her sad, until she had me. Why does Easter make people sad, Grand-Pop? Don't you like the Easter Bunny? I do! I always get an Easter basket with candy and chocolates and eggs and jellybeans. Easter's so much fun! Why don't you like Easter, Grand-Pop?"

Robert felt uneasy and wasn't sure how to explain his feelings to his granddaughter, or even whether he should. In her childlike innocence, she made him realize that just like Susan he needed to learn to cope with this holiday instead of allowing it to depress him. At that moment, Bobbie Kay reached out and grasped his hand as if she were trying to pull him out of bed. Robert smiled, but pulled back with resistance. Bobbie Kay glanced over at Kay's picture on the nightstand. "Mommy says Grandma used to take them to church every Easter, so that's why she always takes me, even though we didn't go to church much when we lived in California. I bet if my grandma were here, she'd go with us, too." Bobbie Kay stepped down off the bed and quietly closed the door behind her, looking as if her long, sad face was dragging on the floor. When Robert watched her leave, he almost thought for a split second that he saw a shadow of Kay walking away, looking dejected and disappointed. His heart swelled with shame at his selfishness and a lump formed in his throat. He realized that he could no longer go on grieving and feeling sorry for himself, while causing sadness and pain for his granddaughter. He walked to the door and called down to Bobbie Kay, "Sweetie Pie, Grand-Pop's getting up. Save me some pancakes!"

"Okay, Grand-Pop!" Bobbie Kay responded. She was seated at the table nibbling on a slice of bacon, clapping her hands together with glee. Timmy and Lucela laughed at her antics. They knew all along that if anyone could get Robert to set a foot into a church, Bobbie Kay could.

Lucela proudly walked into the church with her extended family. Mt. Nebo was already somewhat integrated, with the inclusion of Timmy in the choir and Howard Slaton's German wife that he had brought back from overseas. Clarence waved at Robert, Sr. and Susan from the pulpit. Bobbie Kay, who already considered herself a regular member, possessively held onto her grandfather's hand and waved back.

Once Bobbie Kay had entered school, she had quickly formed numerous friendships. Being only five or six, most of her peers hadn't adopted prejudicial attitudes as of yet, and so Bobbie Kay's lineage was not an issue for them. Also, due to the varying hues of the other Black children in her school, Bobbie Kay's skin tone was never an issue. However, when talk on the playground veered towards the children's events at Mt. Nebo, the largest Black Church in town, Bobbie Kay came home expressing a desire to be a part. "Miss Ceel, Rynona told me that there's going to be a carnival at her church next week. She says you attend her church because she recognized you when you came to the school to bring me my jacket last week. She wants me to meet her there. She said there's going to be games, rides, and even animals! Mommy says she can't take me because she has a lot of homework to do. Are you going?"

"Yes, Sweetie. Do you wanna go with me?"

Bobbie Kay's face beamed as if Lucela had offered her a million pieces of her favorite candy. "Yes, ma'am. Can I ask Mommy if it's okay?"

Lucela thought for a moment and decided to handle things in her own quiet way. "Sugar, lemme ask her. I bet she'll say "yes" if I do. Okay?"

Bobbie Kay nodded her head affirmatively and smiled brightly before taking another nibble of her cheese sandwich. She stirred her vegetable soup lackadaisically, as if she dreaded finishing it.

Lucela decided to use her position to her advantage. "Well, you know if you plan on goin' to the carnival you gotta have lotsa energy. Little girls gotta eat all they vegetables to get energy. You be sure to eat all yo' soup. Okay?"

"Yes, ma'am," Bobbie Kay mumbled. Lucela poured her another glass of juice, then rubbed her curly head. Her face brightened and she giggled before responding with a soft, "Thank you."

The next Saturday, Bobbie Kay excitedly ran about the carnival with Rynona, Elizabeth, and Jerelee, her best friends from school. When they first greeted each other with squeals, hugs, and kisses, an onlooker would think that they were long-lost relatives instead of classmates who had seen each other less than four hours earlier at school. Rambunctious Rynona, a brown-skinned girl with short pigtails and two missing front teeth, was the ringleader of the group. When she first saw Bobbie Kay she emitted a high-pitched scream that was impossible to discern from joy or pain. "Bobbbbbbie Kaaaaay!" She grasped the hands of Elizabeth and Jerelee and ran towards her friend, almost tackling Bobbie Kay in a greeting. Elizabeth, a chubby girl with thick, coarse hair and skin the color of a Hershey Bar regained her manners and composure and politely greeted Lucela.

"Good afternoon, Sister Jessup." Her co-conspirators followed her lead and provided their own greetings.

Lucela smiled and responded, "Good afternoon, girls. I 'spect y'all gonna behave like young ladies today, 'stead a runnin' roun' like a group of vagabonds."

All four of the girls nodded their heads affirmatively and emitted murmurs of "Yes, ma'am."

Lucela, satisfied that they had recognized the error of their ways, decided to cut them some slack. "Now girls, how would you like for Minnie Sue to take you on some a those rides? I got a shiny silver dollar for each one of you." The large coins glistened in her large, leathery hands and each girl responded with a series of "oohs" and "aahs."

Rynona spoke for the group, even though it was a struggle for her to remain composed. She had never been given more than a nickel in her life, and was already plotting how she could save part of her dollar to share with her many brothers and sisters. "Thank, you Sister Jessup. Yes, ma'am, we'd love to go with Minnie Sue." The rest of the crew nodded in unison, too shocked to respond.

"Well, alright. Minnie Sue, take these girls around the carnival. When they get hungry, bring them over to the food tent. Me and yo' mama will fix y'all up."

Quiet, timid Jerelee, a slender girl with skin the color of melted vanilla ice cream and long, wavy, auburn braids, was a child of few words. After the ruckus of celebration died down, she tightly clasped her friend's hand and shyly whispered, "I'm glad you could come, Bobbie." Bobbie Kay's face brightened and she felt an inner warmth from the giddiness of friendship. She finally knew what it felt like to be accepted by someone outside of her family.

At the carnival, Bobbie Kay experienced one of the happiest days of her life. She indulged in cotton candy, rode a horse, talked Timmy into winning her a giant teddy bear that was

202

almost twice her size, ate three hot dogs, drank two sodas, and shared two caramel apples and a powdered sugar topped funnel cake with her friends. Lucela and Myrtle had stayed in the food tent and served concessions while the girls were entrusted to Minnie Sue's care. Lucela laughed when Minnie Sue, Myrtle's youngest daughter, told her she was amazed at Bobbie Kay's appetite. Lucela wasn't the least bit surprised; she knew Bobbie Kay was truly her mother's child. She just hoped she wouldn't grow up thinking she had to constantly diet and resort to unhealthy tactics to lose weight like Susan.

After the carnival ended, Bobbie Kay and Rynona were running about in the grass outside the concessions tent while Lucela and Myrtle were cleaning up. Their conversation was periodically interrupted by the girls' giddy screams of enjoyment while playing tag. She knew that she would be leaving the carnival late and had already arranged for Bobbie Kay to spend the night at her house. After the concessions were packed up and the tents were taken down, Bobbie Kay's young body practically collapsed from exhaustion. When they arrived at Lucela's home, Timmy carried her sleeping body into the house and laid her on the daybed in the guest room. Lucela undressed Bobbie Kay and wiped her sticky face and hands with a warm washcloth before covering her with a quilt. As she rose to exit the room, Bobbie Kay reached up and kissed her on the cheek. "Mama Ceel, can I start going to church with you? If it's okay with my Mommy?"

Lucela rubbed Bobbie Kay's thick, curls. "Sure, Sweetie. Lemme talk to her 'bout it, okay? Now you get some rest."

From that weekend on, the routine was established. Bobbie Kay spent two weekends a month at Lucela's, and attended church with her EVERY Sunday. Since she was such an outgoing child, she relished in the opportunities to be participate in the children's activities associated with the holidays. She came dressed as a ghost at the Halloween celebration and ate three caramel apples. She was an angel in the Christmas play, ate half a dozen Christmas cookies and helped pass out presents from under the church Christmas tree to all of the children. She handed out more than 50 Valentines to every friend she had at church and at school, a process that took her three weekends to complete since she insisted on creating and personalizing each one. Finally, she had practiced her Easter speech for two weeks, every afternoon at lunch with Lucela's assistance and every evening in the mirror while she brushed her teeth. She had anticipated this moment for quite some time, and now that her entire family was present, she was going to shine!

Myrtle had sewn a frilly, yellow and pink Easter dress with a matching bonnet for Bobbie Kay. Susan had offered to buy her one from Sears or Pelletier's, but Bobbie Kay had wanted to have her dress sewn by Myrtle just like Elizabeth and Jerelee. Susan didn't seem to understand why her daughter wanted to put everyone through so much trouble, and she expressed this to both Lucela and Bobbie Kay at breakfast. "I don't know why you insist on having someone sew you an Easter dress, Bobbie Kay, when I can just pick you up one on Saturday."

Bobbie Kay, having become acclimated to the customs of the Black church, crumpled her face in frustration at her mother's comment. She wasn't trying to be difficult because she wasn't a spoiled child. She simply wanted to wear a dress that no one else would have so that she could feel special, just like her friends. Each holiday was a celebration and a time for her to receive special attention for looking fashionable. Susan would probably not allow her to get a fancy dress or anything that would allow her to express her creativity. Lucela had allowed her to pick out the material and the color especially to her liking. She knew that if she got a dress from the store, she'd just have to settle for the colors and styles they had available on the rack. Bobbie Kay's bacon began to taste more salty, since it was mixing with her tears. She lowered her head to try in an attempt to hide them.

Lucela decided to intervene. "Miss Sue, she just wants Myrtle to make her dress like she makin' the dresses of her little friends. We've already picked out the material and Myrtle's already cut the fabric, so we can't take it back. Don't worry, I'm payin' Myrtle for her effort. She gon' make her a matchin' bonnet, too!"

Bobbie Kay's face brightened at the thought of her fancy new dress. Susan's heart softened. "Okay, Lucela. It's just that you do so much for her already; I don't want her getting spoiled. But I guess it's bound to happen, between you and Daddy," she shook her head in exasperation before giving a long sigh of resignation.

CHAPTER TWENTY-SEVEN

Easter Sunday finally arrived and Bobbie Kay proudly entered the church with her mother holding one hand and her grandfather holding the other while she strutted down the aisle in her pastel pink and yellow taffeta dress, matching bonnet, white lace socks, and black patent leather Mary Jane shoes. Susan, feeling slightly underdressed among the festive hats and colorful attire of the audience, self-consciously tugged at the collar of her dark, A-line dress. Robert, realizing that less than five White individuals were present, three of whom were from his own family, scanned the sea of Colored faces to locate someone he recognized. His mind rambled while he identified a few friends and acquaintances. *"There's Hank, the handyman at Dibble's Grocery, and Lois, Earlene's housekeeper. . . . oh, there's that preacher, what's his name? Barnett? Burnett? He came by to offer his condolences when Kay passed. . .Oh, there's Myrtle."* Robert waved excitedly at Myrtle, someone he considered a real friend, not aware of the decorum he should have maintained during the slow hymn that was being played at that time. Myrtle smiled slightly and mouthed an inaudible "Hello" in response; Robert realized the error of his ways and dropped his hand at the same time that Bobbie Kay placed her finger to her lips to signal silence. Once the group had arrived at their seat, she tugged on his hand and whispered, "Grand-Pop, this is where we sit."

Once they were seated, fans that were decorated with DaVinci's "The Last Supper" and made available by Gussman's Funeral Home were immediately handed to them, to combat the extremely warm climate of the sanctuary. Although the church's Building Fund had been established to add additional amenities, such as air conditioning, contributions had not reached the required level necessary for this added luxury. Until then, congregants always came prepared with fans, small towels, and handkerchiefs to combat the warmth. Robert loosened his tie, as he felt that using a fan was too "ladylike." (However, as the service progressed he did have to wipe his forehead with his handkerchief periodically.) After a few announcements were given, the usual routine of the service was changed due to the Easter Holiday. Before Clarence's sermon, the children of the church were going to be allowed time to present their performances.

Miss Lawrence, one of the teachers at Bobbie Kay's school who was also in charge of Mt. Nebo's Sunday School Department, stepped to the podium and emceed the brief program. The festivities were a mixture of spirituality, humor, and childlike innocence. Paul's twin girls, Carla and Darla, presented a violin and flute duet of "Were You There When They Crucified My Lord" that caused a multitude of eyes to moisten with emotion. The DuBois boys, all three of them aged 3 to 5, brought the house down with the upbeat "Angels Rolled the Stone Away." The audience couldn't help laughing at the animated antics and dancing of the youngest boy, while his older brother struggled to restrain him. Finally, Bobbie Kay heard her name called. Miss Lawrence had given her the special task of providing the closing speech, one that was quite long for a child of only five. Bobbie Kay smoothed her dress, put on her white gloves, and walked down the aisle to the podium. She politely took the microphone from Miss Lawrence then slightly cleared her throat before beginning her speech.

"We are gathered here to celebrate this Easter day,

Because the tomb is empty, the stone is rolled away.

The angels told Mary that Christ was already gone,

He had risen from the dead on that early morn.

Jesus told them, *"Go tell my disciples in Galilee*

to patiently wait, and they will see me."

When he met his disciples, he told them to spread the news,

"Remember my commandments! Peace be unto you!

I have risen to give life, more abundantly.

I am going to heaven to prepare a place for thee."

Because our savior sacrificed his life,

When we pass away we will reunite with Christ.

We will live forever in a beautiful place,

All mankind of every race."

Once she had completed her speech, Bobbie Kay curtsied politely before handing the microphone back to Miss Lawrence. The majority of the audience gave her a standing ovation, amazed that such a large discourse had been provided from such a small vessel. Bobbie Kay scanned the audience and allowed her eyes to rest on her family. Timmy was standing tall above the group, pumping his fist in the air with enthusiasm. Susan was wiping her eyes with one of Lucela's handkerchiefs, crying from both shock and surprise at her daughter's performance. Lucela smiled proudly, her deep dimples visible even from the podium. Finally, Bobbie Kay heard someone shout, "Sweetie Pie!" Robert waved to her, his forehead dripping with sweat. Undeterred by his unfamiliar presence in the congregation, he began signaling to others around him and proudly stating, "That's my grandbaby! That's my grandbaby, Bobbie Kay Lofton!"

Once the crowd quieted down, Clarence stepped to the podium. The shadow of his large, robed frame covered the crowd like a protective shield. He bent slightly and cleared his throat before starting his Easter sermon. Bobbie Kay's speech appeared to have served as a preface to his message. "Church, we are here to celebrate the life and death of our Savior, Jesus Christ. You know, Christ didn't live a long life, but he lived long enough to complete the work his father sent him to do."

"Amen!" shouted Mother Talley. A few other "Amen's" echoed around the sanctuary. Clarence appeared to receive energy from the audience's acceptance of his words and confidently continued with slightly more fervor in his voice.

"My Brothers and Sisters, we just heard it from a little child; the reason WHY we celebrate the crucifixion and resurrection of Christ. You see, he didn't die to achieve fame, or fortune, but to save a hopeless world from sin. He lived his life as an example of how we should treat on another, with LOVE!"

"Amen, Reverend!" hollered Sister Jackson.

"Preach, son!" followed Old Brother Culpepper. "Bring the Word!"

Robert listened intently with conviction, feeling as if Clarence's words were speaking directly to him.

"I must say, it does my heart good when I look out into the congregation and see that many of you have gathered here because of the LOVE you have for each other. How much money someone has is not an issue. What color they might be is not an issue. What is an issue for you is the LOVE you feel for them and you have placed that first and used it to direct your actions. Just like Christ. It didn't matter to him that some of the sinners he was dying for might have been sick, diseased, alcoholics, prostitutes, gamblers, Black, White, or any other color. What mattered to him was the LOVE that he felt for them. Brothers and Sisters, I wish we could ALL be like Christ!"

The reverend's captive audience responded with applause and a flurry of affirmative "Amen's", "Preach on's" and "Go ahead's" that signaled their agreement.

Clarence wiped his brow before stepping from behind the podium and continuing. "You know, the Pharisees criticized Jesus for hanging around with what we today would call "street people" and going to places on the "bad side" of town. But Jesus told them, "I didn't come here for you! You SUPPOSED to know the way because y'all are all *"church people"* who stay in the temple and make the laws for everyone else to follow. I came to talk to the people y'all think y'all too good to talk to, maybe cause they poor, or dirty, or a different color, or a different religion. That's who I came to save!"

"Yeah!" hollered Bro. Clyde.

"Now we all know, sometimes the folks who make the laws aren't always right. Sometimes they put their feelings into it and decide that some people should be treated different than others. Can I get an "Amen" in here?"

"Amen, Reverend!" responded Mother Talley.

"Sometimes, we have to take the time to recognize that right is right, and wrong is wrong. No matter who does it and no matter why. Sometimes, it's easier to point the finger at someone else, instead of looking at ourselves and seeing where we're wrong. The Pharisees didn't want to look at themselves. They just kept looking at Jesus and telling him HE was wrong. He talked to the wrong people, he ate with the wrong people, he even healed the wrong people. Can y'all believe they even criticized him for healing people instead of resting on a Sunday? And who ended up putting him on the cross? These same high

211

falutin', seditty, proper folks. Not the street people. They loved him because he LOVED everyone. They called him the Christ. Naw, he was crucified by the folks who shoulda known better, who knew all the right scriptures, and the laws, and the rules. And who was the first ones at the tomb? The street folks: the prostitutes, the poor women, the ones everyone told him to pass on by. They were the ones who cared for him, because they had gotten past what others had to say. He was their Lord and Savior and he taught them how to LOVE. They didn't care if everyone hated him, they were motivated by the LOVE they felt for him! They cared so much about him that they got up early to sneak into the tomb. They wasn't going to be nosey like some folks would have been, Mother Talley. "

Some in the congregation responded with laughter at his remark. Mother Talley waved her handkerchief admonishingly at Clarence, then snickered to herself before he continued.

"Why were these women there? They went to show their respect. They wanted to make sure that their king had been buried with dignity, because they loved and respected him. They didn't care about what anyone else had to say, they KNEW he was their Lord and Savior because they had experienced his LOVE. Do y'all know what kind of love I'm talkin' about? I'm talking about the kind of love that is stronger than the love a mother has for her babies!"

"Amen, Reverend!" an anonymous congregant called out.

"The kind of love that is stronger than a father has for his son!"

212

"Yeah!"

"The kind of love that will see past color and see the true person, even if everyone else refuses to simply because the people who make the laws say they shouldn't treat everyone with love."

"Preach on!" said Brother Culpepper.

"The kind of love that will even forgive someone for killing a loved one. "

The audience sat quietly amid a murmur of a few hushed "Amen's."

Clarence wiped his brow, paused, then looked towards Heaven and wiped his moist eyes. "Church, y'all gotta excuse me. But I'm getting a little emotional myself, just thinking about a friend of mine who had this kind of love." He stepped down to the aisle and placed his large hand on the end of the first pew, as if he hoped it would provide him with some sense of emotional support. "You know, when I was a young, young boy in college, I had a friend like that. He didn't care if everyone else said he shouldn't be my friend, he was my friend anyway. My friend, Bobby, took a stand for me and lost his life because of it. He was just trying to do his part to make this world a better place." Clarence's moist eyes met Robert's and embraced them with a quiet nod. Robert wiped his teary face and responded with a soft "Amen" while Susan tightly held his hand and Timmy rubbed his shoulder.

Clarence continued with a renewed strength. "Church, you know, I was angry for a long, long time. I was angry at all those racists who were such cowards they refused to show their faces and hid them behind sheets while they killed innocent people who disagreed with them. They didn't just kill my friend. These cowards were so hateful that they even killed children, once taking the lives of little girls who had gathered to worship on an Easter Sunday just like we are today. Church, I was angry for a long, long, long time. I couldn't understand how a person could hate so strong that they would kill an innocent stranger? I didn't know who did it, so I hated everyone who even LOOKED like them."

Clarence knelt his large frame beside the pew. "Then, one day I got down on my knees and asked God, *"Why? Why did you let them kill my friend? Why did you let them kill all of those innocent people, the young men, the young ladies, the young children?"*

"Say it, Reverend!" shouted Mother Talley.

"Mother, you know what he told me? He said, "Clarence, you ain't the only one who's lost someone because of hate. I lost my only son. But guess what, I forgave them. And he forgave them. He said, *"Father, forgive them, for they know not what they do."* Sometimes, folks do wrong and don't even realize it. You gotta forgive them, too. Cause hating them ain't gonna change a thing. And LOVE and HATE can't dwell in the same place. Your hate ain't gonna bring your friend back. But your LOVE can help someone who's still living."

Clarence stood up and walked down the aisle. "That little girl said it. We will all live together in heaven. Everyone, of every race, living in LOVE and peace. My friend is waiting for me, just like I know some of y'all got loved ones waiting for you. But we can't get there with hate in our hearts. We can't be like the Pharisees." Clarence paused, wiped his brow and smiled slightly before continuing. "We gotta LOVE each other now, y'all, cause we can't be fighting once we get into Heaven."

Some of the congregants laughed. Robert stood on his feet and shouted, "Amen!" Clarence walked over to him and vigorously shook his hand before responding.

"Amen, Brother Lofton, Amen."

That Sunday, Mt. Nebo welcomed their newest members: Robert and Susan Lofton.

CHAPTER TWENTY-EIGHT

Later that day, Marianne busied herself in her kitchen buttering rolls and slicing the Easter ham. Her entire family was crowded into the small dining and living room of Fred's two-bedroom home. Since their marriage, Marianne had gladly moved from her rambling shack into the living quarters Fred had shared with his deceased wife, Margie. A few remnants remained that revealed his first wife's past presence: the shiny, but bare china cabinet, the large portrait over the fireplace that had been a wedding gift from Margie's aunt, and the large rug embroidered with roses that covered the living room area. Initially, Fred had offered to remove these items to please his new wife, but she had seen the discomfort on his face and declined the offer. Plus, Marianne realized that if the items were removed, they would have to go through the trouble of replacing them since the large picture provided a focal point for the living room and the rug covered a spot on the floor that had been badly scorched by a loose fire ember. Besides, the china cabinet brought a certain level of "class" to the modest home even though it was practically empty. Marianne had gladly left her vermin-infested, dilapidated furniture and honestly was not ill at ease with the reminders of Margie's past presence. She figured that the furniture and décor were no more a reminder of Fred's past life than his daughter, Theresa, whom she loved dearly. Plus, Fred had been just as accepting of her twins and her past transgressions, even marrying her after she had mothered five children out of wedlock.

Fred, Paul, Ronnie, and Johnnie were crowded in front of the television and loudly discussing a sporting event. Carla, Darla and Theresa (who was affectionately referred to as "Reesa") were sitting in the corner and playing with a set of paper dolls, while Laurie assisted Marianne with getting dinner prepared. "Mama, I think we've got everything on the table. You ready for me to gather the family for grace?"

Marianne smiled at her daughter-in-law before nodding her approval. The table was covered with plenty of food. In anticipation of Paul's first visit to her home in more than ten years, she had excitedly prepared all of his favorite foods in addition to the usual Easter Sunday dinner. A large, pineapple and brown sugar glazed ham sat in the center of the table, surrounded by the typical accompaniments: fried chicken, sweet potatoes, collard greens, potato salad, macaroni and cheese, and buttered rolls. A few of Paul's favorites were also squeezed onto the table: smothered chicken, creamed corn, and mashed potatoes. The kitchen counter was covered with desserts to please each of the males in the house. A large, two-layer chocolate cake, Johnnie's favorite, sat under a crystal cake dome that had been given to Margie as a wedding gift. Three foil-covered sweet potato pies sat beside the cake, one of which would be eaten by Ronnie alone. Fred had requested a pan of bread pudding and even though he had not requested it, Marianne had made a lemon meringue pie especially for Paul. She had remembered it as being his favorite as a child. Marianne felt her eyes welling with tears as she thought fondly of her oldest son, Curtis, and wondered if he were being provided with a special meal for Easter, despite being incarcerated.

Laurie timidly entered the living room and approached the men of the family. "Excuse me, y'all. Mama said she's ready for us to gather and say grace. Dinner's ready."

217

Ronnie excitedly jumped up and clapped his hands together. "Yes! I'm starving!" Marianne laughed at his never ending appetite before slapping his hand away when he teased her by reaching for a drumstick.

Once the family had gathered, Reesa asked about her beloved big sister, Janey. "Mom, aren't we gonna wait on Janey?"

Janey, her oldest child, had promised to stop by after she had been relieved from her duties of serving Easter Dinner to the family she worked for. "No, Baby Girl. Janey has to work today. She said she'll be by when she gets off in about an hour." The girls jumped up and down in anticipation of the Easter baskets Janey had promised them.

Fred, acting as man of the house, asked for everyone to bow their heads in prayer. "Father, we thank you for allowing our family to gather together. We thank you for the many blessings you have given us, especially the scholarships we received today. We are so glad that you have made a way for both Ronnie and Johnnie to attend college together. We ask you to bless this family, bless this food, and bless the hands that prepared it. In Your name, Amen."

The family busied themselves fixing plates of food. Ronnie hungrily munched on a drumstick of chicken while he heaped his plate with a serving of every food on the table. Paul smiled at his mother when he realized that she had cooked his favorites as his wife fixed his plate. He peeked into the kitchen and saw the lemon meringue pie on the counter. "Mama, you did all this cooking? Did you get any rest this weekend?"

Marianne laughed. "Aw, Son. It wasn't nothing. I just wanted to make sure everyone enjoyed their Easter Dinner."

"Well, I think that lemon meringue pie will surely be enjoyed once I clean this plate, loosen my belt, and come back for seconds. Thanks, Mom." Paul bent down and kissed his mother on the cheek. Marianne, surprised at this uncommon gesture of affection from Paul, absentmindedly rubbed the warm spot where his lips had touched her cheek. The last time she recalled Paul giving her a kiss was when he was eight years old. She had made him a lemon meringue pie to celebrate his placing first in the school's spelling bee.

Marianne became so overcome with emotion that jumbled thoughts floated through her mind like scraps of paper scattering in the wind. *"My son hasn't kissed me in over 30 years. 30 years!. . .The boys are goin' to college wit' scholarships. . .God done blessed me with a good husband and a wonderful step-child. . . So proud when the reverend announced my sons' names, 'This year's scholarships will be awarded to both Ronnie and Johnnie Clark'. . . Sis. Jessup is such a fine woman, looking past all the hurt I caused her to do right by my boys. . . Wasted all those years on Abe and I coulda been Fred's first wife and birthed him a blood child. . . Wish I had been a better mother to Janey, Curtis, and Paul insteada runnin' in the streets. . Mama, you was wrong, I am somebody's wife! . . .My boys is goin' to college just like Boo. . .God is good!"*

CHAPTER TWENTY-NINE

Lucela and Myrtle set the dinner table. Myrtle's two girls busied themselves in the kitchen. Gladys sat in a chair giving directions like a supervisor, even though she hadn't cooked a thing.

"Mabel, you put lots of butter on that cornbread, didn't you? You know Clarence likes to have plenty of butter on his cornbread, especially when he's eatin' his mama's greens. Myrtle, you put extra ham-hocks in them greens, didn't you? You know Harvey always likes to eat the ham-hocks with his potato salad. And Ceel, I hope you made at least six sweet potato pies 'cause Timmy's gonna eat two of 'em by himself. Minnie Sue, you pressed my good tablebloth, didn't you? I don't want any spots on my buffet. Lord, I hope you girls made enough food. I'd a helped y'all but my sugar been actin' up lately." Gladys grabbed her cane and prepared to stand before continuing. "Y'all need any help in the kitchen?"

All of the women laughed to themselves before responding in unison, "No, ma'am."

Myrtle's two daughters, Mabel Jean and Minnie Sue, busied themselves preparing the breads and beverages for the Easter meal. Mabel, who was in her second year of nursing school, was her grandmother's pride and joy. Gladys had made Clarence announce her presence at church, and the entire congregation had applauded a warm welcome. Although Mabel was smart enough to become a doctor, she knew that women doctors were few and far in between and her chances of being accepted into a medical college were slim. So, she settled for the next best option and chose to be a nurse.

Minnie Sue was the complete opposite of her sister. While Mabel Jean was extremely bright and driven, Minnie realized her shortcomings. She was an extremely pretty girl, and took great pride in her appearance. Most of her clothes she sewed herself, and was a very skilled seamstress. Minnie Sue recognized that she wasn't very bright in most school subjects, and preferred to entertain herself with domesticated duties such as cooking, cleaning, and caring for children. In addition to her sewing, she took great pride in her decorative skills. For the family's Easter dinner, she had sewn a new set of curtains with a matching tablecloth and potholders for the kitchen.

While Mabel Jean earned top honors in her science and math classes but lacked the skills to make a basic cake, Minnie Sue earned top honors in her sewing and home economics classes while struggling in Algebra. However, this fact did not bother her in the least. Truthfully, she didn't want to attend college; she wanted something her mother had never had—a husband. Her goal in life was to be a dedicated housewife and mother. She had been dating her boyfriend, Homer, for the past two years and had already accepted his proposal for marriage. He was a mechanic at his father's garage and they were planning a July wedding. Minnie Sue proudly looked at the small diamond chip on her left hand, the symbol of her engagement. As much as Homer pestered her,

Minnie firmly stood her ground. She would proudly wear white on her wedding day and make her grandmother, Gladys, proud.

Since the two graduating children in the family, Minnie Sue and Harvey, Jr. were not attending college, Lucela had surprisingly had an extra scholarship this year. When the announcement had been made for the first scholarship, it was due to Minnie Sue's engagement. However, Harvey, Jr. surprised everyone in the family by abruptly joining the military. At the last minute, Lucela realized that there were *two* scholarships to give. She had a battle with her heart, but realized that this may have been God's doing after all. She recalled her conversation with Marianne and how she had said that she would be praying that God worked a miracle. Lucela pondered on this and realized that she had seen God work in mysterious ways in her lifetime and didn't want to impede on any miracles he was trying to perform. Since the money was available, why not provide it to these boys and give them a chance at a better life? After much contemplation, Lucela's heart softened and she decided to give a scholarship to each of Abe's unacknowledged sons. God knows Abe had never given a penny for them. She felt that this might amend some of his wrongdoings so that God might have mercy on his soul.

CHAPTER THIRTY

After Easter, the weeks progressed and the families prepared for graduations. In Lucela's extended family, there were three graduations taking place: Timmy, Harvey, Jr., and Minnie Sue. In addition, Ronnie and Johnnie were also getting their diplomas, bringing the actual total to five. All of the children excitedly anticipated the next phase of their lives, while the relatives busied themselves preparing for their celebrations.

Lucela had decided to host the celebratory meal at her home on the Sunday before graduation. Abe had voiced his dissension at holding the event at their home. "Ceel, I don't want all these folks traipsing through my house! Why you gotta cook a whole lotta food and carry on just cause them kids is graduating? Schoolin' ain't no big deal. If you wanna have a dinner for anybody, have it for Young Harvey. At least he's goin' to serve his country!" Lucela had laughed and simply ignored him.

Although she had not spoken to Marianne, Lucela sent word through Timmy to Ronnie and Johnnie that they were welcome to come. Surprisingly, it was Ronnie who urged Johnnie to agree to stop by for a moment and pay their respects to Lucela. Usually the hot-tempered one, he realized that her kindness had allowed them a way to attend college together. "Hey, man, let's stop by even if it's just for a minute, just to tell her 'Thanks' for giving us the scholarships." Johnnie agreed.

That Sunday, each graduate attended service in their cap and gown and sat on the front pew, a custom of Mt. Nebo. Clarence announced the graduate's names and their families joined them at the front of the church for a round of applause from the congregation. Both Lucela and Robert stood with Timmy and Marianne and Fred stood with the twins. In hindsight, Lucela was somewhat grateful that Abe had refused to attend church like she usually requested, since it would have added an unnecessary degree of awkwardness to this joyous occasion.

After service, the family proceeded with their caravan to Abe and Lucela's home. Abe, who had not shaved and had barely gotten four hours of sleep, greeted Harvey, Sr.'s thunderous, "Hey, Cousin!" at the door with a grunt. Harvey, Sr., a tall man who was almost as wide as he was tall, playfully slapped Abe on the back before stating, "We missed you at church today, Cousin!" Timmy, stepping in as a gracious host while Lucela busied herself in the kitchen, called out for Harvey, Sr. and Jr. to join him in the living room.

Lucela had cooked all of the meal herself, allowing Myrtle to only help set the table and place the food in serving dishes. Since the meal was a celebration for the graduates, she had taken great pains to include a special dessert for each graduate. She had baked a coconut cake for Timmy, a chocolate cake for Minnie Sue, and had even baked a caramel cake for Harvey, Jr., which required the arduous task of making homemade caramel frosting. Lucela didn't mind, she was proud of each of the graduates in the family and wanted to make each of them feel special.

225

After everyone had gathered, the family proceeded to partake of a feast of turkey with dressing, ham, roast beef, mashed potatoes, macaroni and cheese, cabbage, potato salad, and homemade hot rolls and cinnamon rolls. Harvey, Sr. slapped his son on the back and told him, "Eat up, boy! You won't be getting food this good in the military!" Everyone laughed.

Clarence teased Minnie Sue about the small amount of food on her plate. She responded that she was trying to maintain her small frame so that she could fit into her grandmother's wedding dress. Gladys, who was nearby, butted in the conversation. "That's right, Clarence. Leave her be. She's gonna wear her grandma's dress! Can you believe I used to be so tiny?" She patted a hefty leg and laughed.

"Grandma, you are something else!" Clarence responded.

While the family ate and engaged in witty banter, Abe sat sullenly in the corner, feeling like a visitor in his own home. His inner thoughts of jealousy began to surface due to his anger at not being the focus of his wife's attention. *"Spending all this money to feed these kids, just cause they graduated! So what? Always puttin' on for company! I can't remember the last time she cooked a meal for me! And why did she have to make THREE cakes? These kids is too spoiled! Glad we didn't have any kids together. Ain't no tellin' how theyd've turned out!"*

Abe's thoughts were interrupted by the ringing of the doorbell. *"Who's ringing the door? Family doesn't do that. Must be one of the neighbors, coming to sneak a bite to eat,"* he thought. Abe struggled to rise from his chair. Before he could reach the door, Timmy walked gallantly into the living room and opened it. He was greeted by both Ronnie and Johnnie. Abe, feeling his manhood threatened, stood stiffly and responded to them gruffly, "What y'all want?"

Ronnie tensed up and Johnnie spoke for them. "Hello, Mr. Jessup. We came by to speak with your wife."

Abe stared at Ronnie through the screen, who matched his stare with the temerity to make his threat a promise. Timmy reached around and opened the screen door. "Hey, fellas. Come on in."

Abe was upset. Timmy didn't have a right to open the door and admit guests to HIS house. He bristled as the boys entered and walked past him without saying another word. "Come on guys," Timmy said. "Mama Ceel is in here."

Timmy escorted the boys to the kitchen, where Lucela and Myrtle were busying themselves putting away the food. Surprisingly, Ronnie initiated the conversation. "Uh, excuse me, Mrs. Jessup?"

Lucela and Myrtle both turned from the sink. Lucela paused, then wiped her hands on her apron before responding. "Yes?"

Ronnie continued. "Well, uh, Mrs. Jessup, we didn't mean to interrupt you. Me and my brother just wanted to stop by and personally thank you for the scholarship. My mother and the rest of my family also send their 'Thanks'. "

Johnnie continued, "Yes, Ma'am, we sure appreciate it. Since we both got scholarships, we'll be able to go to school together. If you hadn't helped us out, we would have been separated and my Ma didn't want that. You know, me and my brother look out for each other. Anyway, we just wanted to come tell you that we appreciate your kindness. May God bless you."

Myrtle patted Lucela on the shoulder. She realized her cousin was definitely a true saint. Few women would have overlooked their personal feelings to extend such a strong act of kindness.

Lucela cleared her throat before responding. "Well, boys, my Aunt Saxie wanted me to begin the scholarship fund to help the young people in our community attend college so that they could one day come back and help others. I hope that you boys go off to school and make us all proud. We're all countin' on you."

The boys replied in unison, "Yes, Ma'am. We will."

Ronnie extended his hand to Lucela and she grasped it in a handshake. When she turned to Johnnie for a handshake, he responded with a hug. After their embrace, both had moistened eyes. Johnnie, feeling slightly embarrassed, wiped the corners of his eyes and dried his hands on his pants.

Lucela wiped her eyes on the corner of her apron.

The boys retreated from the kitchen and entered the living room. Harvey, Jr. walked up and slapped Ronnie on the back. "Hey, Man! Good to see y'all! Heard you're going to Florida. Gonna play ball for Bethune-Cookman!

Harvey, Sr. got up from the sofa and walked over to the twins, his large frame towering over them. He stood between the two boys and placed a large hand on each shoulder. "Just wanted to tell you boys how proud I am. Your mama did a good job raising you up, especially since she had to do it by herself. You've got a bright future ahead of you." He grabbed each boy playfully around the neck before continuing. "While y'all are down in Florida, I want you both to remember to focus on them books and leave them fast tail gals alone!"

The boys laughed heartily at Harvey, Sr.'s advice before Harvey, Jr. interjected, "Don't worry fellas. I got the same advice, except he told me to focus on following my officers' orders and leave them fast tail gals alone!"

Everyone joined in the laughter, except for Abe. He sat sullenly in the corner, thoughts of anger clouding his mind. *"Harvey always got to come over here like he's the man of the family. Runnin' off at the mouth about things that ain't none of his* concern. Talkin' bout Marianne like she some kind of saint and praising her for raising up these boys. Hell, she did what she was supposed to do. She was they mama. Who else was supposed to raise 'em?"

Lucela entered the dining area with two plates. Myrtle followed with two glasses of lemonade. "You boys come have a bite to eat. Sit for a spell and visit with Timmy."

Before Johnnie could open his mouth to politely refuse, Ronnie had already sat down and was slicing up a thick piece of sugar-glazed ham. Johnnie resignedly sat at the table and spoke for the both of them. "Thanks, Mrs. Jessup."

The boys ate heartily while conversing with Timmy and Harvey, Jr. about professional football. Afterwards, Ronnie perused the assortment of desserts on the table: pecan pie, chocolate cake, pound cake, and sweet potato pie. Finally, he noticed the white cake under the crystal dome in the middle of the table. He nudged Timmy. "Hey, man. What kind of cake is that?"

Timmy laughed before responding. "That's my favorite: Coconut cake. It's Mama Ceel's specialty."

Ronnie couldn't contain his excitement. "Coconut cake? That's my favorite, too. My mom doesn't cook it because she doesn't like coconut, but my sister-in-law cooks them for me, sometimes. Can I have a slice?"

Timmy gave him a funny look before laughing again. "Man, sure! Do you see all these desserts? Mama Ceel and Aunt Myrtle cooked enough food to feed an army. There's plenty. "

Ronnie removed the lid from the cake dome and sliced a large piece of cake. Abe, who had nodded off briefly, awoke when he heard the clink of the crystal. *"Who's eatin' my cake?"* he thought.

Johnnie stopped talking briefly. "Hey, bro, is that coconut cake?"

Ronnie rubbed his stomach and smiled before responding. "Yeah, it is. My favorite. Haven't had a slice in a while, since Laurie put Paul on a diet. You want some?"

Johnnie laughed, 'You know I do!"

Ronnie cut another large slice and placed it on Johnnie's plate. While handing the plate to his brother, he locked eyes with an angry-looking Abe. Still holding the knife, he maintained his stare long enough for Abe to soften his gaze. He still felt anger towards Abe since their last encounter and wanted to signal to him that they were not amicable, despite his presence in his house.

Lucela entered from the kitchen and refilled the boys' glasses with lemonade. "So, I see Timmy's not the only one who likes coconut cake?"

Ronnie, his mouth full of cake, took a deep swallow before responding. "No, Ma'am. It's my favorite, too. In fact, this is the best coconut cake I've ever tasted."

Lucela smiled at him. "Well, I'll have to wrap you up a large slice to take home."

Abe seethed with rage. *"These little no-count niggas wanna come in MY house and eat MY food without giving me a thanks or a small bit of respect? All three of 'em sittin' there, Lucela fawning all over them like they're special! If Clarence and Harvey, Sr. wasn't here, I'd straighten this mess out!"*

Lucela returned to the table with a small bag and aluminum foil. She removed the cake dome and sliced off two more large pieces of cake, carefully wrapping them before placing them in the bag. Abe cringed when he saw that less than half of the cake remained.

Lucela handed Ronnie the bag and patted him on the shoulder before saying, "You eat as much as you like. I got more food in the kitchen if you need anything."

Abe stamped his 'good' foot angrily on the floor. Lucela petting over these kids and trying to feed the neighborhood was gonna send them to the poorhouse! Abe's mouth suddenly felt dry and longed for a taste of liquor. Although he could have slipped off and drank in another part of the house, he didn't want to drink alone. He wanted to drink with a friend, someone to console him that would understand all of the injustices he had endured today. Marianne had used to be that friend. Now, he longed for her company. He missed her devoted admiration, her constant affirmation of his manhood that assuaged his insecurities.

After a while, the voices in his head convinced Abe to leave. Listening to the laughter and conversation in the house, he felt like an outsider. Looking at the mantel, he noticed Timmy's Trophy and his diploma. Sitting next to the diploma was a small, black velvet box that contained Bobby's ring. Abe slipped the box in his pocket and left without saying a word. *"I'm 'bout sick of these White boys takin' over my house! All I know is, there better be some coconut cake left for me when I get back."*

CHAPTER THIRTY-ONE

Abe entered the pool hall which was slowly filling with the regulars who had finished their Sunday dinner and nap. Bessie, who sometimes still served as a late night companion, excitedly waddled over to him with his regular brown liquor. She anticipated his start on a long night of slow drinking that might hopefully end with him lying in her bed. Abe grunted his thanks and walked over to the pool table. He placed a quarter on the ledge to signal his desire to play the next game.

After losing a few games and a few quarters, Abe dejectedly sat back down at the bar. After Bessie handed him his second refill accompanied with a smile, he leaned on his elbows and began to listen to the voices in his head. *"Look at how Bessie treats you. Ceel used to treat you like that, before that little White boy moved in. You're a man. And a man needs to be treated like one. That's the problem in your house, Abe. You need to let them know what the problem is and how you're gonna fix it."*

Abe, in his escalating state of inebriation, began to converse with himself. "How am I gonna fix it?"

The voice responded, *"First of all, you need to take charge of the money. Ceel controls everything! If you'd been in control of the money, Ceel wouldn't had all those fools in the house today 'cause you wouldn't have allowed her to waste all that money on groceries. Yeah, you get your pension, but what about the rest of the money? If you're the man, you need to control it all."*

Just then, Smitty interrupted the voice in his head by loudly calling out to another guy, "Let's get it on, Man! Come on and let me take your money!" Abe watched a group of men enter the small room in the back. He knew they were about to start a crap game.

The voice spoke to Abe. *"Just think, if you went home with a bag full of money everybody'd have to listen to you then!"* Abe, who rarely played craps, suddenly had the courage to join in. He left his seat and walked to the back room.

After knocking on the door, Abe entered. Smitty, who was about to roll the dice, looked up and acknowledged his presence, "Hey, Crip, Man, it's five dollars to get in. This ain't no quarter pool game, so if you ain't ready, hit the door. I know Lucela probably don't give you enough allowance to play big boy games like this." Smitty and the rest of his sycophants laughed at the joke. Abe bristled with anger.

Abe, who hated Smitty with a passion, wasn't about to let him embarrass him into leaving. He knew he had to save face. He pulled a ten dollar bill from his pocket (his last) and threw it on the ground before snidely remarking, "Is that enough?"

Smitty laughed even louder, anticipating the thrill of taking all of Abe's money. "Sure, Crip. If you got the money, we won't act funny!" His cronies laughed with him at his corny remark.

After a few rolls, Abe was up. He kept rolling and eventually Smitty was out. Abe felt powerful. He was holding close to a hundred dollars. Smitty, who was sore at losing, hung around the game giving remarks and insults. "Hell, Crip, Lucela might not make you sleep on the porch if you show her that handful of money when you get home. But you better hurry out of here before Bessie catches you with it!" The group continued to laugh and began to break Abe's concentration.

After about an hour, Abe's lucky streak ended. He started to lose and eventually he'd crapped out to Big Rob, the fellow who'd started the game with Smitty. Abe dreaded going home broke. Not only had he spent all of the money he'd won, but he'd spent all that was in his pockets. To make matters worse, all the money in Abe's pockets was all of the money he had until the first of the month. As much as Lucela allowed him his freedom to spend his meager pension, he knew she would not provide him with additional funds to spend on liquor and loose women. Goddamn Smitty!

Big Rob, was a large man who weighed about 400 pounds and talked with a strong lisp. Rob looked at Abe and said, "Thassit, Buddy. I'm thaking this money and theeing if I can find me a thweetheart!" Smitty began to laugh and Big Rob joined him. Abe began to bristle with anger once again, now suspecting that the two men were in cahoots.

Big Rob (who had been on his knees in the customary position for rolling the dice on the floor) tried to steady himself and prepared to stand. Before he could move, Abe interrupted him. "Hey, Man. I ain't tapped out. I got something to work with."

Big Rob slumped back down again. "Whathu got?"

Abe reached into his pocket and removed Bobby's ring. He set the black velvet box on the ground and opened it. The bright gold ring beamed from the interior. Smitty peered at the ring. Having played a year of college football in his younger days, he instantly recognized the seal on the box. Usually the jokester, he was at a loss for words. Abe had sunk to a new low.

Big Rob, who was new to the area and failed to see the significance of the ring, said, "Thas no problem! Thas' enough to keep this game rollin'!" The game resumed.

At first, it appeared that Abe's luck was about to change. He felt powerful again, holding a fistful of money while he rolled the dice. He cracked jokes and teased Smitty about being unable to participate in the game. Smitty barely responded and his cronies sat quietly, some bravely snickering at Abe's jokes. However, after a time, Abe was losing again. Eventually, he lost all of his reclaimed money AND the ring. Dejectedly, he stood and moved away from the dice. Smitty and his crew jokingly waved at Abe as he walked away with his head hanging low. Now that Abe had sobered up, pawning the ring didn't seem like a good idea.

Smitty shook his head as Abe limped out the door. As much as he disliked Abe, he pitied Lucela because he realized that she was married to a fool. Having once dated Lucela, he knew that she was a good woman with a good heart that deserved none of the turmoil and heartache that her husband gave her. Smitty decided to make an attempt to rectify the situation. "Come on, Rob, lemme get you a beer."

The men sat a table and sipped their beer. Abe slumped at the bar and drowned his sorrow in drinks that Bessie slipped him, since he was flat broke.

Smitty took a long swallow of his beer before remarking to Rob, "You don't know whose ring you got in your pocket. Do you?"

Big Rob laughed and said, "I thon't care whose thit was, thit's mine now!"

Smitty said, "Man, I understand how you feel. But let me explain to you how Crip got that ring. When I'm done, you tell me if you feel the same way." Smitty explained the story of Bobby's stand for freedom and his merciless murder at the hands of the law. He went on to explain how his team won the championship after his death and how it had been given to his mother while she was on her deathbed. Rob shook his head in disbelief at some parts. Finally, Smitty ended with, "You don't want a dead man or his sweet mama haunting you about no ring, man. It ain't worth it. Now, I know Crip's wife. I'm gonna take the ring back to her. I know he owed it to you, but look at it this way: you leavin' here with more money than you came with. So you're still a winner."

238

Big Rob, who had been raised in Louisiana by his grandmother, had a strong belief in ghosts and other spirits. He didn't want to be chased by any 'haints' and unsettled souls, thus he wanted no parts of the ring. He knew Smitty wasn't lying because although he was one to often joke, this was the most serious Rob had ever seen him. Rob handed the ring to Smitty.

Smitty jumped up quickly. He knew that it was getting late and wanted to deliver the ring to Lucela before Abe made it home.

CHAPTER THIRTY-TWO

Lucela had finished cleaning the kitchen and had settled down in front of the television with a glass of warm milk to settle her stomach before bed. She was sipping quietly and watching an episode of her favorite show, Barnaby Jones. Timmy was sitting at the kitchen table, reading a book and eating a late night snack of chocolate cake and milk.

Suddenly, the doorbell rang. At first, Lucela had thought it was the television, since no one ever visited her home at this hour. Upon hearing the second ring, Timmy called out to her from the kitchen. "I'll get the door, Ma."

Timmy walked past Lucela and peeked out the window. He saw a tall, burly man he didn't recognize and hesitated before calling out, "Sir, can we help you?"

Smitty stood on the porch, shuffling his feet nervously. He recognized Timmy, but realized that the boy didn't know him. "Son, I'm here to see Lucela. Please tell her it's Lonnie Smith. "

Timmy turned to Lucela, who was engrossed in the television show's car chase. "Mama Ceel, there's a man out here that says his name is Lonnie Smith. He wants to speak to you."

"Lonnie Smith?" Lucela thought. "I haven't seen him in years." Big, tall, and handsome Lonnie. He used to keep her in stitches from laughing at his jokes. He was the town's star football player and had even attended college for a while. Saxie used to love having him around because he was always such a well-mannered young man who enjoyed her good cooking. Lucela's first love. Her heart still felt slightly bruised when she recalled him dumping her after a short courtship that ended when she refused to yield to his demands for physical intimacy. *"What could he want?"* Given her history with Lonnie, Lucela knew that whatever brought him to the house must have been serious and she was sure that he meant her no harm. She got up from her seat and told Timmy, "I'll get the door, Baby."

Lucela walked to the door, smoothing her dress and running her fingers through her hair. After all these years, she was still conscious of her appearance around Smitty as if they were still courting.

Lucela opened the door and spoke through the screen, "Lonnie? What brings you here at this hour?" She had loosened her bun in preparation for bed and her locks cascaded past her shoulders. In the moonlight, she looked many years younger and her appearance startled Smitty. He realized that her beauty had not faded and for a second he was at a loss for words. Lucela smiled at him. "Lonnie, is somethin' wrong?"

Smitty regained his composure. "Lucela, I apologize for coming by here so late, but I need to talk to you. Out of respect for Abe, can you step out on the porch?"

Lucela hesitated, until she saw the serious expression on his face. She stepped out onto the porch and sat on the swing. "Okay, Lonnie. Can you tell me what's goin' on?"

Smitty sat in the rocking chair and lowered his voice. He didn't want Timmy to hear what he was about to say. Unbeknownst to him, Timmy was listening from the kitchen window, not to be nosey, but to be protective of Lucela. Smitty cleared his throat before continuing. "Lucela, I came by here at this hour because I got somethin' important to give to you. I hate to be the one to do it, but I feel that if I didn't, you and that boy in there would be really hurt." He removed the ring from his pocket and handed it to Lucela.

As soon as Lucela recognized the box, her eyes immediately teared up with a mixture or relief and rage. She wasn't sure how Lonnie had gotten the ring, but she was sure Abe had something to do with it. Smitty's eyes also watered up when he saw the pain in her eyes. "Ceel, I'm sorry I had to be the one to tell you this, but you have to know. Abe lost this ring in a crap game at the pool hall. I knew the fella that won it, and I convinced him to let me return it to you." Lucela's brow furrowed in worry and Smitty continued before she could question him. "You don't have to worry about paying him back. He agreed to cancel the debt."

Lucela's face softened before she responded, "Please tell that gentleman that I said 'Thank You' Lonnie. And I'd also like to tell you 'Thanks' for bringing this back to me. It means a lot to my family, especially Timmy. I'm not sure what I would have done if it were gone forever."

Lucela burst into fresh tears after her last comment and Smitty reached out and touched her hand. He hated to see her in so much pain because he felt she was too good of a woman for Abe, or even him. However, the difference between he and Abe was that he was noble enough to recognize this fact and thus ended his courtship with her in the hopes that she would find someone deserving of her love. Abe, on the other hand, saw her kind heart as a tool that could be misused because he was an opportunist and a manipulator. For these reasons, Smitty hated Abe with a deep intensity.

Smitty touched Lucela's hand. "Lucela, remember when we used to sit on that swing, many, many years ago when we thought we was courtin'?" Lucela sad expression changed and she began to smile. Smitty slapped his thigh and laughed loudly. "Aunt Saxie would sit in this rocking chair and watch our every move! I could barely hold your hand!"

Lucela covered her mouth with her hand and giggled like a schoolgirl at the fond memory. Smitty continued, "You know, I know you were mad at me when I stopped coming to see you. But the truth is, I stopped coming to see you because I realized that you were too good for me. I was just looking for fast times and loose women. You was a good girl and I just wasn't ready for that. When I look at you now, I'm glad I left you alone. You were too good for me then, and you're too good for me now." Lucela

243

placed her hands in her lap and tried to control her emotions. Smitty's long-awaited apology soothed an old wound. He paused before continuing. "When I saw Abe giving away that ring, I thought about how you didn't deserve that. I know we haven't talked during the years, and I'm sure it was because of how I treated you when we was young. I thought about that tonight and figured that if I was able to return this ring to you it might make up for some of the hurt I caused you when I was young and dumb."

Lucela smiled at Smitty. "I'm not mad anymore, Lonnie. But if this were thirty years ago, I'd probably had taken a skillet to you by now."

Smitty laughed loudly then stood to his feet. "Well, I guess I better leave now before you change your mind. I'm too old to be dodging skillets!"

Lucela got up from the swing. She walked over to Smitty and gave him a hug. Smitty, who was startled at first, felt a flood of emotion as he held her tightly. For a moment, his mind was taken back and he regretted his decision to let her get away from him. Lucela pulled away and said, "Thank you, Lonnie. I appreciate it."

Smitty smiled down at her. "You're welcome, Lucela. You take care." He stepped off the porch, then turned around and remarked, "Now I hope when you think of me, you won't think about getting' your skillet!"

Lucela laughed and went inside. After she closed the door, her whole demeanor changed. She placed the ring back in its usual place and began to ponder on the events that had occurred. As the reality of Abe's transgression set in, a cloud of anger enveloped her. While she knew that Abe could do some very mean things at times, this had sunk him to a new low. Abe had to know how important that ring was to not only Timmy, but to the entire family. It was the only tangible item that remained of Bobby's brief life and it symbolized the events that had led to his death. Kay had willed the ring to Timmy before passing and Lucela had simply kept it in her home so that he could be near it. To think that Abe had disregarded everyone's feelings and attempted to give the ring to a complete stranger was unforgivable. Lucela had accepted a lot from Abe: infidelity, illegitimate children, drunkenness, disrespect, and limited monetary support. However, this time, he'd gone too far. This time, she was going to take a stand.

Lucela decided to settle this matter with Abe when he arrived home: whenever that might be! Normally, she would have retired to bed at this time. Tonight, she decided to wait for his arrival. She had had about all she could take of Abe's foolishness. She cut a slice of cake and sat at the table. She turned on the percolator and prepared for a long night. She had no idea that Timmy had actually heard her and Lonnie's conversation, and hoped that he could be spared the hurtful details of what Abe had done.

Timmy, who had heard Smitty and Lucela talking on the porch, lay fuming in his bed. He couldn't believe Abe had stolen his brother's ring! It was the one item he had left to remember Bobby. While it was real gold, it was priceless to Timmy and something he would never think of selling. If that kind man hadn't brought it back to Lucela, it would have been lost forever. Timmy not sure what he would have done. Bobby's ring meant more to him than anything!

All through the years, Timmy had put up with Abe's rude remarks, indifference, and horrible attitude. As much as he had tried to respect Abe and treat him like family, Abe had always treated him like he was a stranger in the home. Whenever Lucela was not around, Abe would talk about how much food he ate, how he was nothing more than an orphan, and how he hated his intrusion in his home. Of course, Timmy never told Lucela these things because he wanted to spare her feelings. Also, he didn't want to make more friction amongst the trio. Although he had mended his relationship with his father, he still preferred living with Lucela. Plus, he worried about Lucela's well-being, especially when Abe would become drunk and unruly, hollering commands and throwing dishes. While he had never harmed Lucela, Timmy wondered if it might one day be a possibility. A drunk always regrets their loss of self-control once they sober up.

Abe stumbled into the house with the morning sun. After a romp in the bed with Bessie, he'd sobered up enough to drive home. He had decided to tell Lucela that he had taken the ring to show it to his cousin James and had been robbed on the way home. When he walked into the house, he looked to his left and thought his cloudy mind was playing tricks on him. *"The ring! The ring was back on the mantle! How did that happen?"*

Lucela still sat at the table, sipping coffee from her cracked china cup. Her large butcher knife sat on the counter, within arm's reach. She grabbed it when she heard Abe stumble in, and prepared to confront him. Her eyes were tightened from bouts of crying, and bloodshot from lack of sleep. This would be her last sleepless night because of Abe. Lucela had had enough.

Abe walked into the kitchen to get a glass of water. When he saw Lucela at the table, he was so startled that he jumped. "Ceel, what you doin' up so early? You sick?"

Lucela looked at him with reddened eyes. "Yeah, I'm sick. I'm sick of you! Traipsin' in here at the rooster's crow and tryin' to act like nothin's wrong! Where you been, Abe? Layin' up with one of your whores?"

The still slightly inebriated Abe, who in all their years of marriage had never been confronted regarding his infidelities, was unable to form a coherent thought in response. He stammered a response. "What? Huh? What'd you say?"

The emotionally drained Lucela, who in all their years of marriage had never really stood up to her husband regarding his inappropriate behavior, let loose a current of words that spewed from her as if a floodgate had been opened. "You heard me! You been out layin' up with some whore and now you think you gonna come lay up here in my house like you king of the castle? You lowdown, evil snake! I know what you did last night! I know you took that ring and tried to pawn it. How could you? How could you, Abe?"

Abe became indignant as a defense mechanism and decided to respond to her accusations regarding his infidelity in order to evade the issue about the ring. "Look here, woman! I am the king of this here castle and it's about time I started getting treated like one! Ain't nobody been laying up with no woman! I can barely deal with you! What I look like getting another one?" Abe added a snicker to his last remark, trying to get Lucela to laugh and possibly diffuse some of the anger she was feeling. He looked at Lucela. Her face remained stony and her reddened eyes squinted even more, peering at Abe as if he were dim-witted or a stranger she didn't recognize.

Lucela couldn't believe that Abe was picking a time like this to be funny. She also wondered if he was losing his mind, acting as if he hadn't stolen the ring and that it was appropriate for him to be arriving home at this hour. She lowered her voice and squeezed her eyes shut as if she were saying something distasteful. "Abe, why did you take the ring? Don't say you didn't take it, because I know you did!'

Abe wearily leaned against the wall. The events of the past few hours had been a bit overwhelming and he was still recovering from the shock of the ring miraculously arriving home before he did. "Look here, Ceel. I admit I took the ring. But so what? It's my house and I got a right to take anything in it, anytime I damn well please. You carry on about Timmy and the rest of these youngun's much more than you carry on about me. When's the last time you cooked me a dinner? Or made me a coconut cake? You got everybody here in my house, eating at my table, some of 'em who won't even speak to me, but you give 'em the right to come in here and eat at my table." Abe began to choke on his words and a few tears spilled onto his cheeks. "Folks come in here and treat me like I don't even live here. Walk by me without speaking, and eat at my table like they put the food on the table. They don't respect me! You don't respect me! Nobody respects me, but you expect me to be the man of this house!"

Lucela could not believe that Abe was trying to divert her attention from the real issue: his theft of the ring. She shook her head at him before responding. "This ain't about you being the man of this house. This is about you stealing something that was important to this family and taking it to pawn. That ring belongs to Timmy. It's not even yours to take or give. Yes, it's in your house, but it doesn't belong to you."

Abe refused to back down. "It's just a ring. It don't mean nothing. That boy is dead and the ring won't bring him back. I don't want it in my house anyway. That's why I tried to get rid of it!"

At this point, Lucela lost her composure. "You're a liar! You didn't get rid of it because you didn't want it in your house. You tried to use it to win money in a dice game and when your luck ran out you lost it to a stranger. If Lonnie Smith hadn't brought that ring back to me, it would have been gone! Gone forever!"

When Abe heard Smitty's name, his blood began to boil! At the same time, his angry heart was comforted with the fact that he now had a reason to deflect Lucela's wrath. He stood up straight and took a step towards the seated Lucela. Despite his frequent indiscretions, the idea of his wife being unfaithful spurred him into a murderous rage. He hollered loudly, his voice rushing from his body like a mighty wind. "Smitty been in my house? Woman, you had another man in my house? I know about y'all and how he used to court you before I came on the scene. Marianne told me all about it!" Abe grabbed Lucela's arm before continuing his tirade. "Lucela--you taking up with another man?"

Lucela was startled at the unfamiliar discomfort of Abe's twisting of her arm. In all their years of marriage, he had never touched her in anger. The more she struggled to break free, the tighter his hold became. Her veins pulsed with adrenaline and she began to fear what her husband's next response would be. Abe felt a rush of power when Lucela was unable to break free. This unseemly feeling caused him to feel masculine and he oddly misinterpreted these emotions as a confirmation of his manhood. He squeezed Lucela's arm tighter and bellowed out another command. "Tell me the truth, woman! You carryin' on with Smitty?"

250

Lucela screamed, "Abe, no! No, I am not! Lonnie came by here to give me the ring on his own. I spoke with him on the porch. Let my arm go, Abe. You're hurting me!"

Timmy awoke to Lucela's frightening scream. Startled, he jumped out of bed and ran in her direction. He entered the kitchen and saw Abe raising his hand to strike Lucela. He immediately came to her defense.

Timmy grabbed Abe's raised hand and forcefully pushed him against the wall. Lucela stood, shaking and crying, while rubbing her reddened arm. Abe slid down the wall, landing in a weakened heap on the floor. He placed his head in his hands and cried like a baby.

Timmy held Lucela, his tall muscular figure encircling her large frame in a protective embrace. She laid her head on his shoulder and whimpered; her tired soul feeling relieved.

Abe blubbered like a toddler, his tears falling onto his shirt. "Ceel, I'm sorry. I'm sorry! I just wanted to prove to you that I'm a man. You never respected me as a man. I was trying to prove myself to you! I'm a man!"

Lucela pulled away from Timmy and looked at Abe. Sitting there on the floor, wet-faced with his scrawny knees drawn up to his chest, he looked like a pitiful example of a man. He looked more like a small boy that had put on his father's clothes which were baggy and hanging off of him because they were too big. In that moment, she had an epiphany. She realized that for all these years, Abe had been trying to wear shoes that he wasn't big enough to fill. He was a weak and bitter man who responded to his shortcomings by being selfish and responding in anger. He wasn't fit to be neither a father nor a husband and she had wasted more than twenty years being married to him. Suddenly, her anger turned to pity. Cutting Abe with her butcher knife would do no good because he, in his immaturity, would never realize WHY she was cutting him. Cursing him out for taking the ring would do no good because he, who had never loved anyone except himself, would never realize the significance of holding on to a memento of someone greatly loved.

Lucela looked down at her calloused and work-worn hands. She had wasted years trying to build a life with a man that would never amount to much of anything. All of her life she had wanted to marry and mother children and she had mistakenly married and mothered Abe. Lonnie was right. Abe didn't deserve her. However, putting him out would be futile. He was not and would never be equipped to make it on his own. He would either leave and wander back, or suffer and die in the streets. As angry as she was, she couldn't bear the thought or indignity of her childish husband subjecting her to more shame.

Timmy looked at Abe and thought of the words that Clarence had shared with him many years ago. *"He's mean as a snake, but he ain't nothin' but a big coward. He just tries to use his mouth to make himself seem big. . ."* Seeing Abe bawling on the floor made Timmy realize just how small he really was. Despite his

252

anger, he felt pity for this grown man that was less than a man than him. He realized that manhood didn't necessarily rely on physical strength or authoritative assertions, but rather on love and respect for family, two qualities that Abe obviously lacked and would never obtain during his life. Abe was a lost cause that no amount of talking, fussing, or fighting could save. Timmy shook his head and pondered on how to maintain peace in his home. Peace that would protect his mother and provide her with the stability that she needed.

Lucela sat at the table, wiping the tears that intermittently fell on her dimpled cheeks while she sipped her coffee. Abe remained on the floor, his head bent over his knees like a child enduring punishment.

Timmy walked to the cabinet and removed three small plates. He took three forks from the drawer and placed them on the table. He located Abe's coffee mug and filled it with fresh, hot coffee. He placed a spoon and the sugar bowl beside it.

Abe stopped pouting long enough to see the cup that was waiting for him. He stiffly stood up and limped to his usual seat at the table. He absently added sugar to his coffee and took a long, slow sip. Lucela stared at him, her red eyes having softened.

Timmy reached around her and picked up the large butcher knife. He removed the crystal cake dome cover and began to slice pieces of coconut cake. He placed a large piece in front of

Abe and said, "Mama Ceel made us a cake, Abe. Here, have some." He placed the knife in the sink, out of Lucela's sight.

Lucela took a bite of the cake and a sip of coffee. Timmy drank a large gulp of milk before proceeding to eat his slice. Abe, having already finished more than half of his slice, took a long sip of his coffee before picking up the day's newspaper from the table. In an attempt to initiate conversation, he remarked to Lucela in a softened voice, "Hey, Ceel. Looks like Cassius Clay ain't gonna go fight them Viet-Cong. " He turned to Timmy and spoke with more bravado. "Hey, Boy. Did I ever tell you about the time I met Cassius Clay?"

"No, " Timmy replied. He leaned in, showing interest in hearing the story.

Lucela looked up from her coffee and gave Abe a slight smile.

Abe leaned back in his chair and began his tale. "Well, he was a young boy back then, just starting out as a fighter. He was doing an amateur bout with this local boy that everyone thought would win. Well, let me tell you, Clay beat that boy senseless. See, Clay knew that boy was slow on his feet, so he danced around him until he was seeing circles. Had that boy chasing him around the ring until he was dizzy. The crowd was going crazy . . ."

Lucela's Coconut Cake

Heat oven to 350 degrees

Ingredients:
2 cups of cake flour
½ tsp salt
2 tsp baking powder
1 cup of butter (2 sticks)
2 eggs
1 tsp pure vanilla
½ tsp almond flavor
½ tsp coconut flavor
1 cup milk
1 cup shredded & sweetened coconut

Directions:

Mix dry ingredients (flour, salt, baking powder) and set aside. Mix softened butter and sugar. Mix in eggs and flavorings. Set aside. On a low temp, heat milk (do not scald) and coconut. Simmer for 15 minutes. Drain milk and set coconut aside. Alternately add flour mixture and milk. Mix thoroughly after each addition.

Place in two 8-9" round pans and bake for 30-35 minutes.

After baking, let cool for at least 15 minutes before frosting with **Lucela's Coconut Cake Frosting**.

Lucela's Coconut Cake Frosting

Ingredients:
1 block of softened cream cheese
1 TBSP of softened butter
3 ½ cups of powdered sugar
½ tsp of vanilla
½ tsp of coconut flavoring
¼ cup of milk
Moistened coconut (left from boiled milk)

Directions:

Mix butter, vanilla, coconut flavoring, and 1 cup of powdered sugar. Using a blender on low speed, add cream cheese. After blending, add 2 cups of powdered sugar. Finally, add milk and remaining powdered sugar to desired thickness. Frost each cake layer.

Reading Group Guide

1. Can you understand Lucela's exasperation with Abe? Is she too lenient with him? Do you think her response might have been different if the story was set in our current time period?

2. Was it appropriate for Lucela to serve as a surrogate parent for Timmy? Would you ever consider raising another person's child?

3. Was Marianne wrong for having an affair with Abe? Do you think her upbringing played a role in the choices she made in life? Do we see examples of women like her in society and the media, and if so, how are they regarded?

4. Would you consider Bobby to be a purposeful or accidental hero? How would you categorize Willie and Thomas?

5. Was Robert's initial reaction to Bobbie Kay appropriate? Do people sometimes allow prejudice to influence their actions, even when it involves their own family? What made him change his feelings towards his biracial grand child?

6. Do you think Marianne should have requested the scholarship for her sons? Would you have reacted like Lucela if you were approached by your husband's former mistress?

7. How did you feel when Abe stole Bobby's ring? What was the root of his motivation? Have you ever dealt with someone who committed a hurtful act and tried to justify it? What was your response?

8. Was Lucela's decision at the end of the book one that you expected? Would you have done the same or decided to seek revenge?

9. Who was your favorite character from the story? What did you like about them? Is this character similar to you or someone you know?

10. What was your favorite scene from the story? Did it make you laugh or cry? What image did it leave with you?

Now that you have finished Coconut Cake, turn this page for a preview of its sequel!

Banana Pudding

As secrets are revealed, the lives of the Jessup/Lofton clan will be changed forever!

Earl walked into Jefferson High's gymnasium. The bleachers were filled to capacity and the roar of the crowd resonated in his ears like thunder. He scanned the rainbow of faces in the crowd and thought to himself, *"Wow. Jefferson sure has changed since I went here."*

Due to his nostalgic examination of his surroundings, Earl trailed at the end of his family's procession. There were so many Smiths that they gave the appearance of a church choir marching down an aisle. His father, Lonnie, Sr. (whom family referred to as Big Lonnie and everyone else referred to as Smitty), led the line, waving and tipping his hat to friends in the stands. His mother, Bertha Jean, wobbled unsteadily beside him while holding his arm for support. Earl's brother, Lonnie, Jr. (whom everyone referred to as L.J.) and his wife Pam walked behind them, beaming proudly since their son, Little Lonnie (whom everyone referred to as L.L.) was about to be crowned as Homecoming King. Their other two sons and one daughter skipped along beside them. Earl's younger sister, Willene, who worked at the Post Office, proudly walked through the crowd in her uniform. Due to her position, some people greeted her with smiles, others with disdain. His sister, Jeanetta, and her daughter Kizzy walked in front of Earl. Aunt Esther and Uncle Walter walked behind Jeanetta, and their sons Walt and Mike followed them along with their wives and kids. Starlene, Earl's youngest sister, had promised to attend the occasion. However, as usual, she was running late. Willene rushed by Earl and grumbled, "Star better get here. I won't be able to save a seat for her once this thang starts!"

Kizzy, a student at Jefferson, cut out of the line to speak to a few friends, so Jeanetta slowed her pace until Earl had caught up with her. Her eyes twinkled before she whispered to Earl, "Daddy and L.J. look like they about to bust! L.L.'s keepin' up the family tradition by being the THIRD Lonnie Smith to be crowned Homecoming King at Jefferson High School. Heck, Earl, you'd have probably been voted Homecoming King, too, if you hadn't run off and joined the Army instead of finishing high school."

Earl shook his head. "Naw, Jeanetta. I doubt that. I played sports same as L.J., but I was usually riding the bench. He was the football star like Pops."

Jeanetta smiled warmly at her brother. "Now, Earl. You know you was just as good an athlete as L.J. You always kept up with him when y'all played around in the backyard.

But even if he did outshine you on the football field, you always had more book sense. You remember when you got the highest score in the school on that aptitude test?"

Earl laughed sarcastically at the recollection. "Yeah, I remember. But no guy's ever been chosen to be Homecoming King 'cause of his intellect."

One of Big Lonnie's drinking buddies called out to him, "Smitty! Hey, Man! You got a round on me next Saturday!" Smitty aimed his finger like a gun and pointed it at his friend before laughing while Bertha shook her head derisively.

The Smith Caravan finally arrived at the roped off section of the stands, the area designated for the families of The Royal Court. Big Lonnie and L.J. sat beside each other, talking loudly and responding to the congratulatory handshakes and pats on the back. Bertha Jean and Pam sat at the end of the bench, whispering and giggling like school girls. Willene placed her large frame at the end of the bench, before giving one of her nephews a ten-dollar bill and sending him to the concession stand. Uncle Walt and his crew sat behind them. Earl, feeling left out as usual, sat on the last row. Jeanetta, noticing her wayward brother's distance, plopped down beside him and playfully punched his arm. "C'mon', Brother. Don't try to get away from me. I haven't seen you in almost twenty years! I'm gonna get in as much time as I can with you."

Earl laughed at his sister's remark and placed his arm lovingly around her shoulder. Their moment of tenderness was broken by a loud outburst from across the aisle.

"Earl Smith! Is that you?"

Earl looked up and saw a face he vaguely recognized. "Yeah, it's me. And you are---"

"Charlene! Charlene Templeton! Don't act like you don't remember me!"

Earl was puzzled. This couldn't be Charlene! She'd been the prettiest girl in his class, with natural auburn hair and freckles and a Coke bottle shape that a model would envy. The girl hugging him had two missing front teeth, a large mole on her cheek, and a halo of crinkly gray hair. Before Earl could respond, Charlene had embraced him in a tight hug that constricted him inside her massive arms.

263

When she pulled away, he noticed the freckles and slightly auburn roots in her hair. It was indeed Charlene. She'd aged so much that she looked as if she'd went to high school with Big Lonnie and Bertha Jean. Earl caught his breath before he responded with a faint, "Hey, Charlene."

Charlene placed her hands on her enormous hips and flashed Earl a wide, toothless, smile. "Heeeey, Earl," she purred seductively. "I know you remember me! All the time WE spent together! I heard you was back in town. I also heard you was still single. You still in the military?"

"Sure am. I only have about one more year until I can retire. After that I might think of settling down."

Charlene looked at him quizzically. "You mean to tell me you ain't got no wife? No kids? No girlfriend?"

Earl laughed at the question he'd answered more than ten times in the last week since he returned home. "No. No wife. No kids. No girlfriend.Never had time. The Army keeps me on the go."

Charlene raised her eyebrows and looked Earl up and down. He immediately answered her unstated question.

"And no to THAT question, too! I'm straight. That DEFINITELY hasn't changed, Charlene!"

Charlene laughed loudly, a little too loudly for Earl. "Well, I'm glad to hear that. Anyway, I hope we get a chance to hook up before you hit the road again. It would be nice to catch up on old times."

Before Earl could answer, Jeanetta interjected. "'Lene, leave my brother alone! Tryna start up a fire that burned out twenty years ago! We here for the game and you tryna find a stepdaddy for them five kids of yours! Girl, go on back to your seat!"

Charlene's face reddened. "Aw, forget you, 'Netta. I'm just tryna be social!" Her voice softened before she turned to Earl and said, "I'll catch you later, Sugar."

Jeanetta pulled Earl back down to his seat. Earl turned towards her and let out a belly deep laugh. "'Netta, I swear! You ain't changed a bit, Girl! I wasn't even trying to get with Charlene! By the way, where's the father of those five kids?"

"You mean FATHERS! Heck, I don't even know, I know one of 'em is locked up. The daddy of the youngest boy," she responded. Earl shook his head and smirked.

Almost immediately, the band began to play the National Anthem. All attendees respectfully stood, and Earl habitually placed his hand over his chest. Big Lonnie removed his hat, his thinning crown covered in sweat. *"Pops is graying,"* Earl thought. After the first verse, Bertha Jean sat down, her large frame betraying her. She wiped her brow and began to absently rub her leg. Earl noticed that her ankles were swollen. He felt a pang of guilt at having infrequently returned home during his eighteen year absence. As envious as he was of Big Lonnie and Lonnie Junior's relationship, Earl knew that it had become rock solid during his absence and that he had only himself to blame. At that moment, Earl vowed to spend more time with his family. He knew that his parents were getting up in age and that the years left might be few. Life on the road was beginning to take its toll on Earl. Focusing on his career had given him plenty of money and accolades, but he still felt an emptiness that only the love of his family could fill.

After the crowd was seated, the band played a softer tune and The Royal Court proceeded to march in. The first couple, a blond-haired White girl and an extremely light complexioned Black boy with freckles walked onto the field. Charlene yelled, "Ray-Ray!" and the young man blushed and ducked his head. Jeanetta laughed. Earl realized that this was one of Charlene's five children.

Once the blond and Ray-Ray were seated, another couple began their processional. The brown-skinned girl, who stood over six feet, walked clumsily and wide-legged in her heels as if she were a cowboy. A dark-skinned boy walked beside her, his head barely reaching her shoulder. Jeanetta laughed before whispering, "That's Rynona Jennings. She's the captain of the girls' basketball team. Walking in like she oughta be wearing a pair of tennis shoes!"

After the oddly paired couple was seated, the band changed tunes and everyone stood to honor the Homecoming King and Queen. Bertha Jean wiped her tearful eyes and Big Lonnie emotionally shouted, "That's my boy!" L.L. smiled broadly and waved to his family. The beautiful young lady on his arm waved in their direction as well. Jeanetta conspiratorially whispered to Earl, "That's

L.L.'s little girlfriend, Bobbie Kay. You probably remember her uncle, that White boy that got killed back in the day in Alabama, Bobby Lofton. Yeah, she half-White. That's her momma and folks over there."

Earl looked to his left. He saw an older Black lady wiping her eyes with a frilly handkerchief and an old White man who was wiping his reddened face and telling everyone around him, "That's my grandbaby! That's my grandbaby!" Earl looked to the right of the old man and saw a face he did remember from his youth. She'd gained a few pounds and gotten a little older, but still looked relatively the same. Their eyes immediately locked and the clarity of recognition startled the both of them. *That's Sue! I remember her!*

Susan opened her mouth in shock before she attempted to regain her composure. Lucela looked at her strangely. "Sue, Honey, you look like you've seen a ghost!"

Roger, her husband, clasped her hand possessively. "Honey, are you alright?"

Sue smiled wanly. "Yes, Babe .Just a little emotional. I'm so proud of Bobbie Kay."

The crowd cheered loudly, with a thunderous applause that was deafening. However, Earl heard nothing. He was stunned into silence. Big Lonnie was moving his mouth and pointing to the field while 'Netta was mumbling a comment. Yet Earl heard only his own heartbeat in his ears. He was startled into a semi paralysis that was so severe that he swore his blood had stopped flowing and his hands had become limp and numb. As he looked at caramel skinned, raven-haired Bobbie Kay, Earl realized that he was seeing his daughter for the first time. His stomach churned with nausea as he realized the error of his ways. *"She can't be Little Lonnie's girlfriend! She's his COUSIN!"*